THE FATE OF KATHERINE CARR

THE FATE
OF
KATHERINE CARR

❖

THOMAS H. COOK

An Otto Penzler Book

Quercus

First published in Great Britain in 2009 by

Quercus
21 Bloomsbury Square
London
WC1A 2NS

Copyright © 2009 by Thomas H. Cook

Published by arrangement with Harcourt, Inc

without permission in writing from the publisher.

A CIP catalogue record for this book is available
from the British Library

ISBN (HB) 978 1 84724 840 4
ISBN (TPB) 978 1 84724 841 1

Printed and bound in Great Britain by Clays Ltd, St Ives Plc

10 9 8 7 6 5 4 3 2 1

For
Susan M. Terner, without whom, truly, this
book would not have been written

All Nature is but Art, unknown to thee;
All Chance, Direction, which thou canst not see;
All Discord, Harmony not understood
All partial Evil, universal Good.

—ALEXANDER POPE, *An Essay on Man*

PART I

They strike at heat, she said, and so there is no escape. What if evil were like that, too, a heat that rises from the worst of us, its correction like a hawk circling overhead; always present, but unseen in its dive? Perhaps in all such speculations, the question mark alone is relevant, the opening it offers to a strange dark hope.

But heat, at least, is real, and the one that shimmers around me now comes from the building light, the green, turgid river, the dense jungle and . . .

"Always reading," Mr. Mayawati says as he strolls out onto the deck. He is large and slow-footed, his scent a blend of sweat and curry. "I have noticed that you are always reading."

I put down the book. "Yes."

Mr. Mayawati's face is the color of meat slow-roasted on a skewer. He wears a white linen shirt, already moist in the armpits, and baggy flannel pants. "I hope I do not disturb you," he says as he reaches the chair beside me.

"Not at all," I tell him.

Mr. Mayawati grabs the front of his shirt and slaps it against his chest. "So hot so early here."

It is a heat that does not come from the sun above us, I tell Mr. Mayawati, but from the earth below, waves of it rising from our planet's molten core. "A gift from Hell, you might say."

This observation appears faintly to unsettle Mr. Mayawati, so that he quickly moves to a different subject. "What summons you so far upriver?" he asks casually.

"Things I haven't seen."

Mr. Mayawati laughs and in his laugh I see the avuncular charm that is no doubt his most effective tool, a salesman of himself. How could one refuse to go where he directs, accept what he offers, buy whatever he has to sell?

"And you?" I ask him.

"I have been made rootless by circumstances," Mr. Mayawati answers with a sad shake of the head. With a fat man's groan, he lowers himself into the chair and drops his hands onto the great bulk of his stomach. A gold tooth glints brightly when he smiles. "But I was born in Amritsar."

"Where the massacre was."

Mr. Mayawati is quite obviously surprised by the fact that I know his remote birthplace, its history, the savage slaughter that took place there.

"Ah, but that evil was avenged, was it not?" Mr. Mayawati says with a broad grin. "O'Dwyer, wasn't that his name? The Brit who thought it was all quite proper to slaughter Indians?" The smile widens even more. "Shot down in London some years later, wasn't he?"

"He was, yes," I tell him.

"A sweet vengeance," Mr. Mayawati says with satisfaction.

He laughs. "It is a good feeling, is it not, when an evil man does not get away with his crime?"

I nod. "A very good feeling." The smile I offer him has the feel of a forged document. "You've been made rootless by circumstances, you said?"

Mr. Mayawati releases a great sigh and peers out into the jungle thickness. "Yes," he says mournfully. "In my own country I am an Outcast."

His lowly status has made him a vagabond, he adds, so that he now roams the world in search of safe harbor.

"I wish only to live in peace," he tells me. "Is that so much to ask?"

When I don't answer, he glances at the book in my hand. "To my sorrow, I read very little." He thinks I have not heard him, that his voice has died beneath the rattle of the boat's ravaged engine, and so he raises his voice to hold my attention. "I see you read Spanish."

"Yes."

"And the book you are reading, may I ask what it is about?"

"A man who disappeared in Juarez," I tell him.

"An official of some sort?" Mayawati asks.

"No, a man who killed several children," I tell him. "They found some of their bloodstained clothing in his house."

"But the man himself was gone?"

"Without a trace."

Mr. Mayawati waves his hand dismissingly. "No one disappears without a trace." The deck chair releases a little child's weak cry as he shifts his weight. "I give no credit to such stories."

I look over the boat's unpainted rail, the river beyond it, the mist that boils up from its murky depths.

3

Mr. Mayawati swabs his neck with a red handkerchief. His face has the rounded folds of one long unable to control a ravenous appetite. "I prefer happy endings," he says with a robust laugh. He takes off his hat and begins to fan himself. "Perhaps I am fit only for the sort of story one reads to children." He laughs again. "Fairy tales, that sort of thing."

"But there are some stories you can approach only hesitantly," I tell him. "Fearfully." The last ragged tendrils of the river's mist dissolves into the rising heat. "As you would reach out to touch the substance of a ghost."

Mr. Mayawati's hat stops in mid-flight. "The substance of a ghost," he repeats. "Do you know such a story?"

"Yes."

"What sort of story is it?"

"It's a mystery," I answer. "Rather dark."

Mr. Mayawati releases his breath and glances out into the encroaching jungle. "Such a long way to the central station." He smiles brightly. "A fit occasion for a story, is it not?"

"I suppose."

He smiles like one in anticipation of a treat and, without fear, without hesitation, he says, "Would you mind telling it to me, then?"

"Not at all."

And so like a spider spinning the first delicate fiber of its web, I begin my tale.

I

THE STORY CAME to me by way of Arlo McBride, a man whose light blue eyes seemed oddly shattered.

"Sorry about your little boy," he said quietly.

He meant my son Teddy, who'd gone missing seven years before, and who, as it happened, would have turned fifteen the next day.

"So am I," I said dryly.

There'd been the usual community searches after his disappearance, people tromping through the woods, parting reeds and brush, peeking into storm drains. They'd been strangers for the most part, these many, nameless searchers, so that watching them I'd felt a glimmer of that human kinship the Greeks called *agape,* and without which, they said, one could not live a balanced life. That glimmer had gone out at the sad end of their endeavors, however, and since then, I'd hunkered down in the little foxhole of myself, the days of my life falling away almost soundlessly, like an ever-dwindling pulse.

"His name was Teddy, right?" Arlo asked.

"Yes," I said. "Teddy."

His body had been miles away by the time the last search had ended, all further effort given up. It had been weighted with stones and sunk to the muddy bottom of a river, where it fell prey to nature's customary indifference, the rot of bacteria, the hunger of fish. When it was at last discovered by an old angler, there was no feature left that might actually have been identifiable, nor any way to know just how long my little boy had lived captive to the man who'd taken him, nor what that man had done to him during the time they'd been together.

"I'm sure he was a great kid," Arlo said.

And indeed Teddy had been that: a sweet, winsome child, not the consolation prize for the wife who'd died giving birth to him, but a blessing all his own. For a time after his death, living in Winthrop had been like living in his coffin. There were little reminders of him everywhere: the ice-cream parlor he'd favored, the town park where he'd played, the small stretch of Jefferson Street we'd often walked in the evening, usually from the nearby ball field where we'd slung Frisbees at each other. Mildred, the retired schoolteacher who'd lived next door and often served as babysitter for Teddy on nights when I'd had to work late at the paper, had suggested that I move away from Winthrop, perhaps even back to New York, but I'd remained adamant about staying in the town I'd made a home, however briefly, with my wife and son.

"*I'm* not the guy who kidnapped and murdered an eight-year-old boy," I told Mildred. "*He's* the one who should be hounded to the far corners of the earth."

She'd noticed my hands clench as I said this. "But he's not going to be, George," she'd replied. "It's *you* the dogs are after."

Which they angrily were that night, a kind of snarling I could feel in the air around me as I sat in my usual place at the back of O'Shea's Bar, remembering Teddy, the slow burn of his lost life still scorching mine.

"A terrible thing," Arlo said, those little blue circles of cracked sky now gleaming oddly.

I took a quick sip of scotch and glanced toward the front of the bar, the usual late-night stragglers in their usual places, mostly men, any one of whom might have killed my boy. "Yeah." I shrugged as one does when confronted with an un-bearably bitter truth. "A terrible thing."

"No one ever gets over it," Arlo added. "Which makes it even more terrible."

Suddenly I recognized his face. He'd been one of the people who'd organized search parties for my son.

"You worked for the state police," I said.

He nodded. "Missing Persons. I'm retired now." He offered his hand. "Arlo McBride."

He looked to be about seventy, but there was a certain youthful energy about him, the sense of a still-faintly-glowing coal.

"So, what does a cop do when he retires?" I asked idly.

"I read, mostly," Arlo answered. "As a matter of fact, I read the book you wrote." He seemed faintly embarrassed. "The title escapes me at the moment."

"*Into the Mist,*" I said.

As it had turned out, it had been my only book, written be-fore Celeste and Teddy had lured me from a travel writer's vagabond life.

"I liked the section on that little town in Italy," Arlo went on. "The one where that barbarian king died."

He meant Alaric, the Visigothic chieftain who'd sacked Rome.

"Do you think it's true?" Arlo asked. "The way he was buried?"

After his death at Cosenza, the River Busento had been

rerouted, Alaric buried in its dry bed, the river then returned to its course, all this great labor done by slaves who'd subsequently been slaughtered so that no one could reveal where Alaric lay.

"I don't know," I answered. "But it keeps the town on the tourist map."

Arlo glanced at the clock, though absently, a man who no longer had appointments. "Anyway, I just wanted to say I'm sorry about what happened to your son."

I recalled the way he'd looked seven years before, a robust figure, with short white hair, close-cropped military style, clean-shaven, with a ruddy complexion that gave him an outdoorsman's appearance that struck me as entirely at odds with his sedentary profession. Now I saw something else: a curious intensity that attracted me, and which was probably why I pursued the conversation that evening, though it may also simply have been that he was linked to Teddy, my murdered boy, on this, another anniversary of the life he'd never had.

"Missing Persons," I said. "Did you like that work?"

Arlo's voice suddenly took on a quality I couldn't quite decipher: part gravity, part wistfulness, a nostalgia for the dark. "It's a strange kind of mystery, a missing person. Until that person's found, of course."

The memory of what I'd identified as Teddy flamed up inside me. I doused it with a gulp of scotch. "You must have a few interesting stories," I said.

Arlo nodded.

"Is there one that sticks out?"

"Yeah, there's one." Arlo seemed to sense that my gloomy solitariness was not impenetrable and slid into the booth across from me. "Her name was Katherine Carr."

"A little girl?"

"No, a woman," Arlo answered. He appeared to see this

missing woman take shape before him, then like any other such apparition, slowly fade away. "Thirty-one years old. She lived on Gilmore Street, between Cantibell and Pine. Last seen at around midnight. Standing near that little rock grotto over by the river. A bus driver saw her there."

"Very dramatic," I said. "When was this?"

"April 24, 1987."

I had no trouble imagining the subsequent search, some people moving through the woods and exploring caves while others probed the river's watery depths with long, thin poles, or dragged its bottom with grappling hooks.

"She was a writer, like you," Arlo said, "only she wrote poems."

"Was she published?"

Arlo nodded. "In those little poetry magazines. I'm sure you know the type." He added a few spare details. "She lived alone. No relatives left. No boyfriend. She had a friend over in Kingston, but that's quite a ways from here. I guess you'd have to say she lived with her writings."

"And she just vanished?" I asked.

"Like she cut a slit in this world and stepped through it into another one." His eyes drifted down toward the table, the nearly empty glass. "No one ever saw her again."

Arlo suddenly looked like a man weighted with the burden of an uncompleted mission. He drew in a slow breath, then released it no less slowly. "I sometimes wonder what she would look like now."

She would look like Teddy, I thought, reduced to mush, but I kept that thought to myself.

Arlo drained the last of his beer and returned the glass gently to the table. "Well, I better be getting home." His smile was tentative, a cautious offering. "It was nice talking to you, Mr. Gates."

With that he rose and left me alone in the booth, where I finished my drink, then headed to the little apartment I rented a few blocks away.

Outside, a light rain was falling. I turned up the collar of my coat and hurried down the street. The shops were closed, windows unlighted, so that when I glanced toward them as I walked, I could see myself in the glass, a transparent figure streaked by little rivulets of rain. At a certain point, I stopped, though I don't remember why. Perhaps it was a sound, or that eerie touch we sometimes feel, that makes us turn around, only to find no one there. For whatever reason, I came to a halt, looked to my right, and saw the man I was, not a bad man by any means, but one stripped not only of the curiosity, say, of a traveler for new sights or a scientist for discovery, or even a writer for that elusive image, but of that far simpler and more basic curiosity that says of tomorrow, *Let me see it*. In fact, I could imagine only flatness ahead, like a man walking on level pavement, with nothing before or behind or at either side of him, just an illimitable and featureless stretching forth of days.

Once in my apartment, I hung my jacket on the metal peg beside the door, walked directly into my bedroom and climbed into my never-made-up bed. The room's one charm was a skylight, and for a moment I lay on my back and let my attention drift out into the overhanging darkness. The rain had stopped, which somehow pleased me, and the sky was clearing.

The book I'd been reading lay open on the table beside the bed. It was about the Buranni, a primitive people who lived in Paraguay, remote and poverty-stricken, their hard lives ameliorated by nothing but their odd faith in the Kuri Lam, a mysterious presence whose job it was to find the most evil ones among them and cast them into a bottomless pit.

I read a few more pages, then turned off the light and lay in the darkness, my mind now returning to the particular evil one who'd stolen my son, taken him to some horrible place, and done God knows what unspeakable things to him.

These were brutal thoughts, and to escape them, I rose and walked to the window, where I looked out onto the empty sidewalks, followed the few cars that passed by, then returned to my bed and lay down again, knowing, as I had for many years now, that when sleep came it would be in the form of a drifting off, a passing out, a gift of exhaustion rather than of peace.

2

THE NEXT MORNING dawned with me slumped in the chair behind my desk. I remembered getting out of bed before first light, walking drowsily to my desk, and turning on my computer, but the specific thought that had urged me from sleep had vanished. I may have thought of Cosenza with its little wall overlooking the Busento and felt a slight rekindling of the wanderlust that had once sent me tramping across the world. Or it may have been Alaric who came to mind, so long indistinguishable from mud and water, and in that way like Teddy.

I do recall that my waking thought was of Orwell, his early writings, the days of his being down and out in Paris and London or working as a cop in Burma, the legion of nameless souls he'd encountered on his way, the *plongeurs* and tramps and rickshaw pullers, even the gharry ponies of the Far East—not men at all, but animals worked to death, and for whom, as Orwell wrote, the whip served as a substitute for food.

Why did I think of these creatures that morning? I don't know, save that in some way the thought of them directed me to the odd fact that a person once written about, whether a Visigothic chieftain or an old gray-haired rickshaw puller, is never completely missing, while a boy like Teddy, too young to have been recorded by anything other than the memory of those who knew him, is well and truly gone, or at least will be when the last of those who could recall him is gone, too.

This was not a comforting thought, of course, but such thoughts always plagued me on Teddy's birthday, so this particular dark meditation hardly surprised me. And so, as I'd done on other such occasions, I retreated to my work: little articles for the *Winthrop Examiner*, a form of journalism that was far from Orwell, to say the least, but which paid my rent and put a drink on the table at O'Shea's and by its sheer redemptive triviality, daily saved my life.

On that particular morning I had a profile to write for the Weekend section of the paper, this one on Roger Beaumont, the choirmaster of the local Episcopal church. It was the sort of assignment I was usually given at the paper: light stuff, often upbeat, as if Wyatt Chambers, the paper's editor, suspected that my troubled soul was too frail for the dark side, or any story that touched upon it. And so it was the occasional admiring profile that usually landed on my desk, like the one about ninety-three-year-old Eleanor Graham's tireless commitment to her rose garden, or some equally affirming piece, the story, for example, of a hardworking Vietnamese immigrant who'd won the lottery.

The subject of my current piece had enjoyed the rare good fortune of both loving his work and making a living at it. In the slanting light that came through the front window, I typed out the first line of the profile, careful in my initial identification to use the all-but-obligatory phrase "much admired."

I finished the piece an hour later, glanced up from the laptop, and thought suddenly of Arlo McBride, probably because having finished one profile, I was already searching for the next one. In any event, he kept returning to me as I worked on other assignments that day, the opening of a pet store, the proposed restoration of the town bandstand. For the most part, he was like a little tune playing in my head, though at other times his presence seemed more real, like someone watching me from behind the slightly parted slats of venetian blinds or through the tiny crack of a surreptitiously opened door.

Later that afternoon, I turned in my piece on the choir director to Wyatt, then, as always, waited as he read it.

"I hear the triumphant chords of the *Ode to Joy*, George," he said as he placed it in the slot for copyediting. "And you managed to omit the fact that dear Roger is quite the dancing queen." He sat back. "Care for a drink after work?"

"No, thanks," I said, my usual late afternoon numbness coming on. "Maybe another time."

And so, after leaving Wyatt, I drove out to the little cemetery where Teddy's remains, such as they were, had been buried. It was a practice I'd maintained since his death, though a decidedly muted one, void of emotional histrionics, that banging drum of grief. There was no talking to my dead boy, no conjuring up of his spirit.

In fact, I didn't even bow my head when I visited Teddy's grave on these annual occasions, for all sense of prayer had left me the moment I was certain he'd been murdered. Before that time, for all the weeks between his disappearance and the discovery of his body, I'd prayed with the ferocity of a faithless man, prayed for faith and that little sprig of hope that bloomed inside it. I'd pledged all sorts of eternities, a soulful tithe of obedience. As Faust had sold his soul to the devil, I'd offered mine to God, or Providence, or anything else it might be called, but which, for me, boiled down to whatever had the power to intervene on my son's behalf. If it had had an elephant's head on an obese body, as Shiva's son Ganesha does, I wouldn't have cared. I would have bowed to Baal in any form, dropped to my knees before any Golden Calf. I would have lit every candle in St. Patrick's, piled bags of grain on the pagoda scales, marched to Samara with my back whipped raw—anything, anything, for a single answered prayer: *Bring him safely home.*

But all that was over now, and so I didn't linger at the cemetery for any longer than it took to read his name on the stone, have a few grim thoughts, feel that jagged edge of anger that accompanied my every memory of him.

Following that small wrathful interval, I headed home, where I expected to have a quickly prepared dinner, read a while, and after that go to bed, the routine of a solitary. Nor do I think there'd have been any change to that routine had I not glimpsed a road sign I'd never noticed before, but which suddenly flared so brightly out of the descending shade that even its black letters appeared briefly illuminated: *Gilmore Street.*

I recalled that Arlo McBride had mentioned it when we'd spoken briefly in O'Shea's. Gilmore Street, he'd said, between Cantibell and Pine. Perhaps I could begin the profile with that very conversation: how it had happened by accident, just two men who'd run across each other in a bar.

But I knew I shouldn't get ahead of myself. McBride might not be interested in a profile, might be a very private man, or one with secrets. Still, a little background material wouldn't do any harm, showing interest in a story that clearly interested him.

With that thought, I turned onto Gilmore, now looking for another street sign. I found Cantibell after only a couple of blocks, and up ahead, easily visible beneath a pale streetlight, the sign for Pine.

I pulled over to the curb midway between the two streets, then got out and stood looking south, to where Gilmore came to a dead end, then north toward the river. The little rock grotto where Katherine Carr had last been seen was only a short distance away, a stroll I estimated at no more than twelve minutes.

I stopped in mid-thought, surprised that I'd quite unconsciously calculated the time it had taken for a woman I'd never known to take her final walk. Why had I done that? I had no answer, save that the curious impulse I'd followed had seemed to come from that strange inner sanctum where our dearest hopes and darkest fears reside like a quarrelsome couple in a monstrously cramped bed, every movement of the one a discomfort to the other.

I sank my hand into the pocket of my jacket and looked at the houses that fronted Gilmore Street. They were quite unassuming: all of wood, with small front lawns shaded by large trees. A few had painted wooden shutters with matching trim. Most were lined with bushes and shrubs that had been planted along the front and sides. The grass was green and thick, and at one house, a motionless sprinkler rested near the middle of the yard, a bright red hose snaking from it to an outdoor nozzle a few yards away. It was a neighborhood of families: kids playing in the street, parents calling from front porches at the end of day, not the usual choice of a single woman. In fact, it was exactly the sort of neighborhood I'd fled after Teddy's death—fled wisely, it seemed to me, since there is nothing more heartbreaking than the sounds of other people's children when you have lost your own.

I turned back to my car. Before getting in, I looked up Gilmore again, now thinking of Arlo McBride, the missing woman he'd mentioned in O'Shea's the night before. The street's lovely trees and neat little houses gave no hint that anything tragic had ever happened here, an ordinariness that suddenly returned me to a moment years before, when I'd found myself off the coast of Saipan, staring at the cliffs from which Japanese parents, fearing the atrocities they were certain American troops would visit upon them, had hurled their children, then leaped themselves. American sailors had watched through their binoculars as the tragedy unfolded, helpless to save the panicked parents or to draw their eyes away from the dreadful scene itself. But years later, as my ship drifted by, the cliffs betrayed nothing of those terrible events. They were craggy and rather squat, not at all impressive. I had stood on the Cliffs of Moher, tentatively neared the fearful precipice at Slieve League. Saipan's heights were nothing in comparison. It was only my knowledge of what had once happened there that gave them resonance, the suffering that had topped those undistinguished cliffs, parents with babies in their arms or holding the hands of small children, all that pain hovering on that rocky ledge.

But something tragic had also once touched Gilmore Street, and thinking that, my feet now on the same pavement a missing woman had once walked, I suddenly imagined her moving past the same modest houses, the only difference being that it had been about midnight when she had taken her lonely walk, and so most of the windows would have been dark, most everyone inside already sound asleep.

Even so, someone had once known the fate of this missing woman, and for a moment I imagined him waiting behind the wheel of a beat-up old sedan. As if I were an invisible presence in the backseat of that same car, I saw his broad shoulders,

large ears, and thick, muscular neck, followed the curl of cigarette smoke that twined around him, heard the caught breath
when he spotted what had surely been his prey.

But this was, itself, an odd surmise, I realized. For I knew
nothing of how or why or by what circumstance this missing
woman had vanished. And certainly I had no idea if there'd
ever even been such a man lurking on this street, or if so,
whether he'd had any of the stereotypically brutish physical
characteristics I'd given him. I knew only that such men had
always existed and always would, and that many years after
Katherine Carr's disappearance, on a different street within
this same small town, one such man had spotted a little boy
with blond curls standing at a bus stop, glancing about, waiting for his father, wondering how long he'd have to wait in
this pouring rain.

3

GIVEN THE DARK turn of my mind, I might have predicted another sleepless night. The surprise, instead, was that I slept, and that in the torment of that sleep, held captive by it, I dreamed of Teddy's capture.

It was an imagined scene I'd successfully avoided most nights, but which, on this occasion, drifted through my mind as if carried on the same mists that bore the Burannis' mythical child-stealers over the jungle floor.

I saw my son as he got off the bus that gray afternoon, followed invisibly behind as he chatted briefly with a neighborhood friend. In my dream, his lips are moving and his head is thrown back in a laugh, but there is no sound. It is as if I'm watching a silent movie.

The exchange ends with some little grade-school joke and an affectionate tug at the bill of my son's red baseball cap as the two boys part, Jimmy Dane heading off to the right, his home only a block away, while Teddy remains in place, standing near the bus stop, waiting for me because a sudden storm has broken and earlier that morning, I'd promised to pick him up if it rained.

He straightens his cap as the storm intensifies, now with occasional lightning, which always scared him more. In my dream, the streets clear abruptly, people vanishing not into cars and houses, but simply disappearing, as if effervesced by the rain itself, the street now deserted save for Teddy and a figure whose approach I see over my son's shoulder, a man in a yellow rain slicker, his right hand sliding beneath it, as if reaching for something tucked under the opposite arm.

In this vision, I reach for my son's shoulder, but I have no body, no hand to draw him beneath my own protective arm. Again and again I grab for him, but my hand passes through his flesh and so I cry out in warning.

But there is no sound, so that my scream falls silently on a world gone deaf. Then—quite suddenly—I hear the rain thudding against the sidewalk and slapping through the trees. I try to scream again, but before I can release my warning, I am drawn up and away, as if seized by a vertical thrust of wind, Teddy now visible far beneath me, growing smaller and smaller until, like a bird circling high above, I see a red dot touch a yellow slash, then disappear inside it.

I awoke from this dream exhausted by my own powerlessness, all the energy that had been drained by its vision of futility, like an armless man forever reaching and reaching, but with no hope of gaining a grasp.

I glanced at the clock. It was just after midnight, and I'd actually fallen asleep while working on my latest piece, an old woman's triumphant struggle to hold on to her house against the encroachment of developers. She'd been a talkative sort, as I'd discovered, who'd often interrupted the interview with questions of her own, most all of them about my past. I'd told her that I'd once been a travel writer, but that those days were behind me, that I'd settled in Winthrop some years before, and planned to stay here.

"And are you a family man?" she asked.

"I once was," I told her, then quickly glanced at my notes. "So, when did you first hear that Allied Properties was interested in your house?"

And so on and so forth, until I'd gathered enough material to write the piece whose final page had gleamed from my laptop screen as I'd awakened quite suddenly later that same night.

What to do till dawn? More than *to be or not to be,* that is the question. My answer to it had long been O'Shea's.

I was there ten minutes later, in my usual booth at the back, watching the men at the bar, always with an eye to singling him out, something that would catch my eye, some little trinket I might have given Teddy in the past, a piece of jade from Hong Kong, for example, or some figure carved from amber I'd bought at Cracow's central market, cheap souvenirs of my traveling life, entirely unnoticed by everyone else, but to me proof enough of what he'd done to my little boy.

It was a totally hopeless scenario, of course, but I'd never entirely stopped harboring the notion that the man who'd killed my son would one day walk into my sights. I'd even played out the details of what I'd do next in order to make sure that he didn't get away. First, I would engage this man in idle talk, find out where he lived. At some point after that, I would carry out his execution: shoot or stab or strangle him, and by that murder save someone else's little boy as I had failed to save my own. I knew this was a typical Hollywood ending, but fantasy is grief's nearest companion, and this miraculous act of retribution had been my chief fantasy since Teddy's death, the only one that gave me energy, pumped life into my inner world, the prospect of murder working in me like a heater in a stone-cold room.

"My God, George!" Charlie Wilkins came up from behind me and slid into the booth. "Did you sleep in your clothes?"

He was a fellow reporter at the *Examiner,* the type the paper called on for breaking news of fire and accident, but who was never assigned features because Wyatt had never had much regard for him as a writer or a man. He'd been married twice, but had been "bitched out," as he put it, both times, the children he'd spawned with these two women now located at a place he identified only as somewhere out west.

"So, you working on anything?" he asked.

"The old woman who beat Allied Properties," I said. "I finished it a few minutes ago."

"I read your piece on the pet shop." He laughed. "Very cuddly, George."

"For cuddly, I'm your man," I told him.

He laughed again, the easy laugh of a man who considered himself something of a worldling, at least by Winthrop standards.

"I had an idea for a piece on that brothel over in Kingston," Charlie added. "Wyatt said I'd have to find a human-interest angle in it, but I haven't found one yet."

A waitress came over. I was set. Charlie ordered a beer.

"You hit many places like that, when you were globe-hopping?" Charlie asked. "Brothels?"

By globe-hopping, Charlie meant the time before Celeste and Teddy, when rattling trains and chugging riverboats had been my only homes.

"Yeah, I saw a few brothels," I answered.

Some had been more memorable than others, but only one came to mind at that moment, an undistinguished dive in the whorehouse district of Nuevo Laredo, the haunt of bikers and college-boy one-nighters, along with the usual border flot-sam. He'd come in with an eerie sense of being himself un-real, a man, dressed to the nines, his shoes brightly polished, hair slicked back in a full, slightly graying pompadour. For five consecutive nights I'd watched him take the dimly lighted dance floor, wheel and turn whatever bar girls took his fancy, teaching them the steps and in the process irrigating their parched souls with humor and compliments and what seemed a strangely genuine regard. Then, like a prince on the mid-night, he'd leave them with a nod and, strangest of all, a soft kiss on both eyes—not a whoremaster, this one, but a feeder of hungry hearts.

"I read about the ones in Thailand," Charlie said. "Crazy, man. Girls smoking cigarettes with their—"

"At least those girls are inside," I interrupted dryly. "Not like the ones who work along the Trans-Africa Highway."

With that, I told Charlie the story of a truck stop in Uganda, a shack of corrugated tin that dispensed beer, smokes, canned meat, and various supplies pilfered from hijacked trucks bear-ing First World charity, barley, sorghum, baby formula in huge vats. The girls had stretched themselves out on cardboard pal-lets behind a mound of trash nearly six feet high, the grunts of their johns clearly audible above the idle of diesel engines. Since then, efforts had been made to educate them, at least as far as AIDS was concerned, but I had little doubt that the next generation of doomed girls was already at work on the usual cardboard pallets. The people who covered this part of the world had shared a single, hopeless code for the intransigent horror of the place: *AWA: Africa Wins Again.*

I took a quick sip of scotch when I finished the story. "So, what else is new?"

Charlie shrugged. "I had another idea besides that whore-house in Kingston," he said, "but Wyatt wasn't crazy about that one, either." He took a doleful sip from his glass. "There's always something missing in my stuff. That's what Wyatt thinks."

I knew that this "missing something" was the beating heart of a story, and all that bore the reader toward it, a somberness within the pace and a gravity within the words.

"Anyway," Charlie said. "I thought I might write a feature on this girl who has progeria. You know what that is?"

"The premature-aging disease, right?"

Charlie nodded. "Yeah. She's twelve now, but she looks like an old lady." He glanced at his watch like a man always on the clock, though I knew he wasn't. "Heart disease takes them out." He went on with a few more details about the progress of progeria, then added, "Sandra Parshall, the woman who runs Brookwood Residential, she says the kid's brilliant. Reads all the time. Murder mysteries, stuff like that. She likes coming up with better endings than the authors were able to think up." He smiled. "A little genius, that's what Sandra says."

Charlie's beer arrived. He took a sip. "I could tell Wyatt liked the idea, but figured I wasn't the guy to write it." He grew quiet for a moment, thinking something over. Finally he said, "So, would you like to do it, George, a profile of this little girl?"

I shrugged.

"You got something better on the line?"

I'd not planned to say what I said next, since I never talked about Teddy, and didn't on this occasion, either, save that what I said struck me as somehow about him, too. "You know Arlo McBride?"

"An old cop, yeah. Used to work for the state police."

"Missing Persons," I said. "He's evidently still thinking about a woman who disappeared twenty years ago."

Charlie laughed. "Old cops are always mulling over old cases."

"Exactly," I said. "So I thought I might do a profile of him. Just the type you mean: old detective, obsessed with an unsolved case. People can never get enough of that."

"Yeah, but it's not a cuddly piece, George," Charlie said.

"I thought I might give it a try, though," I said tentatively, by no means convinced.

Charlie laughed. "Kiss your St. Jude medal first."

Normally such an allusion would have vanished from my mind, but I suddenly thought of St. Jude, so strikingly handsome in official church portraits, long reddish hair, the glow of health in his rosy cheeks, a serene smile and eyes far too untroubled for the role he'd been assigned: patron saint of hopeless cases.

Then another face abruptly came to mind: my father's, as he lay in his final illness, his white hair combed back, though left with a curl that hung raffishly over his forehead. We'd been talking of his own checkered past when the question came to me: "What did you struggle most against, Dad?"

His answer had struck me as so darkly resigned to the human fate that my eyes had suddenly glistened. "The inevitable," he'd said. Something in my father's remembered tone at that moment reminded me of Arlo, the murky world of missing things, how sad it always is, the unresolved.

"Her name was Katherine Carr," I said. "The missing woman Arlo keeps thinking about. She lived here in Winthrop and was some sort of poet, evidently. Not famous or anything like that, of course. Arlo says she published her stuff in little literary magazines."

"Good name for a poet," Charlie said with a wide grin. "Alliterative."

At that instant, a first line came to me: *Katherine Carr's name was as lovely as her fate was grim.* I knew it wasn't good enough to make the final cut, but it didn't seem bad for a starter.

"Yeah, it *is* a pretty name," I said. "Katherine Carr."

In a certain kind of story, she might have materialized suddenly at that moment, a figure in a shadowy corner, appearing only for an instant, alluringly, of course, like a tantalizing flash of snow white ankle at the hem of a Victorian dress. But the possibility of such apparitions meant nothing to me then, and so I saw only the space where Arlo McBride had once stood, now empty, with no hint of his afterimage in the air, and certainly none of the missing woman he could not get off his mind.

4

IT WAS ARLO HIMSELF who was on my mind the next morning. His name was in the phone book. I waited until it seemed late enough to call a retired man, then dialed the number.

"It's George Gates," I said when he answered. "We talked for a little while at O'Shea's."

His voice was oddly weighted, like one suddenly drawn into a dark contemplation.

"Yes," he said. "About your son."

"And your work, too," I said. "A case you recalled. A missing woman."

"Katherine Carr," Arlo said.

There are certain ways a man may say a woman's name. It can be said with love, either passionate or long-enduring. Or it can be said with bitterness, as the names of women sound in the mouths of scorned men. But it was neither love nor bitterness I heard in Arlo's voice. There was nothing fraternal or

27

avuncular about it, either, and certainly nothing paternal, no hint of the melancholy loss that tinged Teddy's name on the increasingly rare occasions when I spoke of him. If anything, it was a strange uncertainty I heard when he said her name, the way one might speak of something that had both real and imagined qualities, like Innisfree or Xanadu.

"I'm interested in . . ." I stopped because I knew I couldn't say "Katherine Carr," because no magazine, or even the local Weekend Section of the *Winthrop Examiner* would be interested in a case as cold as hers, one in which there was no hope of resolution, thus, from my point of view, a story doomed to hang, with no ending to nail down, and thus, by common lights, unsatisfying. But as I'd said to Charlie Wilkins, there might be interest in a profile of an old detective obsessed with an unsolved case. Such tales were familiar, of course, but they also possessed a certain deathless appeal: elements of mystery and intrigue along with the always-popular notion of a hero-cop, relentless, high-minded, unselfish. I didn't know if Arlo McBride was such a man, but finding out if he were, or at least learning enough for me to write about him as such, seemed worth a try.

"I'm interested in, well, you, Arlo."

"Me? There's nothing interesting about me, George."

It was a blunt statement, beyond further discussion. If I wanted to write about Arlo, I would first have to show some interest in the case that haunted him.

"Okay," I said cautiously. "Katherine Carr. Her case will never be solved, right?"

"Not by me, that's for sure." Arlo's tone was completely genuine, with no hint of modesty, let alone false modesty.

"But you never forgot it?" I asked.

Arlo didn't answer immediately, and because of that I felt

that my hold upon him was tenuous, our discussion one he might at any moment bring to an end.

"Do you ever think of reopening it?" I asked quickly.

"Reopening it?"

I felt a tug on the line, reeled it in gently.

"At least we could talk about it at some point," I said. "You could tell me what you know about her."

There was another brief pause before Arlo spoke again. "I *should* tell you about Katherine, George," he said.

His voice struck me as unexpectedly urgent, but not in the way of alarm. It was too quiet for that, too carefully considered, his urgency not the product of some unanticipated threat or of something coming suddenly to a boil. It was more like the urge to make an admission, though not the confessional sort, a penchant, say, for licking high-heeled shoes. With Arlo, I decided, the secret would more likely be professional, that he'd missed a vital clue, mislaid a critical piece of information, and due to that misstep, however inadvertent, the case of Katherine Carr would forever go unsolved.

"But first you'd need to read her story," he added.

Outside my window, a bird suddenly took flight. I don't recall whether it was large or small, dull or brightly colored, a sparrow or a jay. I know only that as it took wing, I felt rather like a child in a fairy tale, halted where the road forks: one path familiar, the other unknown.

"Her friend Audrey has all the stuff Katherine wrote," Arlo added. "You'd need to talk to her at some point if you get interested."

As if it were being played out in my mind, I watched the child at the fork in the road take its first step down the unfamiliar path.

"I'd like to hear a little more about it," I said.

There was a pause during which I knew that Arlo was considering my answer. I guessed that it was probably some all-but-inaudible tone in my voice rather than anything more concrete that would decide the issue for him.

"How about the Calico," he suggested finally. "At two thirty?"

I arrived at the Calico at 2:15. It was a large steakhouse, but nearly deserted at such an early hour, the only customers a couple of dark-suited businessmen nursing gin and tonics. The lounge was tarted up in cowboy motif, with longhorns bolted to the wall behind the bar. Other ranch droppings were scattered all around, saddlebags, spurs, a rusty hand water pump and trough, even a holstered six-gun, its barrel no doubt run through with a metal screw or plugged with wax. It was entirely phony, of course, and it reminded me of a similar place I'd seen in, of all places, Vienna, only on this occasion there'd been an Alpine motif, with skis and snowshoes and thin layers of ground Styrofoam to simulate snow. I'd come there to meet a doubtful character who'd claimed to be the inspiration for *The Third Man,* a swindler who said he'd run the table on a whole host of prominent Eastern Bloc officials. The scheme had involved a shimmering mother lode of diamonds pilfered from the death camps, already an old, almost-always-false story, but to which had been added a macabre detail, the "fact" that this treasure trove of jewels had been buried in infant caskets in village churchyards throughout Eastern Europe, all under the same name, Otherion, which was, according to this tale, the elf translation for Victor. Elf? It was, of course, a far-fetched tale, but I was young and curious and open to the most outlandish hopes, and so had agreed to the meeting.

The Third Man had never turned up, but during the course

of a long evening, another gentleman had: large and barrel-chested, but with abnormally short legs, so that despite his size, he appeared oddly dwarfish. He said his name was Max, and never went further as far as identification. He'd spoken excellent English, complete with little Briticisms like "ever so much" and "to hospital," without the American "the." We'd hit it off instantly, as strangers sometimes do, especially strangers who are traveling and thus have little time to grow to like one another, so that it is either done quickly, this give-and-take of affection, or not done at all.

In any event, the evening passed into early morning, the streets of Vienna now deserted, I at last ready to depart when Max said, "Do you want to see the dark side?"

"The dark side?"

"Of Vienna." Max smiled. "The Viennese demimonde."

I nodded, though with a twinge of apprehension, now wondering for the first time if this huge man might be the elfish Victor. It was not a question to which I ever found an answer. I know only that for the next few hours Max made good on his promise, leading me past the Plague Monument and far from the grand boulevard of the Ring, into a criminal shadow world, smoke-filled gambling dens and the back rooms of fences and shylocks, the countinghouses and securities exchanges of a secret economy of black-market goods and laundered money, the traffic of arms and drugs and forged documents.

It was dawn by the time this presentation of Max's Viennese Mahagonny came to an end. By then we'd taken a cab into the hills overlooking Vienna, where we stood peering down upon the whole sleeping city as the first rays of dawn rouged the waters of the Danube Canal.

"Thanks for the tour, Max," I said.

He smiled, then waved me toward his little gray Citroën for the drive back into town. As I got out at my hotel, he offered his hand. "Always remember, George," he said. "The Unseen." And with that, he drove away, leaving me with nothing but the dark phantasm of a storied evening made all the more mysterious by the fact that I'd never seen Max again, never heard his voice or received a note in the mail, a character who'd made himself perfect, as it struck me suddenly, by vanishing.

"George?"

Vienna dissolved before me, and I was once again rooted in place, staring up at Arlo McBride.

He was wearing black pants and a light blue shirt, his shoes black and carefully polished, nothing rumpled about him, nothing in disarray. He might have been a retired military officer or the head of a small company. It was the sort of dress that carried a purpose, and in Arlo's case it seemed to insist that he was a down-to-earth, no-nonsense kind of man. That had been my impression all along, however, so it seemed strange that he'd found the need to declare it.

"Thanks for coming," I said.

I'd expected an exchange of pleasantries, but from the moment Arlo took his seat, it was obvious that he hadn't come for an idle chat. Rather, he appeared to be scouting the territory, a man on reconnaissance, the proposed mission by no means certain.

"I worked the original case," Arlo began. "We had a few leads, but nothing came of them, so that in the end all we had left were the writings Katherine left behind."

"Which Katherine's friend has," I said.

"Audrey," Arlo said. "I talked to her last night. She's very wary about giving Katherine's story to a reporter. But I told her about you, about your . . . tragedy. It was something the two of you have in common, it seemed to me, a lost loved one. So she's willing to give you some of what Katherine wrote, but she won't give it all to you because she's afraid you'd leap to judgment."

"Judgment about what?"

"About Katherine," Arlo answered. "Audrey doesn't want anything crazy written about her." He took an envelope from his jacket pocket and handed it to me. "Audrey said I could give you this. It's the opening chapter of her story and a few poems Katherine wrote when she was young. She said the poems would give you an idea of what Katherine was like."

I took the envelope and put it in the now-battered leather briefcase my father had given me years before, and which had tramped with me about the world.

"They found the story and one last little poem in the house after Katherine disappeared," Arlo added now. "The poem didn't have anything to do with what happened to Katherine, but the story did, so that's what we looked at when we were trying to find out what happened to her."

"Did they find anything else?" I asked. "In the house, I mean?"

"You mean clues?" Arlo asked. He shook his head. "Well, there was no sign of a struggle, if that's what you mean."

"So, the cops, they—"

Arlo lifted a hand to silence me. "We'll talk after you've read the stuff I just gave you."

We didn't discuss anything having to do with Katherine after that. Instead we talked quite amiably about his own background, the long years of law enforcement, work he'd found frustrating and at times fruitless, save for occasional moments he described simply as "unexplainable."

"Unexplainable in what way?" I asked.

"The way some kid will turn around at just the right moment, see a guy coming out of the woods," Arlo answered. "That's how they caught Whitey Lombard last month."

The *Examiner* had detailed the arrest of Whitey Lombard aka John Merrill Hersh aka Edgar Price, an itinerant day laborer who'd murdered a farm girl in a neighboring county, and who might have gone on to murder many more had a boy on a bicycle not glanced toward a break in the forest as a man stepped out of it.

"The kid turned around at just the right moment," Arlo added. "He said it was like he got tapped on the shoulder, like someone said, 'Look there.'"

"Even killers have bad luck, I guess," I said.

"Seems so, yes," Arlo said.

Then, as if cued by manners, he turned the topic to me.

"So, what other stories are you working on, George?" he asked.

"I haven't got anything pinned down at the moment," I answered. "But maybe something about a girl who has progeria. Premature aging. A very bright girl, by all accounts. She's over at Brookwood. Doesn't have much time left, evidently."

Arlo's gaze was the opposite of searing, or even penetrating. There was something almost feathery about it, though this seemed carefully controlled, his eyes like heated objects he kept at a distance from whatever he looked upon. "How old is she?" he asked.

"Twelve," I said.

Charlie had added a few other details before I'd left him at O'Shea's, so to keep the conversation rolling, I related them to Arlo: how rare progeria was, only about a hundred people living with it at any given time.

"They have tiny, pointed noses, these kids," I added. "Which makes their eyes seem enormous."

Arlo asked no questions, so I just kept going.

"By the time they get to middle school, they're old," I said. Old, often breathless, I added, and incontestably dying of the cardiac disease that would kill most of them either before or shortly after they reached early adolescence.

"What about their minds?" Arlo asked.

"Clear as a bell," I answered. "To the end." Thus, although old in body and appearance, I went on, a victim of progeria died with all the torridly hopeful expectations of a wildly youthful heart. They did not become forgetful, as old people often did, nor lose a whit of their own identities. To the last breath, they knew who they were and where they were and exactly what was happening to them.

Arlo remained silent for a few moments before he asked another question.

"What is it about this story that makes you want to tell it?"

I hadn't known what attracted me to the story before Arlo's question, but suddenly I did. "Living without hope," I answered.

"Katherine was like that," Arlo said. "At least until—"

He stopped abruptly, clearly realizing, as I saw, that he'd inadvertently returned us to the original subject of our meeting, a place he didn't want to go. "The girl you may write about," he said quickly. "What's her name?"

Her name, as it turned out, was Alice Barrows, and Sandra Parshall, Charlie's neighbor, was very forthcoming about her when I called Brookwood Residential later that day.

"Her father deserted the family early on, and her mother died last year," she said. "Alice has been at Brookwood ever since." There was a pause before Sandra added, "I think you'll find her very interesting."

"In what way?"

"Her intelligence," Sandra answered. "She has a very high IQ, but there's more to her than that. She has tremendous curiosity. She's mature, and she faces the hopelessness of her

35

situation with this"—she stopped and searched for the appropriate word until she found it—"this . . . stoicism."

It was a rather fancy word, I thought, though I couldn't have imagined one more calculated to draw me in. Of course, I also knew that it had a range of interpretations. Alice might simply be shy or prone to silence, either of which could easily be mistaken for fortitude in the face of trouble.

"So, do you want to meet Alice?" Sandra asked.

I knew that it wasn't really my kind of story, a dying girl, even a smart, mature, stoical one, but I recalled my earlier conversation with Arlo, knew that a feature article about him was anything but certain. A fallback position seemed well advised. "I could drop by after work," I said.

It was nearly five when Sandra Parshall received me in her small office at Brookwood Residential. She was a woman in her late thirties with somewhat lusterless brown hair, cut in a way that was ruthlessly indifferent to style.

"I read that piece you wrote about the choir director," she said. "It helped me decide."

"Decide what?"

"That you're the right person for Alice to talk to," she said. "Frankly, I wasn't sure about Charlie, but I wanted someone to write about Alice, and I didn't know anyone else to ask." Her expression had a hint of warning. "I don't want a carnival show made of her. She's not some kind of circus freak." She smiled suddenly. "But like I said, that piece of yours about the choir director, it made me think you're the right person for Alice. One line in particular."

She saw I had no idea what line I'd written in my piece on Roger Beaumont that had convinced her that I was the right person to tell Alice Barrows's story.

"You were talking about the voices of the choir," Sandra

said. "About the voices the choir director brought together, those harmonies, and you said that sounds may go on forever because sound is a wave. And I thought, Alice won't go on forever, not like a beautiful sound, going out into space. But she's here now, and she's a very interesting person, and people ought to know she was here before she goes. I've told her all this, even mentioned that you might be interested in talking to her. She wasn't crazy about the idea, but she wasn't completely against it, either." She leaned forward. "She doesn't want to get close to anyone, and so she keeps to herself. She never goes into the dayroom, and takes all her meals alone."

"So what does she do all day?" I asked, already beginning to doubt that Alice would be a good subject for a profile.

"She reads," Sandra answered.

"Mysteries, mostly, according to Charlie," I said. "He told me that she likes to find solutions that are better than the ones the writers came up with."

"That's right," Sandra said. "But Alice also spends a lot of time on her computer." With that she smiled one of those institutionally bright smiles, all ribbons and bows, the cheery expression of professional caregivers, rosily painted over masks of sheer dread. "She's in her room," she said. "Shall we go?"

She was sitting in her bed, tapping at a laptop, when we came into the room. For a moment, she didn't look up, but instead kept her attention trained on the computer's softly glowing screen, her brow quite deeply furrowed, eyes squinting, like someone trying to bring a blurred image into focus. Teddy had had a similar focus, his concentration oddly like hers, so that quite without willing it, I connected Alice to my lost boy, though distantly, in the way we occasionally glimpse some aspect of a dead person—the glimmer of a smile, the arch of an eyebrow—in the face of a still-living one.

"Good afternoon, Alice," Sandra said in an upbeat tone

that seemed remarkably cheerful in light of what appeared before us, Alice Barrows in the fullness of her affliction, her legs curled beneath her, almost doll-like in her smallness.

Alice slowly drew her attention from the computer, though with a strange sense of this being a worrisome experience, as if she were being forced back into a world she did not welcome.

"Hello," she said coolly.

"Hi."

She said nothing further, though she seemed to be taking my measure in some way. Then, to my surprise, she glanced toward the window at her right in the pointed way that instantly called my attention to its peculiar ironies.

Like one silently instructed to do so, I looked toward where she indicated, and saw several mythical creatures of colored glass, all of them strung from the top of the window, so that the light passed through them, dappling Alice's white hospital gown and bedding and even the room's interior walls with pastel leprechauns and munchkins and unicorns, along with several different renderings of Tinkerbell.

"My mother liked this kind of stuff," Alice said. "I keep them to remember her."

It was not these fanciful creatures that grabbed my attention, however, but a painting, clearly printed from the Internet and taped to the wall beside the window, a grim, Hieronymus Bosch sort of rendering that showed a group of child-stealing changelings, all of them laughing demonically as they stuffed a little boy, terrified and crying, into a burlap sack.

"That's pretty disturbing," I said, though lightly, merely as a way of engaging her.

Alice watched me intently. "It happens, though. Kids *are* taken."

And I thought, *She's looked me up on that computer of hers. She knows about Teddy.*

I decided that if she were baiting me in some way, I wouldn't take the bait.

"Yeah, it happens," I said with an indifferent shrug. "But why dwell on it?"

Alice didn't answer, and so we simply stared at each other until Sandra Parshall leaped into the breach.

"Alice, as you've probably guessed, this is Mr. Gates," she said brightly. "The man I mentioned to you, the one from the paper."

Alice continued to stare at me, though exactly what she was in the midst of evaluating I couldn't guess, for all she could have seen was a man of normal height and weight, wearing a jacket and open-collared shirt, completely ordinary in appearance.

The sight that confronted me, however, was anything but ordinary, for Alice Barrows, twelve years old, looked like an old woman. But that was only the beginning of what progeria had done to her. Her chin came to a point as sharp as a whittled stick, and her head seemed to bloom from it like a misshapen flower from a tiny vase. Her eyes were brown and very large, the skin around them deeply creased, her face a web of wrinkles. It was the same with her hands, blue veins bulging from pale, almost translucent flesh, without liver spots, but appearing ancient nonetheless. She was completely bald, a condition she made no effort to conceal, no hat nor cap nor bandanna, so that the top of her head shone softly beneath the lamp, her skull somewhat oblong, with two delicately molded ears protruding from either side like tiny mushrooms from pale bark.

Sandra looked back and forth between us. "Well, I don't think you need me anymore, so I'll just be on my way."

And with that, she was gone, so that Alice and I now faced each other without an intermediary and with little clue as to how we should proceed, or even if we should.

Finally I said, "I understand you're quite a reader." I glanced at the bookshelf beside her bed. It was about four feet high and filled to overflowing with books, most of them mysteries of the familiar sort: Agatha Christie and Arthur Conan Doyle, along with *Tales of Poe,* the only hardback on the shelf. "I see you like mysteries."

"My mother wanted me to read only books with happy endings," Alice said. Her tone was guarded, as if she were being gingerly probed for information she preferred to withhold. "I do research, too. On the Internet."

"What kind of research?" I asked.

Rather than answer, she asked a question of her own: "Sandra said you wrote a book. Is that true?"

"Yes."

"What's the title?"

I had a feeling that Alice already knew the answer to this question, but I answered her anyway.

"*Into the Mist,*" I said.

"What's it about?"

"Unsolved mysteries," I told her.

"Like murders?" she asked.

"In some cases," I said, "but sometimes it was just a person who vanished, or a body that could never be found. People like Judge Crater."

Before I could say more, Alice glanced down at her computer screen and began tapping. "Joseph Force Crater," she read when the page loaded. "A New York State Supreme Court judge."

"That's right," I said, now quite certain that Alice's only

40

companion was her computer, its mechanical light wholly neutral, an eye that did not look back, see a wizened girl, feel pity or revulsion.

"Disappeared in 1930," Alice added, still looking at her computer screen. "Never seen again." She looked up. "What do you think happened to him?"

"I don't know," I said. "Perhaps he ran away. Perhaps he was murdered. But solving the cases isn't what my book is about."

She looked at me quizzically.

"It's about the need to find an answer," I explained. "Or maybe just to hope for one."

"An answer for what?"

"For things that disappear. Like Judge Crater."

"Or the Lost Colony," Alice said. "Have you ever been there? Where they all disappeared?"

I nodded. "When I was a travel writer."

Alice drew in a long breath, a slight wheeze at the end of it. "I'd like to travel," she said.

"Where would you like to go?" I asked.

She shrugged. "Just away from here."

Her voice was small, a kind of human chirp, and when she spoke, tiny vertical creases appeared above her upper lip. But there was a terrible resignation in it, too, like the voice of an executioner whose condemned prisoner was herself.

"Just away from here," she repeated, then started to say something else, but stopped, her face growing abruptly fearful as her hand lifted slowly to her nose, the drop of blood that suddenly oozed from it. She drew back her hand and stared at the red tip of her finger.

"I'm bleeding!" she cried sharply.

I stood up, but did nothing, so that I must have appeared

entirely frozen as a large black woman in a green uniform rushed past me and swept Alice into her arms. "I'm bleeding!" Alice cried out again as she was whisked from the room, her large eyes peering at me from over her fleeing shoulder, a bloody tissue in her wrinkled hand, reaching out, hopelessly reaching out into nothingness, as I had a thousand times imagined Teddy reaching hopelessly for me.

5

BLOOD IS A GREAT awakener of dormant memories. Driving away from my brief encounter with Alice Barrows, I recalled a murder room I'd once visited as a cub reporter bent on seeing everything a grim world had to offer. "It's a slasher killing," warned the head of the cleanup crew I was writing about. Then he opened the door, stepped back, and let me in. "The messiest kind."

Which was true enough, as I discovered, for the walls and ceiling and bedding of the room had looked not just bloodstained, but lathered in blood, as if the room itself had bled. For an instant, as I'd watched Alice disappear into the bathroom down the hall, I'd felt somehow in that murder room again, her bloody handkerchief mysteriously connected to that earlier blood-drenched room, so that for a dreadful, chilling moment, it had seemed a broken, blood-fed weave, this life, a vast and impossibly intricate system of ruptured arteries and veins.

At home, the small red light was flashing on my answering machine. I pressed the button and listened. It was a recorded message, something about car loans.

I deleted it, walked over to my desk and, as I often did, drew open the drawer and stared at Celeste's wedding ring, remembering her, then Teddy. Often these were pleasant memories, though tinged with loss; remembrances of trips I'd taken with Celeste, or of little outings with Teddy. But that evening, it was the day of Teddy's disappearance I recalled, the promise I'd made to pick him up at the bus stop if it stormed, the unavoidable fact I hadn't, and that that decision, taken casually as it had been, had made all the difference.

In the midst of this memory, I glanced at my briefcase and seemed to feel something stir inside it, stir almost physically, like a tiny, long-dead animal now mysteriously returning to life.

I opened it and took out the envelope Arlo had given me earlier that afternoon. Inside the envelope, I found two other envelopes, one marked "poems" and the other marked "story." I opened the poems envelope first, probably because it was considerably thinner, or perhaps because I'd never been a particular fan of poetry, and like one who prefers icing and so eats the cake part first, I wanted simply to get through the poems in order to get on to the story.

There were only seven poems inside the envelope, all of them photostats of handwritten manuscripts, so I had no idea if any had ever been published. None was dated, but the poems themselves had the feel of youth about them. For the most part, they were nature poems of the type familiar to anyone who'd read Wordsworth's "Daffodils." Reading them, I imagined Katherine in anachronistic hippie attire, skipping through flowery fields in an ankle-length peasant skirt. She didn't claim to wander lonely as a cloud, but forest rambles

44

and bird sightings punctuated her poems, and she often lapsed into adoration of a natural world whose beauty and benevolence she apparently did not doubt.

Were they any good, Katherine's poems? Not particularly, though of the type, they weren't bad, at least insofar as her rhymes rarely sounded forced and she kept the beat of the lines in firm control. Beyond such technical matters, there was a pronounced sweetness of heart in the sentiments she expressed, so that I got a sense of her as a kindly spirit, harmless to living things.

It was all very bright and young and full of extravagant hope, and I expected more of the same when I turned to her prose, but instead found something quite different in the opening section of the "weird little story" she had left behind:

NOW

Maldrow's world is filled with sharp and blunt objects, knives, saws, ice picks, bricks and bats, crude instruments of murder, beside which a bullet, quick and clean, seems almost a leaden mercy. Now various murder scenes wash through his mind, rocky crevices and isolated trails, byways and ravines, rain-soaked fields. He sees a bicycle rudely tossed into a ditch, a small red wagon turned upside down in a rushing stream, a metal merry-go-round creaking in a deserted playground, carrying like the last offering of a lazy Susan, the gutted remnants of a beheaded doll. With these scenes, he recalls the ones suffocated by pillows and the ones hung in cellars, the ones later sunk in rivers and tossed into culverts, in death mere debris.

It is not for nothing, Maldrow thinks, that all man's fairy tales are crimes.

He closes his eyes. It is so hard now, living in this world's furiously overheated room. He tunes his hearing to its highest amplitude and listens to the heavy rain outside. He hears its countless drops explode on the street beyond the window, hears other drops as they splash into the leaves and branches of the trees that line the street. He hears the drops as they gather in a teeming army and charge down the gutters and into the sewer drains. Grotesquely amplified in this way, the sound of the swirl reminds him of the cheer that rises from the ogling crowd when the guillotine blade whispers down and the head thuds into the basket.

In the beginning, the painful keenness of his hearing had almost driven him mad. Like a man wired to a superpowered amplifier, he'd heard the heartbeat of birds as they soared above him, the gulp of forest carnivores devouring their prey, the scratch of worms as they inched through the soil beneath his feet. But later he'd found this same keenness comforting, a way to clear his head of horror, let him hear the world of ordinary movement: the tunneling of ants, the building of nests, actions stripped of murderous intent.

Now he hears the front door of the bar open, footsteps draw near, a brush of air, the clever ruse of blood and tissue, the whispery counterfeit of breath.

"Maldrow?"

Maldrow opens his eyes, studies the Chief's face, sees other faces, as if in pentimento; all the great criminals whose faces he would recognize instantly should they miraculously rise from their graves and stroll into this bar: Gilles de Rais with his spiked beard, Peter Kürten's clean-shaven features, the flinty stare of Albert Fish.

"You look tired, Maldrow," the Chief says.

Maldrow glimpses his own features in the glass. It is difficult for him to comprehend his years, though he appears a man in his mid-forties, still relatively youthful, a quickness in his eyes. To himself, however, he is not just old, but ancient, a figure carved from long-weathered stone, incalculably aged by the grim archive he carries. Now it is murder rooms that flash through his mind: the dank chambers of Čachtice, the dungeon at Malemort, the crimes committed in these places long ago avenged, though others, committed elsewhere, still await such vengeance.

"She is found," Maldrow tells him.

The Chief appears unconvinced.

"She has great strength," Maldrow assures the Chief. He sees the dead eyes of the survivors, the shine scooped out of them, wounds that never heal. Mrs. Budd stares emptily out her window; Frau Ohliger weeps eternally at the front of the cathedral; the crowd waits silently as the diggers do their work around the tower of Machecoul. "Most people don't."

The Chief makes a small adjustment to his wire-rimmed glasses. "She will need great strength, of course."

Maldrow lowers his gaze to the scarred surface of the table. A name has been carved into the wood, the letters cut deep in quick, violent thrusts. He runs a single finger along the letters of the name, sees the face of the one who carved it, his small, angry eyes, the way his lips curled downward with each dig of the knife.

"So," the Chief says. "Tell me her story."

Maldrow twirls the glass in his hands and watches the amber liquid swirl around inside it.

"Her name," Maldrow begins, "is Katherine Carr."

It was a cryptic beginning, I thought as I turned the page, but not unfamiliar, two men in a bar, engaged in mysterious conversation, the true direction of which would no doubt be revealed in the end. Nor did I find it jarring that "Katherine Carr" had entered the story as a character. Other writers had done the same thing: written about themselves as characters in their own fiction, a familiar device one either found annoying or didn't, and went on from there. As a literary technique, it was far from innovative, and so it didn't surprise me that with the next page, the story took a predictably backward step in time, and with a change from third-person to first-person narrative voice moved us from "Maldrow" and "the Chief" inside a bar to "Katherine" inside her own head:

THEN

I awoke with a start, like a panicked child, and immediately sought the familiar crack of light beneath my locked bedroom door, a tiny slit of light, but reassuring.

You are at home, I told myself. You have not been taken.

A second slice of light inched out from beneath a second door, the bathroom light I also never turned off, brighter and more harsh, like the light of examining rooms and dental chairs.

I drew a deep breath, measured, calming. Look, you are breathing, I told myself, though the air itself scraped against my flesh like tiny needles.

It was always this way in the morning, my first breath a panicked gasp. For I knew that he stood at the end of the bed, loose arms dangling, a glint of metal at the end of his left hand. But he wasn't just at the end of my bed, of course. He also slouched against the window, fingering its drawn curtains, and leaned hard against my closet door, and sat over there with his legs spread in the chair across the room.

I pulled myself to my feet and walked quickly toward the bathroom. I knew he would be there, too, blocking my way, and that I would have to step through him, merge with him for an intolerable instant before I came out on the other side, and that at that instant I would smell his sweat, hear the beat of his heart, feel his blood surge as if it were mine. For they never leave you if they get away with it, and because of that you live imprisoned by an unsolved crime.

But for all that, I did the things I had to do each morning: brushed my teeth, showered, dressed, did all these things beneath his gaze.

48

While he watched, seated idly at the kitchen table, I ate a muffin over the sink, then stepped out into the lighted living room, where this same unknown man stood at the front door, legs spread wide apart, arms casually folded over his sleeveless T-shirt.

I still had to go on, of course, hopelessly go on, and so once again I stepped through him, out onto the porch, then down the stairs, where I turned left and headed down Gilmore Street.

I had made it halfway to Cantibell when I noticed Molly Vaughn talking to a tall, slender young man I recognized as Ronald Duckworth. As I approached, Duckworth said something to Molly, and her face suddenly soured as if she'd been slapped. Duckworth grinned and said something else. Then Molly whirled around and rushed away, moving quickly, fearfully, like some small creature from a spreading fire.

"Hi," Duckworth said as I neared him. His greeting was like a hook in my mouth. "You live down the block, right?"

I glanced away, and saw the same unknown man sitting casually on the hood of a car, slowly scratching his chest. His lean body was visible beneath a translucent shirt, the outline of his ribs pressed against tightly drawn skin. He wore jeans still stained with my blood, and there were small red droplets spattered across his shirt. Only his face, as always, remained a blur.

When I turned back, Duckworth was still staring at me.

"I'm late," I said quickly and rushed ahead, thinking now of a poem I'd once written about how desperately the first people must have needed words, how deeply they must have felt the lack of them, how locked in muteness they must have been, with only grunts to say, "I'm lonely. Please help me. I have lost the gift of hope."

I don't know why but at the moment I put down this first section of Katherine's material, I thought of Maitland Island, a place I'd once written about. All kinds of exotic animals

49

had been brought there, though only to be killed to provide heads for luxuriously appointed trophy rooms. The island had been very small, only three miles long and one mile across at its widest point, the animals set free to roam it, but continually pursued by wealthy, lazy hunters with high-powered rifles. Once released, the animals had darted about Maitland's scant acreage as they were stalked and occasionally shot at. Some were dispatched quickly, while others, the less seriously wounded, had briefly limped from place to place, daubing the ground with little drops of blood before they were brought down. Still others, the smaller and more fleet, had managed to evade the hunters for several hours, traversing the island again and again until it had finally dawned on them that there was no escape. By then they'd learned the island's spare dimensions, how utterly trapped they were, so that no matter what hill they mounted or along what beach they ran, they would never be outside the lethal range of their pursuers. As they tired, a terrible inevitability had settled over them. Some, as a last resort, had waded out into the sea, while others had finally lowered themselves to the ground, utterly exhausted, drawn their legs beneath them, and faced the wind silently.

In the story, Katherine Carr's world was like Maitland Island, I thought, a place in which she darted about, but couldn't hide, and so always remained within range of the unknown man, the character she'd created, whether based upon herself or not, forever doomed prey.

The character of Maldrow was harder to pin down, however, but there were concrete historical references in his part of the narrative, something I could sink my reporter's teeth into, and since I saw no other way actually to work up anything in regard to any later piece on Arlo, I started with them.

I looked up Čachtice first, and found it to be a castle in Hungary that had been presided over by one Countess Erzsébet

Báthory, the Bloody Lady of Čachtice, considered the most infamous serial killer in Hungarian history, a woman who'd tortured and murdered hundreds of young women. Machecoul was the ancestral home of Gilles de Rais, a fifteenth-century slaughterer of young boys thought to be the first recorded serial killer. Albert Fish was also a serial murderer, mostly of children. He'd been captured at last in New York City, and executed at Sing Sing in 1935. "Clean-shaven" Peter Kürten turned out to be the "Vampire of Düsseldorf," a slaughterer of females, though not always children. He'd been guillotined at the comically named Klingelputz Prison in 1932.

I'd just finished the last of my research when the phone rang. It was Arlo McBride.

"Did you read what I gave you?"

"Yes," I said, and rather than add something negative, or at least unenthusiastic about Katherine's poetry, I went directly to her prose. "She uses her own name in her story."

"That's probably because some of it is true," Arlo said. "She was attacked by a man who was never caught."

"Here in Winthrop?"

"Outside town," Arlo said. "Her grandfather had died by then, so she was living alone in the farmhouse."

"When was she attacked?"

"Five years before she disappeared," Arlo answered.

"What was the motive?"

"True evil doesn't need a motive, George," Arlo said. "That's why it's true evil."

"So it wasn't rape or robbery?" I asked.

"The guy took a ring. A gold ring she always wore. It had been her grandmother's. He yanked it off her finger during the attack, but no one ever believed robbery was the motive. He could have robbed her without doing what he did to her."

"Which was what, exactly?"

"He beat her to a pulp. Then he took a knife and cut her upper arms and her legs."

"Why not her throat?" I asked.

"Because he wasn't through with her, I guess," Arlo said. "When he finished cutting her, he said, 'Don't forget me, because I'm coming back. And when I do, I'll finish the job.' My guess is that he said that to terrorize her. And it worked."

"Pretty grim," I said.

"Does that mean you don't want to read more of the writing she left behind?" Arlo asked.

I wasn't sure I did want to read any more of it, but work is work and a man has to have an income. Other than Alice Barrows, I had no other prospects for a future profile, and from my last look at her, Alice might already be dead. And so if I had to read more of Katherine Carr's writings to get to Arlo, then read more of them I would.

"No, I'd like to read some more," I said.

"Okay," Arlo said. "I'll see that you get another installment."

He made it sound like one of those serial novels so popular in the nineteenth century. Dickens had made a fortune stringing out his tales in monthly magazines. Katherine Carr was no Dickens, and although her prose was certainly a tad hothouse for my taste, I hadn't found it unbearably painful. I could take more of it.

"You have a mail slot at your building, right?" Arlo asked.

I was surprised he knew this, but then he'd been a cop for years, probably gone in and out of almost every building in Winthrop. "Yeah," I said. "It'd be okay to leave it there."

We talked a bit longer about nothing in particular, and after that, I made my dinner, then read for a time. In the book the Buranni were carrying out their ancient rituals, reading the names of their murdered innocents and thanking the Kuri

Lam for making the pit bottomless. It was a quite ludicrous ritual, of course, and in its ludicrousness it seemed only to underscore the futility of such primitive hopes for justice.

In any event, I shortly grew impatient with the book, gave in to the same urge that had overtaken me almost every night since Teddy's death, and a few minutes later found myself at O'Shea's.

6

A WOMAN NAMED Stella Owens ran the place, the twice-divorced daughter of Gilly O'Shea. She was a large woman, with stringy red hair and watery blue eyes, exactly the sort of bar matron you'd expect to see in a run-down watering hole like O'Shea's, the one place in all of sunny, prosperous Winthrop that seemed still rooted in its own shadowy past.

"Evening, George," she said as I came through the door.

"Stella."

"Want anything to eat?"

"No, just a scotch."

She poured it for me, then nodded toward the back. "Your booth's waiting for you."

"Thanks."

My booth was empty, but there were a few people at the tables, which was usually the case at this hour. But I was a lone drinker, which my usual slouch made clear, so that I was surprised when someone said, "Hello, George."

I looked up to find Hollis Traylor standing at the booth.

"Hello, Hollis," I said.

We'd briefly become acquainted after Teddy's death, when I'd tried to get over it by going to the Little League games he'd have played in that season had he lived. It hadn't worked, and I'd stopped going long before the end of the season. Hollis had been the coach of a rival team, and I wasn't sure we'd ever actually met, but he'd clearly recognized me from those games, mine the face of the stricken father he'd no doubt often seen on local television or in the paper.

He slid into the booth, took a sip from the beer he'd brought with him, then set down the glass softly. "It's really something about the Wildcats, huh?" he said.

He meant the team he coached.

"They're headed for the state championships," Hollis added.

I recalled him at the Wildcat games, rooting loudly for his team, one of those effusive, energetic personalities who seemed always on the edge of a jubilant cheer.

"Fought their way up from tenth place," Hollis added with a boisterous laugh.

I nodded. "Teddy played them in his last game."

Hollis looked at me cheerfully. "Yeah, I know. He hit a home run."

It was a memory some would have thought sweet, Teddy in his uniform, bat held high, swinging, connecting, the ball rising in a high arc toward center field. But for me it was poisonous, as most every memory of him was, the past a toxic blend of anger and regret.

Hollis clearly saw all this. He shrugged. "No news, I guess," he said softly.

"News?"

"Developments, I mean." Hollis caught the fact that he'd perhaps misspoken. "I mean . . . in the case."

"You mean about Teddy?" I asked.

"I'm sorry," Hollis said. "You probably don't want to talk about it." He waved his hand. "I understand."

"There are no new developments," I said. "And there never will be any." I took a sip from my glass. "He got away with it."

Hollis briefly stared into the sulfurous abyss he no doubt thought I was in, then glanced toward the front of the bar. "Starting to rain," he said, "I better be getting home."

I finished one scotch, then another, the front of the bar slowly filling up with its nightly regulars along with the occasional out-of-towner who happened to have stumbled upon O'Shea's simply because it was near the train station. None caught my eye until, about halfway into my second drink, I noticed a woman in a dark corner near the front of the bar, alone, sitting silently, her dark hair falling to her shoulders in the way of forties femmes fatales. There was something that seemed of that earlier time in the coat she wore, as well, its faintly military cut. Her gestures held the same peculiar aura of the past, the way she kept her hands in her lap, the smooth, steady movement of her eyes, the fact that she spoke to no one and that no one spoke to her, as if she were visible only to me, a woman created from the shattered remnants of my own unsolved mystery.

The only real mystery woman in my life was there when I arrived at my apartment a few minutes later, or at least the second installment of her story was, tucked neatly into the plain manila envelope Arlo had dropped through the mail slot and which one of my neighbors had politely picked up and placed on the small table in the foyer.

Once in my apartment, I walked to my desk and opened it. Just as before, there were photocopies of a few sheets of lined paper, all written in Katherine's now-somewhat-familiar script, neat, but with the letters broken so that no word was ever entirely strung together. I'd done a piece on graphology some years back, and remembered that according to this admittedly far-from-exact science, such writing was a sign of creativity, the sort of fractured cursive one found in poets, writers, fabulists of all kinds, and which signaled that Katherine was, like them, a person who made things up.

NOW

"She lives alone," Maldrow says, as he begins Katherine's story. "She has no one." He recalls the many times he has stood outside the house on Gilmore Street, his gaze always on the door, waiting for her to come down the stairs, then following along, watchful, studying each movement, observing the clipped nature of her gait, noting how she passes almost invisibly among the others, so alone she seems more a distant planet than a person.

"No relatives? No friends?"

He has never seen a visitor from the village at the same house, never seen its door open to anyone save the single distant friend and the young boy she sometimes brings with her. And even then the visits are short, and no one leaves the house to stroll with her down Gilmore or Cantibell.

"She has no relatives," Maldrow answers. "And her one friend lives a long way away."

"How often does this friend visit?"

"Rarely."

"Always a planned visit?"

"There will be no surprises," Maldrow tells the Chief.

The Chief nods approvingly.

"She is completely isolated," Maldrow adds. "There is no one who could help her."

"You're sure of that?"

"Yes."

"But there are neighbors, are there not?" the Chief asks cautiously.

"She's a stranger even in her neighborhood," Maldrow assures him. "People see her on the street, but they have no connection to her." Maldrow recalls his glimpses of Katherine on the street, the quickness of her stride, the sidelong and backward glances, the way she moves like a fleeing deer. "Fear is her only companion."

"Ah, yes," the Chief says softly. "And a cold companion, that."

"There is nothing warm in her life," Maldrow says. "Absolutely nothing to brighten it or relieve it."

"Total shadow."

Maldrow sees her do the things she must, walk the daylight street, make her way into the village, buy the few things she needs to sustain the thin line of her life. "She is like a woman who is already dead."

The Chief glances upward, as if toward notes he expects to find written there, an immemorial catechism. "Is there nothing words can heal?"

"She is beyond the reach of words."

"Is there nothing love can find?"

Maldrow shakes his head.

"What binds her to the earth?" the Chief asks.

Maldrow answers with the lines expected of him. "Her heart beats. She takes in air."

"And beyond this?"

"Nothing but fear and anger."

The Chief glances toward the front of the bar, the few men seated there. "The basic requirements are met, then." He turns toward Maldrow. "But only the basic ones."

"I know."

"So now the hard part begins," the Chief says.

"Always the hardest."

The Chief stares at Maldrow knowingly. "So let us proceed," he says.

THEN

I marveled at the sheer casualness with which they strolled into the parking lot with large bags in their arms, the women of Winthrop. They didn't glance around or behind as they headed for their cars. They didn't hold their children tightly. They were skating over ice, but they were not afraid, because the ice had never cracked beneath them.

But it had cracked beneath me, and since then there was only fear, leadenness, and dark, with everything fixed in heavy shadow, where you wait—in shadow—to be torn, shot, stabbed, beaten, hanged.

I startled and jerked into movement. The task was to dash quickly down the street, dart from shop to shop, buy what I needed but take nothing with me, all of it to be delivered, left by the door, which I would open like a crab, grab with my pale claws, yank into the liquid cave, pull down and suction into my little shell.

I went about my shopping, the unknown man visible at every turn, slumped against the milk case, the bread counter, the produce bins. He stood behind the cashier, watched as she counted out my change, then pointed through the window to the parking lot, where he already stood, leaning on a metal cart. As always, he followed me down Gilmore Street, too, a gauntlet of him, lounging in porch swings, leaning against trees. The multitude of him was like the separate straps of a lash.

By the time I closed in on my house I was breathless, sweating, moving faster and faster until I noticed a car, old and dark and dusty, resting as if abandoned beside the cement curb.

I froze like one suddenly encased in ice.

The man who got out of the car wore a dark suit and a blood-red tie. He came toward me slowly. My mind seized. I steeled myself and waited.

The man had almost reached me when he brought a single out-stretched finger to the brim of his hat.

"Good morning," he said.

There was something in the way he looked at me, searchingly, but with a sense of familiarity, like a man who'd seen me before, or at least knew something of me. I wondered if we'd met, or even known each other at some point in the past. And yet, a sense of distance was still more powerful, and it was this distance that gave him the look of someone who had never lived in Winthrop, or had lived here so long ago that he was no longer accustomed to its people or their ways.

"Katherine Carr," he said firmly, like a man determined to re-mind me that I was precisely who I was.

"Yes," I said. "Do we know each other?"

"I find missing persons," he told me.

His suit was clean, but ill-fitting, and he had the faintly dishev-eled look of one often summoned in the middle of the night.

"I don't know anyone who's missing," I told him.

"Yes, you do." He looked at me with a terrible stillness. "He's been missing for five years."

Odd though it seemed, I knew exactly whom he meant.

"My name is Maldrow," the man added. "I'll talk to you again soon."

With no further word, he walked back to his car and got in, fac-ing forward the whole time, never looking back as he drove away. Watching, I felt my imagination flicker to life, and at that instant saw other conveyances trailing like prisoners behind him—car-riages and wagons, horse-drawn coaches, then finally cars, all in a ghostly procession, without drivers, as if borne on an invisible wave, different years and models, foreign and American, going back for decades, some shiny new, others eaten through with rust, each of them fleeing some dreadful carnage, a slaughtered family or butchered child, their trunks packed with rope and masking tape and small strips of electrical wire, in one the rusty handsaw someone had neglected to wipe clean.

It was indeed a weird little story, I thought, as I put the pages down, written with what seemed a great personal need to tell it. I'd seen this before, of course, writing as therapy, to fend off demons or keep one's center from exploding. I'd done a little of it myself after Teddy's murder, penned brief remembrances of him, imagined the life I thought he might have had. I'd held the Frisbee we'd tossed as if it were a magical door through which I might reach him, and even taken Celeste's wedding ring from the top drawer of my desk and turned it in the light like a man conjuring up the spirit of our lost child. But everything I'd ever written about Teddy had ultimately gone into the wastebasket, writing powerless to ameliorate the brutality of events or return a single particle of what had been lost, a grim lesson I was certain Katherine would ultimately have learned, and under the hammer of that lesson either stopped writing or changed the subject, perhaps penned a memoir or a mystery, her prose finally cooling like a body after death.

Which was precisely what I told Arlo when I called him a few minutes later.

"But Katherine was doing more than just *writing* about the way she lived," Arlo said. "She was *changing* the way she lived."

"In what way?"

"Well, for one thing, she went back to the farmhouse."

Back to the place where she'd been attacked? That struck me as very strange indeed, considering the fact that if the first-person parts of her story were autobiographical, then Katherine had barely been able to summon the courage to walk the crime-free streets of Winthrop, much less revisit the place where she'd been attacked by the now-ubiquitous unknown man.

"When did she do that?" I asked.

"Not long before she disappeared," Arlo answered. "She told Audrey she had to do it."

"Why?"

"It was part of gaining her strength back," Arlo answered.

"A pretty hard way," I said. "Of course, being a writer, she might have gone back to the farmhouse only in her imagination."

"That's not what she told Audrey," Arlo said. "Katherine said she actually went back to the farmhouse."

"But Katherine makes things up, doesn't she?" I reminded him. "She's a storyteller, after all."

Rather than address this point, Arlo said, "You should go there, too. The scene of the crime."

During my traveling years, I'd visited Drogheda and Auschwitz, along with countless other scenes of distant or more recent slaughter. I'd even found a strange allure in such places, as Hardy had found an austere beauty in prison walls. But that had been before Teddy, before the little boat of my life had run aground upon its own tragic shore.

"I've lost my taste for murder scenes," I said.

"Katherine wasn't murdered at the farmhouse," Arlo reminded me.

"You know what I mean."

"Yes, I do, but I still think you need to see it, George," Arlo returned insistently. "A sign of her character."

I held my ground and said nothing.

"Would it matter, George, if I told you that this sign was written in her own blood?"

7

STRANGE, BUT ARLO'S mention of Katherine's blood immediately returned me to Alice Barrows, a vision of her as she'd disappeared down the corridor and into the bathroom, a small, wrinkled face with blood dripping from her nose. It had not been the smoothest of first meetings, of course, and initially I'd even sensed something rather confrontational about Alice, or at least something that drove her to warn others away. But that had changed with the appearance of that first drop of blood, so that I'd seen the young girl in the old woman's body, the youthful panic beneath the ancient face, and in that sighting, brief though it was, felt something in me go out to her.

And so, after making an appointment to go with Arlo to the farmhouse at which Katherine had been attacked, I hung up and dialed Sandra Parshall.

"Is Alice okay?" I asked when she came on the line.

"She'll never be okay," Sandra said. "She gets weaker with every episode."

"Why does she bleed?" I asked.

"Coumadin," Sandra answered. "It's a blood thinner she has to take."

My father had taken the same drug, but it was not his long illness I recalled at that moment, but Teddy's, the one time he'd suddenly run a high fever, and briefly been hospitalized, how bare his room had looked when I'd entered it, how dim the light, the frightened look on his face before I came through the door, the vast relief that had swept over him when he saw me, how sweet it had seemed to me, the power to release him from his terror.

"I'd like to visit Alice again, if she's up to it," I said.

"I think she'd like to see you again, too." There was an unmistakable sense of surprise in Sandra's voice, as if she'd considered Alice's isolation unbridgeable before. "I think she liked you, George." Her words turned very nearly imploring. "And so I hope you come back to see her again soon, because at this stage . . ."

Sandra's voice trailed off but her point could hardly have been more darkly blunt: like the tiniest microbe and the largest galaxy, Alice Barrows was dying at the hands of Time.

"When can I see her again?" I asked.

"Whenever you like," Sandra answered. "I wouldn't limit Alice's visiting hours."

I'd heard a certain urgency in Sandra's voice as she'd said those final words, and so I left for Brookwood Residential as soon as I hung up the phone.

Alice was reading when I came into her room.

"Hi," I said.

She was quite obviously surprised to see me.

"How are you doing?" I asked.

She lifted the book, a thin little paperback, and said, "It's not very good."

I took the book from her hand. "Nero Wolfe," I said. "He's a detective, right?"

Alice nodded. "But this other guy does most of the work. Wolfe mostly *thinks*." She drew the book from my hand and laid it down beside her. "Sorry about the other day." She seemed embarrassed by what had happened, though less for the bloody nose than her reaction to it. "It's this medicine I take."

"Coumadin, I know," I told her. There seemed nowhere to go on such a grim subject, so I returned to the book. "Wolfe lives in New York City, doesn't he?"

Alice touched her finger to her nose, checking for blood, as I supposed, a gesture she often repeated as we continued to talk.

"In a brownstone," she said. "With ten thousand orchids." She frowned. "His address isn't the same in all the books. And I looked at this street map of New York on my computer, and if he really lived at some of those addresses, he'd have been in the Hudson River."

I admired her sense of correctness, the reporter's eye for the careless error, and it struck me that she had no doubt listened to a hundred misdiagnoses, been countless times misinformed as to the full range of side effects, been offered scores of hopeful prognoses her illness had long since proven wrong, and that from these lapses in thoroughness or casual fudging of facts, she had developed a distaste for the slapdash and haphazard, felt affronted by it, knew with crystal clarity when she had been treated with condescension or contempt.

She glanced at the book I'd brought with me. "Is that the one you wrote?" she asked.

I stepped over to her bed and handed it to her. "I hope you like it."

She gave the book a cursory glance, but said nothing.

I took the chair nearest her bed and sat down. "Actually," I added, "I hope you respect it."

She shrugged, and her eyes drifted toward the window like two tiny floating balloons. "It's probably good," she said. "You seem smart."

I drew out a notebook and pen. "So, tell me about these glass figures." I looked from one to the other, taking in this unicorn, that angel. "You said they were your mother's."

Alice looked at me severely. "Why did you come here?"

I stared at her silently.

"Because it's your job?" She saw that I was taken aback by the decidedly negative tone in her voice, but even so she didn't retreat from the demanding nature of her question, so that I saw just how utterly alone she was, visited only by people in white coats who probed and questioned her, people for whom her suffering was a job.

"No, it's not because it's my job," I answered quietly.

"What then?" Alice demanded. "Teddy?"

So I'd been right. Alice had done her research, looked me up, found the newspaper coverage of Teddy's disappearance, knew when and from what place he had vanished, where he'd finally be found, seen the photographs that weren't too gruesome to print.

"Maybe that's part of it." I shifted uneasily beneath her steady gaze. "Maybe I wanted to feel that again. A little taste of fatherhood."

Alice took this admission in for a moment, then said, "I guess that's okay." She smiled softly, and now seemed somewhat more relaxed, as if some secret source of tension had been removed from between us. "Let's go outside."

"Outside?" I asked.

She drew herself up and pressed her back against the pillow. "To the garden. There's no air in here."

There was a wheelchair in one corner of the room. I brought it over, then watched as she eased herself into it. Once this maneuver was accomplished, she plucked my book from the bed and tucked it into her lap. "Ready," she said.

She directed me down the corridor, past room after doleful room of what were surely hopeless cases, the near-dead and the catatonic, people wasted by cancer, stroke victims tangled up in their sheets.

The garden was small but well kept, with short hedges and comfortable wooden benches, all its paths and rest areas built for the wide turning axis required by wheelchairs.

When we reached the garden, she asked me to face her chair away from the little fountain and all the sidewalks, a position she had no doubt chosen as a way of making herself as invisible as possible. Then she glanced down at my book. "So, I guess you've gone to lots of places?"

"Yes," I said.

"Did you go to Lourdes?"

"Yes."

"My mother wanted to take me there. What's it like?"

"It's very sad," I said. "Particularly the evening procession, when the people come hoping to be healed."

"Where's the saddest place you ever went?" Alice asked.

It seemed odd that we were discussing my life rather than hers, but it was clearly the way Alice wanted it, so I went along.

"Kalaupapa," I answered for no real reason other than it was the first place that popped into my mind. "It's in Hawaii. It had been a leper colony since 1869, but there were only about fifty lepers left when I went there."

It struck me that Alice might be in need of grim antidotes to her mother's determined and incessant upbeat. I had seen the same reaction in my father, his rejection of any comforting vision of this or any future life, an armor no hope-tipped arrow could penetrate.

"It's a beautiful place, actually," I said. "Which makes what happened there all the worse."

"Tell me about it," Alice said.

And so I did.

For unknown centuries, Kalaupapa had been a very remote and largely inaccessible fishing village on the island of Molokai, I told her, and it had been precisely this remoteness and inaccessibility that had made it so attractive as a leper colony. The sea cliffs that cut the village off from the interior were the tallest on earth, a full sixteen hundred feet. There were no roads leading out of the village, and for lepers, crippled as they were, with gnarled hands and feet and utterly wasted muscles, the narrow mountain trail that was the only route of escape would have been impossible.

"So it was a prison," Alice said.

"Yes," I answered. "With prisoners who arrived by boat, though it couldn't really be thought of as an arrival, since they were sometimes just tossed overboard."

Alice stared at me gravely, but said nothing.

"And it was salt water they were thrown into, of course," I added. "So, what with open wounds, the swim to shore must have been very painful—for those who could swim."

But that had been only the beginning of their suffering, I told Alice, for once ashore, the lepers had found no shelters built for them, and so had lived huddled into small crevices cut out of the rock cliffs, with nothing but piles of leaves to protect them from the elements. There was no medicine, and often their supplies were thrown overboard rather than

68

delivered, so that many of their provisions had either sunk or been swept out to sea.

"And so they died of hunger and exposure," I said. "As complete outcasts."

Because Alice continued to be interested in this narrative, I went on about the conditions at Kalaupapa, then brought the story around to the arrival of the saintly and celebrated Father Damien.

"Things improved at Kalaupapa after he came there," I said. "He built homes and a church."

At Damien's death, a similarly saintly priest had taken over Kalaupapa, I told Alice, and with him there had been further improvements until at last the ban had been lifted and the lepers allowed to leave.

"Did they?" Alice asked.

I shook my head. "Not many. By then most of them were quite old, and they'd lost touch with their families. A few left, but most of them never returned to their villages."

"It's just as well," Alice said with a shrug.

"Why do you say that?" I asked.

She seemed surprised by the question.

"Because if they'd gone back to their villages," she answered, "they'd have been the village freaks."

8

Village freaks.

They weren't the last words Alice said to me that evening, but in one of those tricks of association by which thoughts are mysteriously linked, they brought me back to Katherine. Had she been a village freak, I wondered, made one by what an unknown man had done to her? It was the sort of question that only emphasizes how little one actually knows about any particular subject, of course, and it certainly had that effect upon me as I headed for work the next morning.

Our search for knowledge is a great thing, of course, but it is also a peculiar one, rarely engaged in for its own sake. Certainly my decision to go to the town library to find out what I could about Katherine was anything but disinterested. For the most part, as I well knew, it was an effort to remove any doubt Arlo might have as to my interest in her, though at that point I still remained far more interested in him.

The Winthrop Library was located in a stately mansion the

Winthrop family had donated to the town to which they'd also given their name. Great Georgian columns rose high above a wide portico decked with white rockers in which readers lounged in the warm summer air. The building sat on a high hill, and from that position gave off a sense of peering dully down at the village in the way the billboard eyes of Dr. Eckleburg, Fitzgerald's bankrupt optometrist, symbolically survey the "valley of ashes" at the tip of East Egg. It had the same unsettling silence, too, a passive, indifferent God distantly observing our felonies and misdemeanors, the great sprawling train wreck of human life, though not particularly interested in how it happened or why, nor in the fate of those on board, God as the "absentee landlord" of deist theology, either unwilling or unable to intervene in the poor play of earth.

I had no trouble finding what I needed. I simply typed "Katherine Carr" into the Search Catalog blank, and a short list of citations popped onto the screen. The first mention of her was far from unexpected: GIRL POET WINS TRI-COUNTY CONTEST.

The year was 1973, so that my first glimpse of Katherine showed a slender teenaged girl in a white blouse and dark skirt. She was standing on a small stage, clutching a plaque to her chest, smiling. She'd won the "Eighth Grade Creative Writing Competition" with a poem called "My Grandfather's Eyes." In a sidebar, the paper had printed her poem in full:

All his history is there,
In little orbs of cracked blue sky,
A farm boy's blink, grain in his eye,
And in his mouth and hair.

Before Ardennes and Belleau Wood,
Where mustard smoked the blue to gray

His eyes had sparkled with new day
As such a boy's forever should.

But fire and gas and rifle shot
Blew out the light that twinkled there.
Smoke now sole tenant of his hair,
Eyes he cannot talk about.

And so in spring, as things renew,
He sits in silence as he stares
At flowers blooming in red flares,
With eyes of shaded, shattered blue.

I had no idea what middle-school poetry should be like, though I could see plenty wrong in Katherine's poem: lines of awkwardly inverted syntax, strained rhymes. But "sole tenant of his hair" showed promise in a girl of twelve, and so it didn't surprise me that the next citation had her winning another contest a year later, and after that, at seventeen, a scholarship to the state university.

Six years passed before she appeared again, this time on the pages of the newly established *Winthrop Examiner*. She was now twenty-three, and in the photograph she stands before a modest farmhouse, her arm embracing an old man in a wheelchair. The headline reads LOCAL POET GROWS OWN FOOD, and the accompanying story details Katherine's return to Winthrop after college, the fact that she has begun to publish her poems in small literary magazines, "a simple life," as the profile writer rather bucolically describes it, "lived at the pace of the seasons, where words are allowed to grow slowly, like the crops."

It was a typical local-color puff piece, clearly admiring of Katherine's embrace of rural life, complete with an inventory of her garden vegetables, even a recipe for what the writer called "poet's stew." It was all quite idyllic, with no hint that Katherine was anything but a small-town girl who'd made a tiny mark, was living as she liked, and seemed happy to be doing so.

All of which made the next reference more jarring: LOCAL WOMAN VICTIM OF ATTACK.

It had occurred on August 27, 1982, at the farmhouse where she'd lived alone following her grandfather's death. The time was approximately six thirty in the evening, and she'd just gotten home from taking her friend's son to a local fair. According to the article, Katherine had been attacked in the garage, her friend's son asleep in the backseat of the car. She had been assaulted with a knife, the paper said, but gave no further details of the attack. The "unknown man," as the paper called the assailant, had worn a black ski mask and had evidently left her for dead on the cement floor of the garage.

Subsequent editions dealt with the investigation, which had turned up nothing, so that within a few weeks all references to the crime had faded from the pages of the *Winthrop Examiner,* save a strange little summation of the case, an article by—of all people—a summer intern with the paper who seemed, at least from the sadly sympathetic tone of his report, to have been moved not only by what had happened to Katherine, but also by the terrible nature of what had followed:

This may well be the last you hear of Katherine Carr, for according to her friend, she no longer writes poetry. Miss Carr, herself, refused to be interviewed for this article, but we are informed that she has sold the farmhouse she once shared with her grandfather and now lives in town, at an address we have been asked not to disclose. Although not technically housebound, she is variously described as

73

"enclosed," "reflective," and "reclusive." Thus, although she remains with us, it might be said that Katherine Carr has vanished.

Not a bad final line, I thought, staring at the byline, so that it didn't surprise me that the reporter who'd written it had later risen to become the *Examiner*'s editor-in-chief.

"So, did you ever meet her?" I asked Wyatt in his office an hour or so later.

He shook his head. "No, but the people who did said nice things about her."

"Like what?"

"Well, the way she took care of her grandfather, people admired that," Wyatt answered. "That's the sort of person she seemed to be, a natural caregiver."

"She sounds a bit saintly," I said suspiciously.

"She must have had her faults," Wyatt said. "But when I did the piece on her—that little one you read—I couldn't find anyone who had anything bad to say about her. They just said she was 'nice' or she was 'kind.' The way people speak of the dead."

"*Someone* must have known her," I said.

"Yeah, who?" Wyatt asked. "Katherine's parents were killed in a car accident when she was three. After that she lived out in the sticks with her grandfather. She was homeschooled for the simple reason that he'd been crippled in World War I. Bad legs. Bad eyes. She was with him all the time." He looked at me pointedly. "But the old man had died, and Katherine was beginning to come out into the world. That's what makes what happened to her such a lousy break. Because she'd started to come into town, attend concerts, chat with whoever was around. You know, have a normal life." He shook his head. "Then she got traumatized by some bastard, and after that she was sort of a ghost." With that, Wyatt gave me one of his worldly reporter sighs. "You'll never get ride of human violence, George. But take heart, the animals have it even worse."

Now clearly launched into another subject, Wyatt had gone on to give a particularly lurid account of the animal world, the gang rapes carried out by mallard ducks, the murder rate among ground squirrels, and normally I would have gone on with my daily routine after leaving his office, perhaps headed directly to my desk and put the finishing touches on a piece about the town's new candy store. But something about Katherine—or perhaps about Alice—had gotten under my skin, so I strolled out of the office and sat down in one of the little benches at the side of the building. The town was at its customary level of bustle, and the ordinary noise and traffic, the flow of people, the sound of idle chatter, should have drowned out any further thought of anything save the day ahead, the tasks before me. And yet I found myself thinking about Wyatt's last remarks, his assumption, all but universally agreed upon, that nature is morally blank, the animal world simply a matter, as Wyatt said, of fang and claw.

Which it certainly is, and yet, with Wyatt's voice still echoing in my mind, I suddenly recalled a moment when something unexplainable had happened in that world. At the time I'd hardly noticed it, so that recalling it so vividly now struck me as mysterious in itself, our memories like ghosts in a million-roomed house, wandering purposelessly until suddenly, miraculously summoned.

It had been late in the day, in a Ugandan village where my bus had broken down. I'd long ago forgotten the name of the village, but the windless, stifling heat had been impossible to forget. It had risen in hellish waves from every available surface, the flat clay square of the market, the hoods and fenders of the few disabled cars, the corrugated tin roofs of the houses and vegetable stands. I'd just slumped beneath the paltry shade of the appropriately named fire tree when I first caught sight of the dogs, a pack of them, scrawny and ravenous, their eyes ablaze for the smallest rotten morsel or rancid drop of water. It was the leader of the pack that held my attention. He seemed to take no notice of the small army of gnats and flies that swarmed about his long black snout, drinking when they could from whatever tiny pool of moisture his mouth provided. The other dogs trotted behind, a minion of short-legged, pug-faced mutts, not one of whom bore a shadow of their leader's bearing, the way he sometimes stopped abruptly, held his head very still, his ear cocked attentively, as if listening to the distant muezzin's call to prayer.

For a time, the pack loped along the periphery of the square, sniffing the ground, the entrances of shacks and stalls, seeking whatever tiny residue of nourishment that had survived the heat and dust and endless trample of the crowd. They found nothing, but kept looking, sniffing the earth desperately as they made one round, then another, in a fruitless circle that seemed driven by nothing beyond the simple, unwilled drive to live.

"Did you know that mallard ducks rape their females so ruthlessly they're often drowned in the process?" Wyatt's voice came to me as if from some middle distance between where I sat on a bench in immaculate Winthrop and the dusty swelter of that now-vividly-recalled Ugandan afternoon. "And did you know that if we applied the same murder rate to squirrels that we do to humans, they'd annihilate a city the size of Houston every night?"

Wyatt had said these things as I'd sat in his office moments before, and they were no doubt true, but even as I recalled them now, I saw the kitten appear as it had those many years before, a tiny ball of complete innocence that inched out from beneath one of the matoke stalls, pink, hairless, with eyes that had not yet opened, so that it had no idea of the famished world it had crawled into, nor the stark gaze of the dogs when they caught sight of it.

The stillness of the dogs lasted only the barest instant before they bolted forward, blurred by speed, a cloud of toxic dust blowing across the arid square.

The kitten had managed to angle halfway back under the floor of the shed when the first dog came in at a low crouch, snarling madly as it grabbed the kitten by the ear and flung it to the side, where it rolled into the open air, the rest of the pack now spiraling around it, but without attacking, as if in the throes of some sacrificial rite, circling and snarling with heads thrust upward into the stifling air, poised to make the dive, tear their helpless prey apart, but somehow relishing their power in a malevolent instant of suspension.

Suddenly the leader burst through their circle and stood over the flailing kitten, staring at the other dogs with a look of unyielding authority. The dogs first slowed, then came to a halt, waiting now, shifting left and right, heads bobbing, staring at the kitten but afraid to fall upon it.

For a moment, everything seemed to stop. Not just the dogs in their confused shifting, nor the kitten as it pawed the dust blindly, but the whole agitation of the village, the shuffling feet, the rippling air, even the great white clouds that floated above it all.

In that stillness, the leader communicated his command, and on it, the other dogs turned reluctantly and broke free of the circle and went about their rounds again, sniffing and growling among the now-reanimated village. He did not look down at the kitten, nor make any gesture toward it. He didn't lick it or nudge it back under the shed. After all, he was not Lassie. Instead, he simply stepped away from it and continued on his way, now trailing the others, and never looking back, so that I was left to ponder what might explain such unexpected behavior, save the existence somewhere deep within the animal darkness of a spark inexplicable to us, an unseen star within the moral void.

"George?"

The voice whisked me back to the cooler reaches of North America. "Yes?"

"What were you thinking about?"

It was Arlo. He'd spotted me sitting in front of the newspaper office and strolled over.

"You looked like you were in a trance," he added now.

"I did?"

"What were you thinking about?"

I could have said "Uganda" or "a dog," but it seemed to me that I'd been thinking about neither of these. "How little we know," I said. "I was thinking about how little we know . . . for sure."

But even this didn't seem exactly right in terms of the true direction of my mind.

"How little we know about what?" Arlo asked.

I knew the answer that would most appeal to him, and so, quite cynically, I gave it.

"About Katherine," I said.

Arlo smiled appreciatively. "Well, why don't we try to learn some more?"

9

A FEW MINUTES LATER, we turned onto an unpaved road that wound along a small stream lined with dry reeds. There was no discernible breeze, but they swayed anyway, and a whispery moan rose from them, barely audible, but insistent, like long rows of mourners locked in eternal grief. It was an unsettling vision. To avoid it, I switched my attention to the road ahead, watching silently as it continued along the course of the stream then curled abruptly back upon itself and disappeared into a high green wall of forest.

The farmhouse was a plain wooden structure with a low roof and attached garage. It was typical of the time in which it had been built, with a low ceiling and small windows, not a place for weekenders in need of a summer house, but what remained of a working farm, with a barn at some distance behind the main house, along with various pens and stalls.

We got out of the car, and the sheer richness of the air swept over me: the smell of grass and fields, the thick forest beyond them. I recalled how often smells returned me to places, and sometimes even to people, the dusty smell of Spanish villages, the flower shops in Paris. Celeste had used a particular soap, which had coated her body with the subtle aroma of lavender. Teddy's breath had been buttery, like movie-house popcorn.

However, it was Katherine who came to me now. I could almost feel her in the little breeze that whirled around me, a farm girl who mowed the lawn and gathered eggs and probably napped in the hayloft of the old barn that stood not far from the house.

But there was also a disturbance in this idyll, one that had to have been there for anyone who read, who peered out at the horizon, felt the wonder of the world.

"I'll bet she was tired of this place," I said. "I'll bet she wanted to travel around, see Paris, Rome." I looked up into the wide blue sky. "I can almost feel it."

"Feel what?" Arlo asked.

"Her yearning," I said. "To get away. A feeling that she was trapped."

Arlo looked at the farmhouse. "Audrey owns the place now," he said. He began walking toward the house. "She comes up here from time to time." He stopped and nodded toward the garage. "There's where Katherine was attacked." His eyes grew quite intense, like a slow-burning ember. "She started to put the key in the door. That's when he came up behind her."

We reached the entrance to the garage and stood, facing the door that led into the house.

"Audrey's son was sleeping in the back of the car," Arlo went on. "She didn't want to wake him. They'd had a long day, going to the fair just outside town, doing the rides, cotton candy. He fell asleep on the way home."

"So he didn't see anything?" I asked.

"Slept through it all," Arlo answered.

He moved forward, and I followed him until we reached the back of the garage. He pointed to the step that led into the house. "This is exactly where the attack took place." He nodded toward the front of the garage, a distance of perhaps forty feet. "That's where Katherine was when Cody finally woke up and found her. In the police photos, there's a wide swath of blood that leads from the step here to the front of the garage." He looked at me. "Katherine had dragged herself all that way." He seemed briefly in awe of this feat. "Her tracks told the story. She was chasing him. For all she knew, she was bleeding to death, but she kept chasing him, George." His tone hardened. "And she never stopped chasing him."

I recognized Arlo's admiration for Katherine's determination. This was the mysterious "something" Katherine had written in her blood, a heroic, but probably dazed attempt to pursue the man who'd attacked her.

"Katherine wasn't the usual victim," Arlo added. He remained silent for a time, as if studying the distance Katherine had dragged herself in fruitless pursuit of the unknown man who'd attacked her. "Do you ever go back to Jefferson Street, George?" he asked finally. "Jefferson between Park and Lansdale?"

Teddy had disappeared between these two streets.

"No," I said.

"I think Katherine would have gone back to Jefferson Street if Teddy had been her son. I think she would have revisited all the places that reminded her of him. Just like she came back here."

"But why *did* she come back here?" I asked.

"To get her strength back, that's what she told Audrey."

Arlo only watched silently as I glanced about.

"Maybe she was looking for clues," I said. "Actually trying

to track down the guy who attacked her. Like finding a match-book he left behind. Some hopeless thing like that."

"Well, it's true," Arlo said. "You always hope that you might stumble onto something." He looked at me disconsolately. "Or maybe it's just a hope for hope you're looking for."

With no further word, he returned to the events of the at-tack, walking me through it step by step before he stopped suddenly, drew a photograph from his pocket and handed it to me.

It was a picture of Katherine after the attack, lying in a hospital bed, her head bound tightly in white cloth, little visible but her purple, swollen eyes.

"It's the last photograph that was ever taken of her," Arlo said. "After the attack, she wouldn't allow anyone to take pictures of her. Not even Audrey."

I tried to imagine Katherine from the little I'd read of her story: a young woman just on the verge of living a full life, but whom an unknown man had cast into a darkness as deep as a bottomless pit.

"She must have been very angry," I said.

Arlo nodded. "Like you are, George," he said.

And he was right, of course. Rage had long seemed the only emotion I had left, and it was perhaps that still-burning fuel that urged me to Jefferson Street an hour or so after Arlo dropped me off at the paper.

Normally, I would have gotten in my car and gone directly home. But the visit to the farmhouse—my first visit to an ac-tual crime scene in many years—turned my thoughts not just to Teddy, but the last place he'd been seen alive.

But why had I come there? That was the question I asked myself as I got out of my car and looked up Jefferson Street that night. Had I come in a hopeless search for clues? No, not at all. For I well knew that the man who'd taken my little boy was far beyond my reach, perhaps had never been within it save for those few brief moments when he'd actually been on Jefferson, somewhere between Park and Lansdale, or on some nearby side street, a man on foot, draped in a yellow rain slicker, passing this house, then that one, converging on a distant corner, a briefly halted school bus, two little boys, both laughing, one reaching to pull the bill of the other's red baseball cap, then one little boy, left behind by the other, waiting for his father as the storm raged around him. But Teddy's father had remained at 237 Jefferson, a tiny pink Victorian, where he'd stood in the front room, staring out the window, thinking not of the promise he'd made to his little boy that very morning, nor of the present rain and thunder, but of distant Extremadura in the desert wastes of Spain.

The house where I'd stood at the window that afternoon was still the same shade of pink as when I'd left it, "cake-icing pink," as Celeste had called it. But now it reminded me of the pink of Casa Rosada, the government house in Buenos Aires before which the Argentine mothers had marched year after fruitless year, carrying pictures of sons and daughters who had disappeared. Like them, I wanted to lift a portrait of Teddy into the air, remind my former neighbors on Jefferson Street that they had lost one of their own, that there had been a crime in the neighborhood, and thus for all the sameness of this place, and at least for as long as I lived, it would never be the same any more than the farmhouse would ever be the same for Katherine.

Suddenly, as if carried on that thought, I imagined her at the grotto, alone, her body almost motionless, eyes steady and unblinking. It was a melodramatic rendering, of course—and yet, by its very drama, this figment of my imagination urged me back to Katherine's peculiar story, so that when I finally returned to my apartment that night, it picked it up again:

NOW

Maldrow rolls the glass of bourbon between his hands, listening as a gust of wind splatters rain against the bar's front window, the sound of muffled gunshots. How many thousands has he heard, shots fired from rifles, pistols, tiny pearl-handled derringers yanked from ankle holsters? How many has he seen clutch the spouting wound as they fell over stools, tables, beds? How many have stumbled back into ditches, wells, pits, clutching at throats, chests, elbows, knees?

"Katherine must feel it all," the Chief says gently.

Maldrow glances down at the table. The jabs of the knife thrust eerily, and with each thrust he recalls the long hours of his education, the Chief beside him, taking him through vast epochs of travail, a river of blood they swam in together. Ages had seemed to pass while he listened, and now he suddenly feels the accumulated weight of that long absorption, a world of unhealed wounds, people pulled like stragglers from the herd, devoured by the wolves. The boiling flasks of François Prelati flash in his mind, the murder house on Bluebird Lane, the small chair that graced the living room of Ed Gein. How comfortably he must have sat in it, looking at his many souvenirs.

The Chief watches Maldrow silently for a moment, then glances down at his hands. "Skin like jelly. Light goes through it. Not much left of . . . what is it called? 'The vital spark.'" He looks at Maldrow pointedly. "Everything must be renewed, Maldrow."

Maldrow straightens the photograph that rests on the table. In it Katherine is five years younger than she is now.

84

"They look different after something happens," the Chief says. "Like people after a storm. Everything scattered, torn apart."

Maldrow suddenly sees Katherine as she was a few days before, emerging from her house. At the edge of the porch she stops and looks across the street. He brings her face in for a closer view, notes the minute constriction of her eyes, the infinitesimally slight parting of her lips. "She sensed something on that first morning."

"About you?" the Chief asks.

Maldrow recalls the way Katherine looked as he approached her that same morning. "No, about herself." He sees Katherine's eyes suddenly fixed on him, her shoulders as she comes toward him, straightening her body and holding it firm, as if in preparation for some still-unknown task. "I could tell by the way she moved toward me that morning that she had learned something about herself."

"What had she learned about herself?" the Chief asks.

"That she wanted a different ending," Maldrow answers quietly.

"To what?"

Maldrow immediately sees it not as it was—an empty field—but as it had been that day five years before: Katherine strolling with a little boy, the swirling blue of his cotton candy, the flow of her long hair. "To her story."

THEN

I recalled the madly spinning lights, smelled the sugary sweetness of cotton candy, heard a calliope's jangling music.

"This is where it was," I said.

I could barely accept the fact that I was here, that Maldrow now sat beside me in the front seat of his car, that together we had driven through a morning fog, arrived at this place. He had called that morning, asked if he might pick me up. There was something he wanted to show me, he'd said. I'd agreed, then waited by the window, watching as a fog rolled in from the river, and out of which his car seemed suddenly to appear. He'd watched as I came down the stairs and gotten in his car. Then, without a word, he'd driven down Gilmore Street to Main Street, then out to where the fairgrounds rested in a morning haze, its abandoned field exactly what I now faced.

"This is where it was," I said fearfully.

Maldrow nodded, then got out of the car and strode a few feet away.

I noticed that the last of the fog seemed to pull back as he made his way toward it, so that he looked like an old ship, battered but still pressing into a retreating harbor mist.

"The entrance to the fairgrounds was over there," Maldrow said when I came up beside him.

He placed his hand at my back and urged me forward, the two of us now making our way through what was left of the fog, so that for a moment I felt myself floating a few inches above the ground, rather than walking.

"Your friend's son was with you," he said.

I looked at my hand, astonished by the way the memory had returned to me not only through my mind, but physically, as well, the actual touch of Cody's small hand as he'd slipped it into mine, a touch so real I lifted my right hand and peered at it as if I expected to find the imprint of Cody's tiny fingers on my skin, miraculous as the Stigmata.

"Tell me what you remember," Maldrow said.

I closed my eyes and saw a short, plump man with a handlebar mustache.

"He looked like he was from another century," I said, "the man who guessed Cody's weight. He was wearing a straw bowler."

Maldrow nodded and together we moved forward again until I

stopped at what seemed the exact place where Cody had paused at the entrance to a ride.

"The man at the bumper cars was very friendly," I said. "Very tall. With a gap between his teeth." I played the whirl of the cars in my mind, Cody as he spun around its course, the wild excitement in his eyes. "I think that was his favorite ride. He looked disappointed when it was over." I glanced out over the field, the slowly dissipating fog. "After that I bought him a cotton candy." I recalled his small, delighted face as the man swirled the sticky, sugary mass onto a cardboard cone and handed it to him, a frothy mountain of blue. "Then we walked on down the fairway and stopped at the shooting gallery."

Maldrow's eyes were deeper now, more sunken, as if the nearer we drew in upon the final moments of that day, the more solemn he became.

"The sun was beginning to set," he said.

I instantly felt the air cool around me, saw the air darken just a shade.

"It was just after six when you and Cody headed back to the car."

It was the last moment I'd felt at home in the world, the last time I'd felt the sun on my face.

"Why did you bring me here?" I asked.

His answer confirmed what I'd just felt. "So you could remember what you lost."

I put down the final page of this last installment, rose from my desk, went to the window, and looked out over the same streets Katherine had walked some twenty years before. She had made a lonely reach to reclaim them, I supposed, though it was hard to grasp the mental rearmament she was attempting, her particular way of reentering the world, using a story as her portal, and in that story creating a man whose real

87

purpose—regardless of how she had styled him—was some-how to rescue her from the clutches of the unknown man. I knew that in some way, Katherine's effort to write her way back into a normal life could be regarded as heroic. But in an-other way, it struck me as dismally inadequate. For what pur-pose could it serve to imagine a world more hopeful than the real one, where strangers swam out of the blue to offer a help-ing hand?

I reached for the phone, planning to call Arlo, perhaps talk through this point, but the phone rang before I could make the call.

"George?"

It was Alice, her voice clearly weaker than when I'd spoken with her earlier.

"Are you okay?" I asked.

"I'm in the hospital," Alice said, "I started bleeding again."

There was a pause, during which I sensed that Alice was un-clear as to how to proceed, or even what I was to her that she should have called me. Then, as if carried on a faint breeze, I heard Teddy's voice, the last words I'd heard him say, *Will you come for me?* and which seemed at that moment to be Alice's question as well.

And so I said, "I'm on my way."

Winthrop Hospital lay in a great expanse of open field about ten miles outside of town. It was built of pale yellow brick and had a flat institutional plainness despite the small circu-lar fountain someone had had the foresight to place out front. The walls of the reception area were painted with a large mu-ral that was meant to depict a beach at sunset, but whose jar-ring reds gave off an apocalyptic vision of earth abandoned af-ter some hellish onslaught of war or natural calamity.

People of various ages slumped in bright orange chairs,

flipping through magazines or staring vacantly, like stunned animals. They had the look of people expecting either bad news or the darkly ambiguous sort, waiting, like their stricken loved ones, to find out the true constriction of the arteries, the size of the tumor, the spread of the disease, whether hope was real or false. Curled forward or slouched or nearly prone, with legs stretched like disembarking ramps across the rust-colored carpet, they seemed equally burdened by the very scheme of things, like prisoners sentenced for crimes they had not committed, nor in which they had even been complicit.

"May I help you?"

The voice came from a large man whose eyes were made unnaturally large and owl-like by the thick lenses of his glasses.

"I'm here to see Alice Barrows," I said.

The man clicked a few keys with his chubby fingers, the image of the console glowing eerily in the thick lenses of his glasses.

"Pediatrics," he said. "Room 406."

Pediatrics was a separate unit of the hospital, reached, as it turned out, by a wide corridor lined with stretchers and hospital beds and the slender chrome towers I recalled from my father's final hospitalization, a small city of them that had held instruments and monitors and all manner of plastic bags and tubing, and which he'd flailed against before his last sedation, hallucinating whole armies of wildly charging "Japs," a terrified young soldier, hopelessly hurling imaginary grenades and thrusting imaginary bayonets in these last moments of his consciousness, so that here, at the farthest reach of his life, he'd seemed still to be fighting hand to hand.

Alice's room was at the end of the corridor, the door ajar, so that I heard the drone of a television. I knocked softly, then eased the door open and stepped into the room.

"Hi," I said.

Beneath the covers, Alice appeared even smaller than before, her eyes correspondingly larger, though her nose now looked more like a fleshy beak.

"Hi."

She nodded toward the television, where I saw one of those periodic Amber Alerts, the face of a young girl, this one from Kansas, around eight years old and smiling in her school photograph. "A kid is missing," she said. "They say that if they don't find her in twenty-four hours, she'll probably be dead. Is that true?"

"Yes."

Alice looked at me darkly, so that I knew she'd heard the sudden spark of anger in my voice. She started to speak, then stopped, thought something through, then drew my book from beneath the covers and peered at the jacket. "What kinds of stories do you like to read, George?" she asked.

It struck me as an odd question, and I would have had no answer for her had I not in one of those peculiar movements of the eye, as if some invisible witness said, *Look there,* glanced out her window and caught the figure of a little boy in the distance, about four feet tall, with hair that blinked blond as he passed beneath a streetlamp.

"I guess I like a story that has something mysterious about it," I said.

A black car was parked a few feet ahead of the boy, but he moved toward it without noticing it there, his attention on something in his hand, a marble, perhaps, or a stick of gum.

". . . mysterious."

A man sat behind the wheel of the car, very still, his head lifted slightly so that he seemed to be watching the boy's approach in the car's rearview mirror. As the boy drew closer, he scooted over into the passenger side of the car, the one nearest the sidewalk, and waited.

"And something . . ."

The passenger-side door of the car swung open when the boy reached it, and the man scooted back behind the wheel to let the boy inside, the man, now quite obviously the little boy's father, come to retrieve his son from the bus stop and bear him safely home, as I had not done for Teddy.

". . . dark."

"Are you reading a story like that now?" Alice asked.

I thought of Katherine, the odd tale I'd been reading for the last few days, how peculiar it all was, the creepy conversation she'd written for Maldrow and the Chief, the ubiquity of the unknown man she had portrayed so forcefully, the way all of this suggested a life lived in a kind of no-man's-land between constant dread and sudden panic.

"I think so," I told her.

"What's it about?" Alice asked.

What Alice wanted seemed very little, just a few added details about a story I'd been reading, and yet I was afraid that this particular story, with its flickering horrors and talk of blood, was too grim for a girl whose own dark fate was approaching quickly.

"It's by a woman named Katherine Carr," I answered cautiously. "She wrote it, then disappeared."

"My mother read me stories," Alice said. "Did you read to Teddy?"

"Yes."

"Will you read to me?"

I saw a great yearning for connection in Alice's eyes, and knew absolutely that I felt the same, that in different ways both of us had been stripped of a vital spark that needed to be rekindled.

"Katherine's story," Alice added. "Will you read it to me, please?"

The forces that propel us toward this act or that one are unseen. For all their power, they remain intangible and invisible. We know only that they move us, as I knew at that moment that one of them had moved me; knew this absolutely and without the slightest doubt, though the only physical evidence I could have given for its unseen power was the promise that I made.

"Yes," I said. "I will."

PART II

"Ah, so it is really Alice's story you are telling," Mr. Mayawati says with a show of literary insight. "Not Katherine's, but the little girl's." He smiles in proud appreciation of his discovery. He seems relieved that the story has moved in this direction, taken on a familiar form, strapped itself down, hemmed itself in, will now proceed in the lockstep of an established formula. "Nancy Drew, is she not a famous girl detective?"

"She is, yes."

"And little Alice is to be like her in your story, no? She is to be a 'Nancy Drew'?"

Monkeys frolic in the trees on the near bank of the river, shrieking loudly and flinging themselves from limb to limb, so close to the boat I can almost hear their madly throbbing hearts. But it is Mr. Mayawati's unknowing heart that interests me now, the story he believes himself already to have figured out.

"Nancy Drew," Mr. Mayawati says with a laugh. "She is very popular in my country. All the little girls read her adventures." He stops, as if to correct himself. "Of course, Alice is not pretty."

"No, she isn't," I tell him.

"But it is the heart one must look at," Mr. Mayawati adds quickly.

"The heart, yes. Hers. Mine." I allow a dark glimmer to invade my gaze. "Yours."

He looks at me with a sudden wariness, as if some unsavory aspect of himself has been revealed to me. "And all children are beautiful inside," he says.

A crested eagle lifts from the green glove of the forest and begins its slow circle above us.

"A girl of my village was a great reader of these stories," Mr. Mayawati goes on. "She was always in the park. Always with her head in a book. It is a beautiful thing, is it not, a child reading?"

"Beautiful, yes."

Most of the morning mist has burned off now, the opaque green of the river flowing softly around us. Even so, enough dissipating fog remains to shroud the far shore in ghostly whiffs of cloud. It strikes me that I am no longer troubled by fog, or mist, or anything unseen.

"And mystery games. She was fond of games, this little girl," Mr. Mayawati adds. "Perhaps your story is like a game of Clue."

I offer no assurance that his supposition is correct, nothing in my voice or in my eyes that affirms what he clearly assumes. Mr. Mayawati sees this, and his confidence that he knows where the story is going instantly vanishes.

"Or am I mistaken?" he asks cautiously.

He notes the gravity of my gaze, its hint that the story's dark core has yet to be revealed. The bait I toss him is as old as Scheherazade. "Do you want to hear more?"

Mr. Mayawati does not answer immediately, and in his hesitation I sense a subtle dread. "I hope I shall not be disappointed," he says distantly. "With the ending."

"What ending do you want?" I ask.

"The sort we all hope for," Mr. Mayawati says. "That the evil ones do not get away with their crimes."

"Then you won't be disappointed," I assure him.

"But there are many evil ones in this story," Mr. Mayawati says doubtfully. "None will escape?"

My smile allays Mr. Mayawati's doubts and gives him hope that the story will have a happy ending. "Not a single one."

IO

I ONCE DROVE UP the Amalfi Coast, a road of legendary hairpin turns with little visibility ahead and a deep precipice alongside. At the end of that treacherous drive, at the top of a steep hill, there was a place known as the Terrace of the Infinite that looked out over the Mediterranean. On a clear day, it was impossible to tell where the sky met the ocean, so that you stared out into a perfect blankness, neither land nor sea. You knew that it was still out there, a whole vast world, but you couldn't see any of it. I remember thinking of Max as I stood there, what he'd said to me in Vienna: *Always remember, George, the Unseen.*

I thought of him again when I headed for my car the next morning, and in thinking of him, considered just how crowded life is with unsolved mysteries: some trivial, that misplaced pen you never find; some far more grave, the murder of a little boy, the whereabouts of a missing woman.

The road out of Winthrop took me along the river, past the

little rock grotto where Katherine had last been seen. I imagined her shrouded in a melodramatic fog, arms folded over her chest, pacing back and forth before the grotto. Why had she gone there, I wondered, though without any actual expectation that I would ever know, and with the sense that my purpose that morning had little to do with the real Katherine, anyway. It was the rest of her story I was after, partly to keep Arlo on the hook, I suppose, but more because I'd promised Alice to read it to her and so now needed to get hold of it.

I'd rarely been to Kingston. There was nothing there to attract the eye or the mind, and sad though it is, the story of a dying factory town is hardly news, the death throes of such a place no less familiar, empty stores on a once-thriving main street, the remaining commercial space given over to used clothes or pawnshops or storefront religion.

As it turned out, Audrey lived outside town, in one of the few middle-class neighborhoods of this otherwise-declining town. The wood-framed houses of the surrounding neighborhood were quite large and sat on spacious lawns, everything neatly trimmed and well maintained, and which, in their false sense of invulnerability, reminded me of the life I'd lived briefly on Jefferson Street.

Audrey's house occupied a corner lot. For a time, not knowing exactly how to approach her, I simply sat and peered at it. As a writer, I'd been a great visitor of houses made famous because some august person had lived or died there, but it was the Winchester Mystery House that came to mind now, that strange, rambling edifice that had once belonged to the heiress to the Winchester fortune who, after her husband died, had come to believe that she would live only as long as the house remained uncompleted, and so over a period of thirty-eight years, had obsessively added rooms, windows, staircases. By the time she'd died, the house had become a crazy warren of stairs that twined to nowhere, doors that opened onto walls, windows in floors and ceilings, the house at last nothing more than the weird architectural rendering of its owner's extravagantly funded hope for eternity.

Even from the outside, Audrey's house offered a similarly odd sense of reflecting the mental state of the woman who lived inside it. The porch was adorned with sculpted figures, most carved from wood and more or less totemic. A large African mask hung beside the door, the face of a chieftain, predictably severe. The windows were hung with beaded curtains, rather than cloth, and instead of a traditional wooden swing, two brightly colored hammocks hung in either corner of the porch, though even these were different from the usual, brightly colored with thinner and more elastic strands, like the ones I'd seen in Cozumel and along the Yucatán.

"I'm George Gates," I said to the woman who opened the door. "Arlo spoke to you last night, I believe."

"Yes, Arlo called me," Audrey said. "He said you were interested in reading more of Katherine's writings."

"Yes, I am."

She was a tall woman, slender and elegant, with graying hair coiled in a neat bun. I don't know why, but I'd expected someone smaller and more ferocious, like a little dog that bites, so that Audrey now seemed less formidable and at the same time sadder and more resigned.

"I don't let people read Katherine's story in order to mock her," she warned. "She made mistakes. But she doesn't deserve to be mocked."

Arlo had told me very little about Audrey, that she'd married and had a son, then divorced and never married again. She had the firm look of a woman who could not easily be swayed from any set belief.

"I thought you'd be older," Audrey said. "An older man."

I shrugged. "Sorry."

"Katherine would be in her early fifties now, had she lived."

There was a sense of great loss in her tone, so that I naturally thought of Teddy, and at that moment imagined him not as he was at the time of his murder, but as he would be now, a blond-haired boy of fifteen.

Audrey appeared to sense that I was thinking this, or something like it, that I'd returned to a tragedy that was closer to me than Katherine's.

"You lost your son, Arlo told me," she said.

"Yes. He was murdered seven years ago."

"And they never found who did it," Audrey said, a fact Arlo had also clearly shared with her.

"That's right."

"Do you have any hope that he won't get away with it, the man who killed your son?"

I shook my head. "No, I don't have any hope of that."

Audrey opened the door farther and stepped back. "Good," she said. "It's better that way." She saw the quizzical look in my eyes. "To give up hope for some miraculous solution," she added. "Which is what Katherine should have done." She shook her head. "She'd be alive today if she'd been able to do that, Mr. Gates. She would have been alive and flourishing, but she chose the dark side, and fell in love with it."

This was a cryptic remark, but one I thought it better not to pursue at such a moment, with the two of us still standing rather stiffly in the foyer, an atmosphere so brittle I found silence the best option.

"Come in, then," Audrey said.

I followed her down a short corridor and into a room furnished with heavy wooden furniture, a table with claw legs, a cabinet with beveled glass doors. A hooked rug woven in dark colors covered a good portion of the floor. Everything seemed weighted, somber.

"You've read Katherine's early poems?" Audrey asked.

"Yes, I have."

"So you know that as a girl, she was all feathers and light," Audrey said in a tone that seemed less disapproving than melancholic, the regret of a grounded friend for the fate of a flighty one. "I used to call her that. Feathers and Light. A nature poet." Her features abruptly turned grim. "But Katherine discovered that nature had bacteria, viruses, that it kills you in the end. Being attacked taught her that life wasn't feathers and light. In that one regard, perhaps it was a good thing."

I let this remark go by without comment.

"You were a travel writer, I understand," Audrey said. "So you must believe in the kindness of strangers. Travelers have to depend on that sort of thing, isn't that true?"

"Often, yes."

Audrey shook her head. "But not all strangers are kind, are they?" She drew in a long, sad breath. "Katherine found that out," she added. "And if she'd lived long enough to say so, she'd have been a great writer."

It was clear that Audrey ascribed great gifts to her vanished friend, had gone far in the way of mythologizing her. It was a common response to sudden loss, and I immediately recalled a woman whose son had been killed in the World Trade Center. "He would have changed the world," she said. But he'd been in his mid-thirties at his death, a bond salesman, and perhaps a fine man in his own right, but surely not a maker of new worlds. I had tried to do just the opposite with Teddy, keep him in perspective, his later potential well within the human scale, his loss made somehow greater and more poignant to me because it was *his* loss of himself, and *my* loss of him, not the world's loss of someone who would have changed it.

Audrey pointed to a chair. "Please," she said.

I took the seat she indicated, then watched as she walked to the cabinet, drew open a drawer, and retrieved a thin stack of papers I recognized as more of the same type that Arlo had given me, photocopies of ordinary notebook paper, the original manuscript no doubt tucked into a locked drawer or closed up in a safe. To this she'd added a few photographs of Katherine at various ages.

"It's always good to have a sense of what a person looks like, don't you think?" she asked.

"Yes," I said.

"But it's really *what* Katherine wrote that matters." Audrey nodded toward the pages she'd just given me. "There's not much of it, as you can see." She returned to the sofa and sat down. "Do you know what her favorite poem was when she was a little girl?" Before I could answer, she began to recite: "'Yesterday upon the stair, I met a man who wasn't there.'" She stopped and looked at me sternly. "The problem is that this man *was* there." She saw that I found this remark perplexing, and drew the top sheet from the stack of papers in her lap and handed it to me. "This should explain it," she said.

It was a poem called "Munch's Title," and it was clear that I was being instructed to read it before any further discussion would be allowed.

> A *dealer called it* Vampire,
> *There was blood in her hair, he thought,*
> *Her embrace a death-grip,*
> *Fangs in her unseen mouth,*
> *The man draining pale*
> *As she held him, his ebbing life*
> *The food of her eternity.*
> *But Munch called it* Love and Pain,

Saw nothing supernatural in
Our need to hold,
No noose in circled arms,
No brutal weaponry
Behind the curtained lips.
Love was sharp enough for Munch.
No need for deathless spirits,
Immortals spinning plots.
As we are, we were enough for Munch.
Perhaps even more than he could bear.

"It's a love poem, don't you think?" Audrey asked when she noticed I'd finished reading it.

"In a way, yes."

"It's at the Metropolitan Museum in New York, the painting Katherine is talking about," Audrey went on. "Katherine's grandfather took Katherine and me there. It was the last trip she ever took. After that, he became too weak for travel." She shrugged. "Anyway, the painting isn't all that much. It's quite small as a matter of fact. There's a man and a woman in it, just like Katherine says in the poem. They both look like they're sitting in the dark. The woman is sort of holding the man. She looks like she's comforting him. Which Katherine would do for anyone who needed it." She stopped, eyed me closely, then added, "You should take a look at that painting because you can figure a lot out by studying it closely."

"A lot about what?" I asked.

"About Katherine," Audrey said.

Katherine's poem rustled softly in a breeze that suddenly swept gently through the window; nothing but a breeze, and yet it had the ghostly effect of those invisible fingers that dance along the keys of a player piano.

Audrey settled the pages with a firm hand, and in that gesture

I saw the hard realist Arlo had sketchily described when we'd talked the previous night, this woman who had worked in the slums of Hartford and New Haven, who had no doubt seen a great deal in life that was neither feathery nor light. There was nothing about her that seemed in the least fanciful. Rather she appeared almost to resent Katherine for vanishing, a hint of blame in almost every word she said, Katherine somehow the author of her own destruction.

"Arlo never told me why you got in touch with him," I said.

"Because I believe that the police were wrong," Audrey said. "In their eyes, Katherine was a female stereotype. A girl poet. A recluse. She couldn't have been stranger to them if she'd come from Mars. And so I wanted to give a different view of her. For the record, you might say." Her gaze grew intense. "What do you think happened to Katherine, Mr. Gates?"

I shrugged. "I have no idea. I didn't know her. All I have is her story."

"Her story, yes," Audrey said. "Other than one little poem, that was all she left, so the police focused on it right away."

"And found nothing, I suppose?"

"Nothing they could believe," Audrey said. "And so they decided Katherine had killed herself. Case closed." She watched me cautiously for a moment, then added, "The police thought he was just some character Katherine made up in her story. But what if he wasn't? What if he was real, the man she calls 'Maldrow'?"

In the little I'd read so far, Maldrow had emerged as a vague figure, more or less fantastical. Audrey was clearly alluding to a very different type of character: not only real, but darkly so.

"What if it was a con job?" Audrey asked. "This whole business of finding the man who attacked her. A con job from start to finish. Maldrow—or whatever his real name was—what if he was after her money? She didn't have any, really, but he may not have known that."

I found that I had nowhere to go with this, for it all seemed too speculative, a reading of signs.

"You can imagine how vulnerable Katherine must have been," Audrey said emphatically. "Lonely the way she was. Easy prey for a man like that." Her eyes glimmered with a spark of pride. "At least, at first. But Katherine would have caught on to him in the end." She pulled herself upright and her features grew stern. "And when she did, she'd have gone after him."

I thought of the bloody crawl Katherine had made in pursuit of the unknown man who'd attacked her, and at least this last of Audrey's statements struck me as very likely true: that Katherine would not have allowed a second unknown man to escape her wrath.

"That would be his motive," Audrey added grimly. "Because she saw through him and would have exposed him to make sure he never did it again, never took advantage of another woman. That would be the reason he killed her, because he knew she'd go to the police."

To my surprise, I immediately imagined this hypothetical murder in a decidedly melodramatic scene: Katherine confronting her deceiver, revealing the whole scheme in what must have been a violent paroxysm of fury and hopelessness, the man who had betrayed her now fully exposed, listening as she raged, knowing he could do nothing to quell her anger, and so at last deciding what surely must be done.

"But he'd be smart about it, wouldn't he?" Audrey continued. "He wouldn't have done it at her house, or anyplace around here. He had a trailer. It's in her story. My guess is that

Katherine went there and told him she knew what he was up to. That's when he killed her. He did it in his trailer, then drove away. Later he buried her or put her in the river."

It was the sort of explanation—a plausible motivation for murder combined with the opportunity both to commit and get away with it—that one might find in a typical murder mystery, but that didn't make it any less possible in real life.

"Of course, that's not how Katherine's story ends," Audrey added with obvious reluctance. "In the story, Katherine never stops believing in Maldrow. As you'll see, when you read it."

With that, I knew that she'd decided to let me read the rest of what Katherine had left behind.

"But I don't think Katherine wrote that ending," Audrey added quickly.

This was a supposition I hadn't heard before.

Cautiously, I asked, "Well, if you don't think Katherine wrote the ending, who did?"

Audrey didn't say the name as she handed over the rest of Katherine's tale, but I instantly envisioned it written on the walls and floors and mirrors and doors of countless murder rooms, the dying effort of innumerable murdered women to identify one they would not let get away, the letters of his name crudely drawn, glistening, forever dripping red: *Maldrow*.

11

IT WAS A NOIRISH little scenario, Audrey's portrait of Maldrow as a con man who'd chosen the wrong mark in Katherine and had consequently found it necessary to kill her. But that didn't matter to me as much as the fact that she had given me the rest of Katherine's story, a tale I could unwind to Alice, discuss and analyze as amateur detectives, perhaps conclude that it had been Colonel Mustard in the billiard parlor with a pistol, the two of us smiling at the end of it like satisfied players of Clue.

Alice was not in the dayroom when I passed it, but other children were, mostly six- or seven-year-olds, though some were younger still. A few sat at tables, working puzzles or arranging blocks. Others were on the carpeted floor, playing with the various toys the children's ward provided. Their laughter was the laughter of children, bright and airy, but it didn't hide their grave infirmities, nor the effort they were making to put all that briefly out of their minds, to lose themselves in play. Watching them I could hardly imagine the crime that had been committed against them: murdered by their own bodies, so that they lacked even the figure of a stranger fleeing from them, someone still out there, whom they might yet track down. It was nature's bloody hand that attacked these children, and so in the darkest, deepest sense of things, no one would ever be made to pay for what had been done to them.

Alice's eyes shot over to me when I came into her room, though with an energy that seemed already to have dissipated slightly by the time she spoke. "Did you bring the story?" she asked softly.

"Yes," I said. I drew over a chair and sat down. "But I need to bring you up to speed on what I've read of it so far."

Alice reached for the laptop on the table beside her bed, her slender arms little more than pale reeds, the weight of the machine almost too much for them to bear, though they did, in fact, manage to draw it into her lap.

"Okay," she said as she turned it on. "I'm ready."

For the next few minutes, and orchestrated by the steady tapping of Alice's fingers on the keyboard, I told her everything I'd learned about Katherine's life, all Arlo and Audrey had told me, along with what I'd picked up in the *Winthrop Examiner*. Then I went through everything I'd read in Katherine's story up to the point of meeting Audrey.

Alice listened very attentively, rarely looking down to type. There was a strange hunger in her gaze, an eagerness to absorb each detail, so that I felt her mind had long been starved for such exchanges, the sound of a voice other than a doctor's, someone beside her in other than a professional capacity, speaking of something other than her affliction.

Because of that, I found myself going over what I knew of Katherine's story more slowly than normal, elaborating conversations and giving more detailed descriptions of various places, Audrey's house, the diner where I met Arlo, the look of Gilmore Street the night I'd visited it, the stone grotto by the river where Katherine had been seen last.

"Any questions so far?" I asked at one point.

Alice shook her head. "Not yet."

And so I continued my narrative, now breaking to read the sections of Katherine's manuscript Arlo had given me, or to answer the questions Alice at last began to ask, most of them quite concrete, and usually about the identity of some arch-villain mentioned in the "Now" section of Katherine's story, Maldrow's criminal archive.

Most of the time she seemed deeply concentrated on whatever I was saying, but she would occasionally draw her gaze over to the window and stare out into the middle distance. She rarely spoke during those intervals, but I sensed a purposeful silence, that within this oddly focused quiet, Alice was assembling pieces of a puzzle, perhaps even beginning to arrange them in an order she had long ago devised.

Finally she asked, "Do you think Audrey's right about Maldrow?"

"You mean, that he's a con man?"

She shook her head. "No, that he was a real person."

Her inquiry was quite fundamental in that it touched upon the essential question of whether Katherine's narrative was fiction or nonfiction or something in between.

I offered the only answer that seemed reasonable at the time: "I don't know."

Alice appeared entirely satisfied by this answer, so that I suddenly realized that I should never read ahead of her, know more than she knew, that from here on we should explore the twists and turns of Katherine's story, if there were any, like two people winding down a river on the same boat.

"Do you think you've caught up with me now?" I asked. "Anything else before I start to read?"

She straightened her shoulders slightly, drew in a short anticipatory breath, and placed her fingers in position on the laptop keyboard.

"Ready," she said.

NOW

"You seem to have won Katherine's confidence very quickly," the Chief says. "But then, you are good at winning trust."

Maldrow sees Mrs. Budd staring angrily out her window, her white hair trembling, unable to focus on anything but a little cottage in White Plains, the terrible walk her daughter took, holding Fish's hand. So many like her. Drained by anguish, ready for his approach.

"Of course, rage makes one vulnerable," the Chief adds. "We've learned that much, Maldrow."

Maldrow recalls Katherine's eyes as she'd stared at the magazines that lay scattered across the floor. The fury of her gaze had reminded him of Yenna, emboldened by what she'd learned, her green eyes forever after searching for some murderous figure in the village square, following him as he ambled among the crowd, buying cheese and bread, stopping at the tradesman whose trade it was to sharpen knives. Had it not been for Stanovich, she would be with him now—partners, as it were, in crime.

"Especially futile rage," the Chief adds.

Maldrow recalls the legion of others who lived inside that furious futility, unable to go on, their lives lived in fruitless contemplation of some unknown man, his freedom an endless torture to them, a pain mercy could not ease, nor forgiveness in any way deflect.

"Does Katherine know this?" the Chief asks emphatically.

Maldrow recalls Katherine as she came out of the bus, a smoldering ruin, charred by what she'd seen, but moving forward anyway. "Yes," he answers. "She does."

The Chief's gaze drifts down to Maldrow's long fingers, the rhythmic way he squeezes and releases them. "You are in an odd condition."

Maldrow massages his fingers. "I'm anxious to close Katherine's case."

The Chief's eyes glitter with a distant sense of approaching trouble. "Then let us determine if she is truly found. For there can be no mistake in this."

"I know."

The Chief regards Maldrow with a stern gaze. "Does she believe in you?"

"Yes, she does."

The Chief sits back and draws in a long, thoughtful breath. "So did another at one time."

Maldrow sees Yenna's body facedown in the flowing river.

"Tragic, all of them," the Chief adds. "You felt the weight of them." He thinks a moment, then poses the question: "But you never considered any of them after Yenna, did you?"

"Not until now."

"Why?"

Maldrow sees scores of others who never made it beyond their despair, people who leaped from bridges or hanged themselves from rafters, or placed the cold steel barrel between their lips and pulled the trigger. Others had been lost to alcohol, to madness, or perhaps within the folds of their own enveloping grief.

"Because they didn't love life anymore," Maldrow answers. "You have to love life for it to matter if you lose it."

"But even that is not enough," the Chief says.

"No, it isn't."

"Then what makes Katherine different?"

Maldrow recalls the look in Katherine's eyes after he'd finished his story of that filthy old child murderer. It was the same broken-yet-forbidding look of people on the witness stand, victims of some dreadful atrocity whose perpetrators they were now in fearful position to identify. *There he is, the one who bashed my baby's head against a wall.* It was the look of the people who'd identified Eichmann in Jerusalem, the look of people who knew that if justice were for mortals, eternal as they are not, then other witnesses even now would be pointing to King Leopold or the Duke of Padua along with legions of equally unpunished slaughterers, the swordsmen of Jericho, the gunmen of Babi Yar. More than anything, it was the dark look of those who knew the dreadful truth that Heaven could be made Paradise only by tribunals long and grim.

"Her darkness," Maldrow answers.

A darkness that had been even deeper than Yenna's, so that he'd known how mercilessly she would have faced them: Lawrence Bittaker washing pliers in a metal sink; John Joubert stuffing rope and a hunting knife in his army locker; Vladimir Ionosyan buttoning his false uniform from Moscow Gas.

"Ah, yes," the Chief says quietly. "And what is more desirable than that?"

I stopped and sat listening to the tap of the laptop.

"How do you spell those last names?" Alice asked after a moment. "The ones you just read."

I handed her the page, then watched as she typed the names carefully. After typing them into her notes, she checked the spelling by looking from the text to the screen, a thoroughness that reminded me of my boyhood, the great drive I'd had to get the facts right in my school papers. When she'd finished this process, she looked up with a visible eagerness.

"That's the end of that section," I said. "Is there anything you want to talk about?"

"Who is Yenna?" Alice asked.

"I don't know," I answered.

"She's connected to Stanovich, somehow, and they're both connected to Maldrow."

"Yes," I said. "My guess is that we'll see the connection later in the story."

"All right," Alice said. "Then let's read on."

THEN

I imagined them in their endless travels, eternal vagabonds trudging through fields of windswept wheat, leaning wearily against crumbling earthen walls, squatting beside fence posts. I saw them tirelessly searching waist-high grasses, slogging down sodden roads, following muddy footprints; saw them barefoot, in tattered sandals or worn-out shoes, jostled in wooden carts, weaving in the sweltering steerage, clothed in baggy suits, soiled robes, hair shirts, tattered muslin; saw them bone-thin and squinty-eyed, studying some incriminating object through a pair of wire-rimmed spectacles.

"Tell me again about Stanovich," I said.

Maldrow smiled softly. "It is what you hoped for, the end of his story. It is what all of you hope for."

"Is that why you do what you do?"

"It is the only reason."

"When was it offered to you, this . . . job?"

"A long time ago."

He rose, and as if suddenly called to action, I got to my feet and we walked out onto the porch. It was a cool, beautiful night, bright stars and moon, the town visible below, fixed in a bluish light.

"Everything seems so full," I said.

Maldrow gazed toward the town and seemed to see everything within it, all its many rooms. Then he glanced toward Main Street, to where it ended at a little rock grotto.

"What are you thinking?" I asked.

"About a man," Maldrow said. "His name was Albert Fish. He murdered a great many children."

Then Maldrow meticulously described the horrible things Fish had done to the children who'd fallen into his hands.

"Did he get away with it?" I asked.

"No," Maldrow answered. "He was caught and executed."

"How?"

"Electrocution," Maldrow answered.

But it had been a botched execution, Maldrow told me, hideous in its details, Fish the recipient of a truly dreadful death.

"And so, you see," Maldrow said when he came to the end of Fish's story, "Fish didn't get away with it."

But I knew he had.

I stopped again. "That's where this section ends," I said.

Alice stared at me thoughtfully. "Why does Katherine think that Fish got away with it?" she asked. "I mean, if he was executed."

I shrugged. "I don't know. But Fish was a real person, and he was executed. That much of what Maldrow tells Katherine is true."

I started to turn the page, prepared to go on, but Alice stopped me.

"Can I have the first part?" she asked. "The part you've already read."

She meant the sections I'd told her about, the ones Arlo had given me initially, and from which I'd read excerpts, an updating process she now appeared to find incomplete.

"Sure." I took the pages I'd already read and handed them to her.

For a time, her attention was focused on Katherine's manuscript, studying its first page with her old-lady eyes. Then she glanced up suddenly, as if something had occurred to her, though not something she was prepared to share. "Would it be all right if I kept them?" she asked.

"Sure," I said.

She returned to the pages, studying them so intently that I thought it a good time to leave her, and on that thought, got to my feet.

"Where are you going?" she asked.

"Home," I answered. "I thought you might prefer to be alone."

"Why would I want to be alone?" she asked. "Is it because you want to leave?"

"No," I said. "Not at all."

I sat back down and waited for Alice to speak, curiously unable to initiate conversation myself, so that I again felt the weight of just how long it had been since I'd talked to a child.

Alice clearly sensed my unease, returned quickly to her computer, made a few taps, then turned the screen to face me.

It was a ghastly serial-killer Web site, the faces of the men lined up in rows, like mug shots, faces of every color, race, ethnic type, their names and the countries from which they came written in a black, vaguely gothic script, a skinny Korean, a pockmarked Slav, all of them with at least one thing in common other than their maliciousness: STILL AT LARGE.

"Why are you looking at that sort of thing?" I asked.

"Because I read your book," Alice answered. "And I wondered if you'd ever written about people like this."

"You mean, murderers?" I asked.

"Murderers who never got caught," Alice said.

"Why would I write about people like that?" I asked.

She seemed somewhat disappointed by this answer, like one who'd hazarded a move and been blocked.

"No reason," she said as she turned the screen back around, made another tap, then turned the computer off altogether.

She said nothing for a moment, but merely held her gaze on the blank screen. Then, as if prompted by the recognition of some dreadful failure, she said, "Maybe you should go now. I'm tired."

It was an abrupt change of mood, but one I had no choice but to accept.

"Okay," I said. "See you tomorrow."

"Tomorrow?" Alice asked doubtfully.

"Yes, tomorrow," I assured her. "So we can read some more of the story."

She was clearly surprised that I intended to come back so soon, and in that surprise, I saw how many people had come and gone in her life, the many faces that had lingered briefly by her bed, sweet and solicitous, promising to care, then vanished.

"We have to find out what happens in Katherine's story, don't we?" I added. "Who Yenna is, for example. And Stanovich. Why Katherine thinks Fish got away with it."

Alice smiled. "Yes, we do."

"See you tomorrow, then."

With that I rose and headed for the door. When I reached it, I turned back to say good night to Alice. But her head was lowered, her hairless pate shining softly in the light as she studied Katherine's manuscript, turning the pages with her tiny, wrinkled fingers, slowly, one by one.

12

PERHAPS IT WAS that last look of Alice studying Katherine's story that returned me to its long-missing author as I headed for my car that night. For as I drove back to my apartment, I could almost feel her around me, though oddly so, like someone who disappears as soon as you turn, darts around a corner or into an adjoining room, a figure gone so quickly, you're not sure it was ever there at all.

It was a presence that wasn't present, and I suppose it was my feeble effort to conjure her up that sent me to my computer when I returned to my apartment. There was no way to get an image of Katherine, of course, but there was an image that had intrigued the woman herself, and about which she'd written, and with a few taps at my own keyboard, it flashed onto the screen.

Munch's painting, whether called *Vampire* or *Love and Pain*, looked much as Audrey had earlier described it. It was small and dark, with only two figures. But it was also highly dramatic, a captured moment in which a man and a woman seem locked in a fierce grief. The cause of this grief, whether death or loss or rejection, was impossible to decipher, but the intensity of it, bleak and inconsolable, was etched in both faces. Even so, the man and woman were different. The man seemed in grief for an unknown reason, while the woman appeared to be grieving for the man, cradling him in her arms; a broken man, as he seemed to me, and thus hardly the sinister figure Audrey had painted of Maldrow.

In fact, the man in Munch's painting struck me as far more similar to the Maldrow Katherine had portrayed in her story, only half-visible, his features cloudy and indistinct, a character she'd rendered too insubstantially to be pinned down by anything I'd ever come across in literary psychology.

But if he'd existed at all, I told myself, Maldrow might well have been a dark manipulator of the weak, the vulnerable, the innocent, just as Audrey believed. I knew that throughout history such unconscionable deceivers had existed, sometimes on a monumental scale.

But more than that, reading Katherine's story aloud had given it an added eeriness in tone, particularly the scene where she'd stood with Maldrow on the porch of her house, her eyes cast up toward the order of the firmament, his down to the chaotic world of man. His tone had been oddly instructive at that moment, his worldliness far deeper that Katherine's, so that he'd seemed almost her teacher or mentor . . . or guru.

But would Katherine have been vulnerable to such chicanery? And if so, how would it have resulted in her death?

I considered the police theory first, the one Audrey had so vehemently refused to accept, that Katherine had taken her own life. To my surprise, I found it quite easy to think of Katherine exactly as the police had thought of her, a woman lost in upheaval, seeking deliverance, finding none, and in the terrible aloneness of her despair, walking directly into the water. Emily Dickinson's famous lines occurred to me: how after great pain a formal feeling comes, one's tormented emotions finally at rest. Surely it was reasonable to suggest that Katherine had come at last to precisely that dark serenity, her jangling nerves, in Dickinson's words, "sitting ceremonious, like tombs."

I thought of the little rock grotto by the river, the place where Katherine had last been seen. She'd been alone, according to the Route 34 bus driver, her shoulders wrapped in a long dark shawl, her hair falling in a thick black curtain over her shoulders. By such a description, she joined the legendary suicides of her sex: Ophelia floating among the flower petals, Eustacia Vye leaping into a raging stream, unable to be saved, as Hardy said, by earth's fettered gods. And of course there was Virginia Woolf, tucking stones into her pockets, then wading out into the River Ouse.

For a moment I wondered if this were indeed the fate I preferred for Katherine, literary as it was, and oddly haunting, a woman walking into the water. For what end could be better for her than a willful death, carried out in sober sorrow, and with a backdrop of natural beauty?

I imagined the lapping water, the peaceful shore. At night it would have been even more lovely, and I knew that in this aspect, as a suitable place to take one's life, it neatly fit a universal pattern. For one thing was clearly known about suicides: they often liked to die in beauty, the panorama of the Golden Gate Bridge, the cliffs of England's Beachy Head, or within the beguiling depths of the Aokigahara Woods, where the Japanese killed themselves in striking numbers. As locations, these most popular of earth's suicide sites had all shared a stunning beauty that powerfully contradicted the prosaic signs and notices posted all about, pleas to "phone a friend" or "think of your family."

Audrey would clearly not accept such a death, and so—almost as an act of fairness—I turned to her own idea of Katherine's end: that Katherine had discovered the truth about Maldrow, an evil truth, and had threatened to expose him for the charlatan he was.

I sat back and studied Munch's painting again, but found nothing there that could take me to the next step. I knew I couldn't read ahead in the story, for that would have been unfair to Alice.

Luckily, however, the story was not my only source.

Arlo's voice was drowsy, so that I knew I'd roused him from his bed.

"Sorry," I said immediately. "I didn't notice how late it was."

"Audrey called," Arlo said. "She told me she gave you the rest of Katherine's story."

"That's right," I said. "But I can't read it right away."

"Why not?"

"It's a little game I'm playing with Alice," I said. "The kid with progeria. We're reading the story together, and I don't want to get ahead of her. You know, because we're trying to solve it. She likes doing that sort of thing."

"There is no solution," Arlo said. "There is only . . . hope."

Hope. It struck me as a curious word, though one often repeated in Katherine's tale, a strangely vague minor theme. "Hope for what?" I asked.

"Hope for hope," Arlo answered.

"But what is—"

"You'll see," Arlo said quickly, obviously determined to cut me off. "Or not."

He had quite obviously erected a wall to any further inquiry along this line, so I returned to my original purpose. "Audrey says the police believed that Katherine committed suicide."

"That's right," Arlo said. "They figured she probably walked into the river, swam out, drowned. The current is pretty swift. The body could have been carried a long ways."

"But Audrey thinks Maldrow murdered her."

"Audrey is a devout Catholic," Arlo said. "She doesn't want to think of her best friend in Hell."

"So what do *you* think happened, Arlo?" I asked. "You've never actually told me what *you* think."

"Because I don't know."

"But you must have run a few scenarios through your mind," I said insistently.

"Well, she may have simply left town," Arlo said. "People disappear like that all the time. Just vanish. Never seen again. But why would she have wanted to do that? And why would she have left that story behind?"

"So, do you think she killed herself?" I asked.

"She may have done that," Arlo said, "but if she did, where did she do it? Maybe she swam out into the river, but we never found her body, and we dragged that river again and again."

"That leaves murder," I said.

"Yes, that's true," Arlo admitted. "She may have been murdered, just like Audrey thinks, by a guy who drove away in a trailer or a car, then buried her in some remote place or simply dropped her into a river or a lake."

"Lots of possibilities, but where do they leave us?" I asked.

"They leave us with a mystery," Arlo answered quietly. "For you and Alice to solve."

A mystery to solve.

They were intriguing words, the sort that draw you in, and they lingered with me not only after I'd hung up the phone, but in bed later that night. In fact, they were still with me the next day, as I worked on a piece about summer gardening Wyatt had tossed me nearly a month before. Between the annuals and the perennials, heather and purple violets, I thought of Katherine walking into the river or, if not that, then of her shot, stabbed, bludgeoned, in just the ghastly way, and with almost the same dread, as I'd repeatedly imagined Teddy's murder both before and after his body had been found.

Once again, I recalled the bloody room I'd visited years before, the "slasher murder" that had been committed there, how its reek had lingered in the air, weighted it and shaded it and given it a troubling and unquiet feel, not exactly eerie, and probably more figurative than real, but a distinct sense of people at the jagged edge of things, a fatal instant of closed options.

I had no way of knowing if Katherine's life had been terminated by some similarly abrupt closure, though it would later seem to me that the possibility that it had had steadily deepened in my mind during the next few hours, sent me out walking briefly as evening fell, with no direction in mind, then out driving with the same sense of having no destination, a trail of thought and movement that ultimately wound me back to Gilmore Street.

Night had fallen by then, the street fixed in a darkness that was broken only by the faintly illuminated windows of other houses, along with the more distant light from the streetlights at nearby Cantibell.

I don't know how long I sat in my car that evening, staring silently at the house from which Katherine had vanished. I knew that criminals often returned to the scenes of their crimes, sometimes to relive them, sometimes to gloat at having gotten away with the terrible things they'd done. But I also knew that others returned for a completely different reason, returned, as we so often do in memory, because it was at this particular place that our lives veered off, sharply and irrevocably, and from there went wholly wrong.

"Are you looking for someone?"

An almost-blinding light suddenly hurtled toward me from the left, illuminating the interior of my car, a beam so intense it seemed almost instantly to raise the temperature of the air around me. The voice behind the light carried hints of both fear and aggression, like a small animal making a great, but empty show, before a vastly larger one.

"You've been sitting here a long time."

I shifted my head, trying to see a face behind the light, but the surrounding halo was too intense to penetrate.

Then the light pulled back and shifted to the right, revealing the face of a woman or, I should say, half a woman's face, as her right side was cloaked in the darkness of the hood.

"Neighborhood watch," the woman explained.

I knew that the *Winthrop Examiner* followed the police blotter carefully, reported every little blip of crime. There was no reason to keep watch on Gilmore Street.

"I'm George Gates," I told her. "I work for the *Examiner*."

The light drew back a bit farther, then angled away and toward the ground, the two of us now fixed in a faded beam. I got out of the car and nodded toward Katherine's house. "I'm working on a story about the woman who used to live in that house. Her name was Katherine Carr."

The light flicked off, so that we now stood in darkness, the woman's face visible only as a grayish smudge. We remained in the darkness for only the briefest moment; then the light came on again, but oddly angled, so that I could see only the right folds of the woman's hood.

"Have you lived around here a long time?" I asked.

"Always," the woman said. The gray blur of her face emerged from the blackness, lingered there briefly, swam back into darkness, then reappeared, now slightly more distinct so that I saw the creases at her eyes and around her mouth. "They never found her, did they?" she asked.

"No, she vanished."

The woman smiled, but faintly, edgily, without the slightest sense of amusement. "'The neighborhood freak' he called her."

"He?"

"The man who used to follow her," the woman said. "He lived on the other side of Gilmore Street. At the very end." Her voice tightened. "He called her a freak, but he didn't get away with it."

"What do you mean?"

The woman's smile did not so much trail away as drop off precipitously, like a body over a cliff. "I mean he didn't get away with it," she repeated.

I felt the small chill one sees in old detective movies, when the story opens slightly or takes an unexpected turn, usually by accident or coincidence, but at the same time in a way that seems eerily ordained, as if it were here, at precisely this spot in the tale, that the puppet master jerked the string.

The woman jiggled the light briefly, slices of her face dancing in and out of its yellow glow. "They found him all balled up in the alley behind O'Shea's." The lamp drifted to the right, leaving the woman in utter darkness. "After that he became sort of a hermit."

"Where is he now?"

"Potter's Lake," the woman said.

I knew it well. The police had dragged it in their hopeless search for Teddy.

"Does this man have a name?" I asked.

"Ronald," the woman said. Nothing broke the blackness that deepened around her, so thick and impenetrable she might, at that moment, have been only a voice. "Ronald Duckworth."

13

He wasn't hard to find, but it wasn't until after work the next evening that I headed for the house on Potter's Lake. I'd worked all that day in the midst of an ordinary world, surrounded by small-town merchants and laborers and politicians. I'd attended a meeting of the Chamber of Commerce and duly recorded its many services, then gone on to watch the mayor break ground for the new city hall. It was in every way a life lived in the open, the one I'd spent the day recording, and it was perhaps its stark visibility that seemed in gravest contrast to the man who drew back the door of the house on Potter's Lake, a man so gaunt he seemed almost intangible, the vague transparency of himself.

"Ronald Duckworth?" I asked.

He nodded very softly, barely a movement at all.

"My name is George Gates," I told him. "I'm a reporter for the *Winthrop Examiner*."

He said nothing, nor made any move to step away from the

door, allow me into the ramshackle house, little more than a fishing shack, he occupied on the banks of Potter's Lake. I was not even sure he'd heard me. More than that. He seemed in some way not actually to be there, a creature truly in the world, so that I recalled a story Celeste had once told me. She'd been standing along the sidelines of a college football game, glanced up into the bleachers, and seen a young man with hair so blond it was very nearly white. She'd smiled and waved to him warmly, a greeting he'd returned with no less a sense of old familiarity. A few minutes later, he'd joined her on the sidelines, where they'd talked just long enough, as Celeste said, to realize that they'd never met. There'd been no hint of flirtation in any of what passed between them. It was all, as Celeste put it, "like family." His last name had been Hamsun, like the famous Norwegian writer, and as their talk continued, they'd laughed at how strong it was, this feeling that they'd always known each other. Then they'd parted, never to meet again, so that it was years later, when Celeste was going through her dead mother's old letters, that she'd realized that her maternal grandfather had changed her name upon coming to America, changed it to Harris . . . from Hamsun.

Facing me silently through a rusty screen door, Ronald Duckworth had that same sense of being more the faintly remaining residue of some long-ago eeriness than an actual flesh-and-blood human being.

"I've come to talk to you about Katherine Carr," I told him.

He started to close the door, but the door stopped, as if an unseen bolt had shot up from the floor to keep it in place. Duckworth released an exhausted sigh, like someone giving in to a vastly unpleasant certainty, and with that, he stepped back and the screen door glided open smoothly, effortlessly, almost as if in response to the pull of something other than Duckworth's hand.

"Come in, then," he said in an utterly resigned tone.

I stepped inside and was immediately taken aback by the sheer austerity in which Duckworth lived, a single room with a wood stove, walls hung not with family portraits, but with hooks and nets and coils of fishing line. There was not so much as a calendar by which he could record the passage of his days. A few shelves held his store of canned goods—mostly beans, along with a few tins of coffee, salt, sugar. Everything in the room, the shelves, the few chairs, the two small card tables, lay beneath a gloomy patina of dust, and the single light that hung from the water-stained ceiling was without a shade. Small mounds of rusty hooks were scattered across the top of one of the tables. They'd been arranged by size, but none was very big. A rifle leaned in one corner of the room, but it was only an old .22 caliber, fit for nothing beyond birds and squirrels. Ronald Duckworth had clearly spent his life in pursuit of pitiably small game.

"I got a smoker out back," he said, like a man attempting to demonstrate that he had more than what he could show, a richer reserve of options, greater possibilities. "Who told you about me?"

"Someone I met on Gilmore Street."

Duckworth looked at me doubtfully. "There's nobody left on Gilmore that'd remember me."

"It was a woman," I said.

"A woman?" Duckworth dropped into one of the two chairs, a spindly rocker that like the other furniture in the room appeared to have been retrieved from the local dump. "Must be Edna May Gifford. Crazy old bat. That's the only woman I ever knew on Gilmore Street."

"Except for Katherine Carr," I said.

Duckworth winced, as if the sound of her name worked like a knife I'd jabbed him with. "I didn't know her. I just knew what everybody else knew about her."

"Which was what?" I asked.

Duckworth's small eyes narrowed, and for a moment I thought he might roll them toward the ceiling in a parody of thoughtfulness, but they held to me steadily, like tiny vises.

"I knew she kept herself locked up most of the time," he said. The thin slit of his mouth turned down at the edges, but it was not a sneer or a smirk, and there was nothing angry in his expression. Instead he seemed infinitely weary, though of what remained unclear. When he spoke, his voice held the same ragged emptiness. "She didn't go out except for these short trips to buy food and things. She was afraid of everything."

"Was she afraid of you?" I asked.

Duckworth glared at me. "I was in the hospital when she disappeared," he snarled. "I was there for nearly a week."

"Did the police ever talk to you about her? Were you a suspect?"

He shrugged. "She had my name in some writing she did. The cops came to see me, but I was in the hospital, so I couldn't have had nothing to do with whatever happened to her."

"Why were you in the hospital?"

"Because I got beat up." He appeared to be gathering the loose strings of a story in his mind, one I sensed he'd rarely told, so that as he began to tell it, I took out my notebook, suspecting that he was making it up as he went along and would tell it differently the next time, changes my notes would reveal easily. "Because this guy beat me up."

He stopped, took a quick breath, almost a gasp, like a swimmer coming up for air. At that instant he seemed like a man who felt himself utterly outside the world other people knew, his life lived at the whim of something beyond him, himself powerless against its brutal but unseen sway, waiting for it to come for him again as a man might wait in his cell for the torturer's return.

"He came out of nowhere," he said. "Just swooped down on me." He appeared to be astonished by his own words, like a man telling a story he knew to be true, yet could not believe. "That's what it seemed like, anyway. I was just going home from the bar."

"What bar?"

"O'Shea's," Duckworth said. "I used to work there, clean up the place. I was going home from work when he just swooped down."

Swooped? As a description it was so odd that I found myself imagining not a man at all, but some murderous bird of prey.

"It was in that little alley that runs from Pryor to Gilmore Street," Duckworth continued.

It was as if a terrible weight had fallen upon him from a great height, he said, a weight that had pressed him flat onto the gravelly earth of the alley, so that he'd felt his entire body reduced to powder beneath its enormity.

"I felt like a cracker in somebody's fist," Duckworth added. "Just a little cracker all crumbled up."

But the weight had pressed him down and down farther, until he'd felt "deeper than people in mines. Deeper than people under caved-in mountains and mudslides."

So deep, he'd begun to suffocate.

"I couldn't breathe. I was . . . dead."

Then—abruptly—he was in midair, hurtling toward the cement wall that bordered the alley.

"It felt like I stuck to that wall, like a piece of gum, or like a tomato would, just smashed and sticking on the wall,"

Duckworth went on. "And while I was smashed up on that wall, it was like I was being shot and stabbed and strangled, all at the same time. Like I was being beat over the head and kicked in the ribs and had my knees busted with a hammer. And there was things being pulled over my head and tied around my eyes and stuffed down my throat, old rags that smelled like they was dipped in kerosene, and they exploded just like that, and it was like my whole face was peeling off in fire. Which I thought it was until—"

It stopped—abruptly stopped—the whole murderous machine suddenly turned off, all its gears stilled, no humming motor, no whirling blades and blunt instruments, an infernal mechanism now motionless and silent.

"I wasn't getting hit with bricks and bats and hammers," Duckworth said. "No more stabbing me with knives and broken bottles or strangling me with all those different cords and ropes."

And so I thought Duckworth's strange story must surely be over at that point, but it hadn't ended for him yet.

"Then it was just the cold," he said. "This awful cold." He lifted his hand to the side of his face and jaggedly drew down a faintly trembling finger. "And it was like I was bleeding out. I could feel blood pouring down my face and soaking my shirt. It was like I was being drained." He turned his hand slowly toward me, the fingertip he dragged down the side of his face completely clean yet oddly glistening. "Then I just . . . waited." Duckworth gazed at me with dark wonder.

"For what?" I asked.

He looked like a man confronting a truth almost too brutal to confront. "For nothing," he said. "From then on . . . for nothing."

14

THE DRIVE FROM Duckworth's shack to Winthrop Hospital took me through the center of town, past the park, where the little rock grotto's appearance struck me as curiously sudden, almost like an apparition. I'd passed it many times, of course, but on this occasion I noticed its peculiar design for the first time, that it was not just a vaguely conical pile of stones, but a kind of outdoor chapel with a stone table at the center. There was a kneeling bench before it, also made of stone. There were no religious images in or around the grotto, but even so it gave off the sense of a place one might go in spiritual distress, so that I once again imagined Katherine on the last night of her life, pacing back and forth as the river fog closed in around her.

In an instant, I'd swept by it. The grotto vanished as quickly as it had appeared, and yet its afterimage was still floating through my mind when I got to Alice's room.

"Hi," I said.

She glanced at the clock that hung opposite her bed. "I didn't think you were coming." There was an unmistakable tone of resignation and acceptance in this, so that I sensed that she was long accustomed to promises made but not kept.

"I thought maybe you were too busy," she added.

"No, I'm not," I assured her.

She struggled to straighten herself, which clearly required considerable effort, and watching this struggle against such close physical restraint, I thought of how different Katherine must have been from Alice at the same age, strolling around her grandfather's farm in the bright sunlight, reading nature poems, writing about a natural order she'd evidently thought totally beneficent.

"I looked them up," Alice said, some measure of energy returning to her. "The men in Katherine's story." She handed me a page, the names written in her neat script: *Bittaker, Joubert, Ionosyan.*

"They're all murderers." She groaned very softly and shifted again. "The thing is, how would Katherine have known about them? She didn't have the Internet, so she couldn't just look things up. And even if she'd gone to the library, how could she have found out about all these foreign crimes?"

I knew that even now the Winthrop Library had a limited collection on such subjects, and that twenty years before, that collection would have been even more limited, if it had existed at all.

"So where do you think she got all that information?" I asked.

"Could it have been from Maldrow?" Alice asked tentatively, a mere testing of the speculative waters. "He told her about Albert Fish, remember?"

"Yes, he did."

She looked at me wonderingly. "But that means he was a real person. That Katherine didn't just make him up."

"But if he were real, wouldn't someone have seen him?" I asked.

"I looked back over everything we've read so far," Alice answered. "And I noticed that except for the first time, Maldrow comes to Katherine on foggy days or at night. Or they go to a place that's deserted. Like the fairgrounds."

"But that's the way people write these weird type of stories," I said. "Always fog, stuff like that."

Alice took this in for a moment, then said, "But maybe, in his line of work, Maldrow has to come and go . . . unseen."

There was an argument to be made for this, though it seemed to rest upon an eerie foundation.

"Because what he does can't be legal," Alice added. "Unless he's a bounty hunter."

"A bounty hunter." I smiled. "Very good, Alice. You could be right."

She nodded toward the pages I'd already taken from my briefcase. "Let's see if I am," she said.

NOW

"So you told her about Fish, that filthy old child murderer," the Chief says quietly.

"Yes."

"And it was the story of Fish's execution that first showed you her potential," the Chief adds. "Tell me what you think she got from that story. This 'something' that makes her different."

"She saw that Fish was unreachable," Maldrow answers gravely. "That he was beyond punishment."

The Chief peers at Maldrow quizzically. "Beyond punishment? He was electrocuted. Isn't that punishment?"

"Not for him," Maldrow says. "That's what Katherine realized. That's what she sensed about his death." He leans forward. "When I described what happened to Fish—that he was electrocuted—she reacted . . ." He stops, considers his words. "She felt his dying . . . felt it physically."

The Chief looks at Maldrow intently. "And learned what?"

"You know what happened," Maldrow continues. "How Fish had inserted all those metal sewing needles into himself, how the needles shorted out the electric chair the first time they tried to kill him."

"Katherine felt that?" the Chief asks. "Fish's pain?"

"Not his pain, no," Maldrow answers. "That's what was unusual. She felt the pain the way Fish must have felt it. And so it wasn't really pain at all. Not for him. For him, it was the ultimate pleasure, and because of that, he was beyond punishment."

"Because he felt pain as pleasure and relished it," the Chief says.

Maldrow nods. "And since Fish loathed himself, he welcomed death. That means that he was beyond anything that could be done to him. He would delight in punishment and find joy in oblivion, and because of that, he would always win."

Maldrow waits for the Chief to respond, but there is only silence, the Chief's eyes now more somber than before.

"Shall I go on?" Maldrow asks.

"Yes."

Maldrow draws the photograph from his jacket pocket and places it faceup on the table. "The picture was taken before she was attacked. One week before."

The Chief looks at the photograph, Katherine in the front yard of the farmhouse, the garage to her right, dark, empty.

Maldrow points to a spot in a shadowy corner where the blurry image of a life jacket hangs on the plain wood wall. "There's where it was done."

The Chief bends forward, places his right index finger on the photograph, and draws it down slowly. "No wonder she lost hope."

Suddenly Maldrow recalls the Chief's first assignment, the man he had described, as vicious as he was cunning, skilled in murder and evasion, despair like a dark wake following behind him. He could still recall the Chief's final words: "Depart now and restore the balance."

"Yes," Maldrow says.

"Then you know that . . ." the Chief begins, then stops as the barkeep moves toward the booth.

"What'll it be?" the barkeep asks when he reaches it.

"Same," Maldrow says.

The barkeep nods coolly, takes the glass, turns back toward the bar.

Maldrow watches as the bartender trudges down the aisle, his head slanted to the right, as if trying to get a better view of him, but slyly, without being noticed. When he is out of range, he looks across the table to where the Chief sits, facing him.

"You know that nothing can be allowed to interfere once the choice is made," the Chief continues.

Maldrow recalls Yenna's body floating in murky water only forty yards from the railway station. It turns slowly, the dark cord trailing at her throat, an abandoned corpse, Yenna, edging toward the riverbank, where it snags upon a floating branch and finally comes to rest. "Yenna," he says softly.

"Is there any danger of such a thing happening in Katherine's case?" the Chief asks pointedly.

Now Maldrow sees the young man as he moves ever deeper into the alley's darkness, knows the evil he had done, and the greater one he'd intended. "Not anymore," he says.

• • •

I stopped, suddenly struck by a way I might find to make Katherine's story even more intriguing to Alice, an element I could add to the mystery. "How odd," I said. "This young man that Maldrow's thinking about. The one moving into darkness. The one Maldrow seems to think might somehow interfere."

Alice watched me silently.

"I went over to where Katherine once lived," I told her. "A woman was there. We had a little talk and she mentioned a young man who'd once lived on Gilmore. His name was Ronald Duckworth."

Alice peered at me with razor-sharp acuity, and in the passionate involvement I saw in her eyes, I felt that I had surely done the right thing: Katherine's story, for all its weirdness and gore, was perfect for her.

"I found him living out by Potter's Lake," I continued. "And what he said had happened to him was strange. Someone had attacked him a few days before Katherine disappeared. A very bizarre attack, from the way he described it. He said it was like being stabbed and beaten and strangled all at once." I looked at Alice gravely. "It makes me wonder if Duckworth and this guy Maldrow just thought about are the same. And if it was Maldrow who attacked him."

"But why would he have done that?" Alice asked.

"Maybe because he thought Duckworth was going to interfere with . . ." I stopped, pondered the issue a moment, then said, "With their plan. Maldrow's and the Chief's."

"Their plan for what?" Alice asked.

"For Katherine," I answered.

I had meant all this as something added to our experience of reading Katherine's story together, an intriguing little supposition that upped the stakes a bit, but I suddenly saw the two stories come together in Alice's mind: the story Katherine was writing and the one she was living, so that at the instant she'd feared for the fictional Katherine, she'd feared also for the real one, a sense of impending danger, of imminent tragedy, of Katherine's helplessness in the face of it.

"But, of course, we don't know if they have a plan," I added.

Alice looked at me gravely. "Then let's go on," she said.

THEN

I opened the door and felt the odd force of a once-violent but now-dissipating power, like the aftershock of an explosion.

"Come in," I said, then stepped back and let Maldrow pass in front of me.

He took a seat and looked at me calmly, without speaking, like one long accustomed to stillness.

Watching him, I felt the exhausting nature of his labor, forever tracking down the ones who harmed us, who raped and murdered us, who stole our children and invaded our homes and claimed our space and in doing that took something essential from our lives, something that, in the aftermath of this damage, would always be missing.

"People believe that nothing gets in their way," I said. "That no one is coming for them."

Maldrow smiled softly. "But someone is," he said.

For a moment, he was silent, and during that silence, I felt a great sense of purpose take shape in me, unseen and unspoken, but becoming ever more real.

"What must I do?" I asked.

"Make others believe."

"Believe what?" I asked.

He touched my face. "Your story."

I put down the page, now persuaded that Maldrow would not turn out to be the dark figure I had earlier believed him to be, and thus that Katherine's story might have a considerably less-disturbing resolution than the dreadful irresolution that was the story of her life.

"Looks like I was wrong about Maldrow and the Chief," I said.

Alice glanced toward the window and looked out as if in search of some phantasmagorical version of Maldrow's dusty old sedan.

"I'm being moved," she said. "To a hospice." Her eyes drifted over to me. "They do that when there's no more hope."

I felt a dreadful pall settle over me, the full weight of her impending death. "Where?"

"Not far from here," Alice answered. She smiled softly. "I can go out, though. I don't have to stay in my room, the way I would if they kept me in the hospital. So maybe we could go somewhere, George."

"Where would you like to go?" I asked.

"Someplace in Katherine's story," Alice answered. "Someplace where something happened. Like you went to the places in your book."

"All right," I said. "We'll do that."

I expected that in the methodical way she did things, Alice would immediately tell me the place she most wanted to see, Gilmore Street or the grotto by the river, for example. But instead she leaned back in her pillow, and said, "Tell me a story about a place you went to."

There were scores of places that might have occurred to me, but when I looked into Alice's large, nearly motionless eyes, one place and story rose from all the rest.

"It was July in Granada," I began. "Very, very hot. My sister started vomiting, so my father and I left her and my mother in our steaming hotel room and hailed a cab. My father's Spanish wasn't great, but he explained the situation to the driver as best he could, that his daughter was very sick and that he needed to get to a pharmacy as quickly as possible."

Alice stirred slightly, and in the stirring, as I saw, winced painfully, then instantly lifted her hand. "No, it's okay," she said. "Go on."

"Well, it was a Sunday," I continued. "Most of the pharmacies were closed, so the driver had to race from one to another before he found one that was open. He finally found one, though, and my father went in and bought the medicine, and after that the driver took us back to the hotel. My father handed me the medicine and started to pay the driver. He pulled out some money and started peeling off bills, but the cab driver sat back and wouldn't take anything. *'Por qué no?'* my father asked. 'Why not?' The driver looked at my father as if he knew nothing about life, for all his money and all the places he'd been and all his education. He just shrugged and said, *'Porque tengo hija.'* '*Because I have a daughter.*'"

I glanced toward the window, looked out into the darkness for a moment, then shifted around and faced Alice once again. "I wanted to tell my son Teddy that story," I said before I could stop myself. A sulfurous wave washed over me, dark and murky as the waters into which my son's body had been sunk. "But someone murdered him and got away with it, so I'll never even know what happened to him."

Alice looked at me piercingly. "But you imagine it, don't you? What happened to Teddy."

She was right. I had imagined Teddy's murder many times. The mush he had become by the time he'd been found had revealed nothing concerning the actual manner of his death, and because of that, a hundred different murders had unfolded in my mind: a little boy stabbed, strangled, shot, but before that terrorized, perhaps tortured. I had imagined him curled in a closet, strapped to a board, lashed to a pole, hung on a hook. Nothing had not occurred to me, no carefully prepared dungeon too dark for my imagination to penetrate, and in that slowly accumulating light, I had seen my son's blond hair eerily aglow, frail as a flickering candle. In my final vision, he was always in a basement, with small square windows covered in black plastic, always naked, inhumanly pale, already half a ghost, shivering in the cold, his arms tied behind the back of a splintery wooden chair. Always he turned to me in that building light, always he looked at me, always he asked me, *Why didn't you come for me?*

"Yes, I do." I shrugged. "Anyway, I'd wanted to tell him stories." I walked back to my chair, picked up the manuscript, thinking to read the next section.

"No, let's wait," Alice said. Her voice was quite weak, and her skin seemed to have drooped slightly, as if she aged by the hour. "Tomorrow we can read some more. I'll be at the hospice by then." She drew in a long, labored breath. "It's on Gladwell Street."

"I'll be there tomorrow evening."

She smiled, but the smile itself seemed quite heavy, a burden difficult to lift.

"I should probably rest now," she said.

Her energy had flagged noticeably during the last few minutes, but it seemed to me that it was more than her fading strength that had prompted her to ask that we not continue reading Katherine's story until the next day. She wanted to string out the tale, to slow our journey to its end, and by that means hold on to this last element of suspense life offered her.

"Okay," I said. "But tomorrow let's read at that little grotto by the river. Where Katherine disappeared."

"That would be nice, George," Alice said softly. "That would be a good place."

She added nothing to this, but only eased herself back into the pillow and closed her eyes, her body so small and motionless, sunk so deeply into the enclosing folds of the pillow, that by the time I got to the door and looked back at her, she seemed hardly to be there at all.

15

Driving home that night, I recalled the story I'd just told Alice, along with the dark circumstances under which I had told it, and in recalling both, felt myself strangely submerged in my own history, like a man deep beneath the waves, exploring caverns and old dead ships, not at all concerned that in all his earlier dives, something had been missed.

I remembered being frightened by gypsies in Portugal and the swarms of traders in Tangiers, and being saved by a man who'd appeared suddenly at a border station in Czechoslovakia and by whose near-miraculous intercession I'd managed to cross over into Poland on an otherwise-terrifying night. I remembered a rainstorm in the Carpathian Mountains and tramping among the northern fjords, the Terrace of the Infinite, night-bound Vienna, Max.

Then, quite suddenly, I remembered a time in Guadalajara, a fiery summer day, the little square deserted save for a single pigeon, its diseased feathers ruffled and untended, like a man with a bad haircut, and moving so crazily, with quick spins and abrupt halts, that I came to suspect that its tiny bird brain was like mine, disoriented by a heat so intense I'd later recalled it as physically visible, a scrim of infernal waves.

The pigeon took wing just as the man appeared, so that briefly they seemed simply to have exchanged shapes. He was probably the town lunatic, I'd thought later, the man who'd strolled with a vaguely dancing step into the square that afternoon, but I'd been only a day or two in Guadalajara, and so hadn't run across him before that steamy afternoon. He was dressed as a harlequin, in colorful tights and a cap with bells at its tips. It was the bells that had first drawn my attention, though their tiny tinkling sound would hardly have been audible if, at that moment, everything else had not been so deathly still. He'd brought a brightly colored wooden box with him, and after glancing about, he popped onto it with an airy, weightless leap, then on one foot began to twirl, full turn, then stop, each time repeating one of two phrases: *Soy alegría. Soy tristeza.* I am joy. I am sorrow.

Another's grim misfortune comes to us in many forms, but for some reason, driving back through Winthrop that night, recalling the madly spinning figure in that hellish square, I suddenly felt Katherine's tragedy as I thought Alice might think of her own; not as the product of some terrible confluence of events, but as something cruelly embedded within the scheme of things.

This was hardly a comforting thought, and I knew that in the way all such thoughts had done during the last seven years, it would finally bring me to Teddy, the promise I'd made to him, then broken, and that at last I would relive the moment of that promise-breaking, when I'd stood at the window, looked

143

at the rain, seen a man in a yellow rain slicker, then turned away from the window and gone back to my little article on Extremadura, a line I couldn't finish, and had never finished.

It was a bleak, oft-repeated journey, the reliving of that moment, and I had no wish to make it yet again that night. Anything was preferable, even a high-toned book about a primitive tribe. I retrieved it from the little table beside my bed, walked to my desk, and read again of the seesawing spiritual life of the Buranni, sometimes in despair at their powerlessness before the "evil" Nemji Gai, sometimes hopeful of miraculous intervention on their behalf, realism at one end, superstition at the other, a perpetual imbalance I once again found vaguely disquieting, like a man who'd lost purchase, sought stability, but couldn't find it.

For that reason, probably more than any other, I welcomed the sound of the downstairs buzzer, walked to the window, looked out and saw a figure at the door, held in shadow, with shoulder-length hair so luminously black, so much the shimmering curtain that was said to have been Katherine's, that for a single miraculous instant, I thought, *She's found.*

"Mr. Gates," the voice said over the intercom. "My name is Cody. I'm Audrey's son. I was with Katherine when she was attacked."

"Cody, yes," I said. "I know about that."

"I wonder if we could talk," Cody asked.

"All right," I said, then pressed the buzzer.

A heavy tread sounded on the stairs, then on the landing that led to my door.

"Sorry to bother you," Cody said when I opened the door.

"No bother," I told him. "I was just reading."

"It's just that I know you've talked to my mother about Katherine, and so I thought I should speak to you about her, too."

I could see that something of life's ineffable vitality had been stolen from him. He didn't appear as one who'd been touched by the sort of evil Katherine had experienced, but something just as powerful had left its mark, one I'd seen in people who'd had to confront some dreadful truth about themselves. But I'd also seen the same look in those who'd suddenly had to recognize the culpability of a loved one, a son who'd raped a neighbor's child or a daughter who'd joined some mind-robbing cult, the sense that an invisible malevolence coiled deep within the heart of the very things that had previously seemed utterly benign.

"It isn't easy for me to talk about this," Cody added. "It's never been easy."

I led him into the tiny living room that overlooked the street. There was a sofa and a couple of chairs, a small table, a lamp, all of them scavenged from local thrift shops, a stripping down that no doubt appeared consciously imposed, like a punishment.

"Please, sit down," I said.

Cody lowered himself into one of the chairs. "Mother told me that you were looking into Katherine's case. I'm sure you'll be the last person who does that, so I wanted you to know what I think about it."

I knew a story was coming. I leaned back in my chair, as if with a book in my hands, the first page not yet open.

Cody's opening line was better than I'd expected.

"You know, Mr. Gates, with a small turn of the screw, anyone can do anything."

Then he took me back in time.

It was late on a summer day twenty years before. He'd come to spend the weekend with Katherine, something he'd often done as a boy.

"My father and mother got divorced when I was three,"

he said. "After that my father more or less disappeared." He glanced toward one of the photographs on the little table behind my desk, Teddy and I making a snowman on the front lawn of the house on Jefferson Street. "So Katherine did a lot of the father-son things with me. She'd come over to Kingston and take me to the movies or to a ball game, things like that."

On the day of the attack, she'd picked him up in Kingston, he said. Then they'd driven back to Winthrop.

"There was a fair going on," Cody said, "one of those traveling things, with rides and games. We got there late in the afternoon."

He was clearly conjuring up that moment twenty years before, a dark return, as I could see, but one to which he appeared to have grown accustomed, like a man grown used to a cave he'd first entered fearfully, but now could navigate without dread.

"I remember that I was a little afraid of the whole thing," Cody went on. "The people and the noise. So I grabbed Katherine's hand."

"Just like she writes in her story," I said.

"Yes," Cody answered. "A lot of what she writes is true."

"But not all?"

He was clearly surprised by my question. "Well, the ending, for example."

I told him that I hadn't yet read the ending, and why, that a little girl and I were reading it together and that I thought it best not to get ahead.

"You want to keep the mystery going, I guess." Cody smiled. "Don't we all?"

I shrugged. "Anyway, I promised myself that I wouldn't skip ahead."

"Good," Cody said. "I'm glad you haven't. Because it'll

make what I have to tell you more . . . believable." His expression turned quite grave. "Because there are things Katherine left out, Mr. Gates. Things that aren't in the story she left behind."

But rather than go further into the "things Katherine left out," Cody returned to the day in question, the day of the attack, detailing his and Katherine's movements through the fair, then their return to Katherine's car for the drive to the farmhouse, where he'd curled up in the backseat and gone to sleep.

"I remember that she closed the car door very softly," Cody told me, "but I was always a light sleeper, and it jarred me awake. You know, it was just that little click a car door makes. But it was enough. I don't know if I opened my eyes, but I know I was awake."

Awake enough to hear Katherine as she made her way toward the entrance to the farmhouse, then to hear another set of footsteps—moving quickly, rushing forward, louder—so he'd opened his eyes.

"I saw a blur," Cody said. "Something moved past the car window. Very fast. Like I said, just a blur. I couldn't have identified anybody. I always knew that." A desperate quality came into his voice. "I was just a kid. I got scared."

And so he'd remained in the backseat of the car and listened, terrified, a shivering little boy.

"I couldn't move," he said. "If I could have moved, I would have looked out and maybe seen his face."

I felt myself hurled back to the very moment I'd tried earlier to avoid, so that I once again heard the thunder that had broken over the little pink Victorian, followed by rain, the way I'd reluctantly gotten up from my desk, walked to the window, looked out to see a figure in a yellow rain slicker, drawing ever nearer as it moved up Jefferson Street, the face too distant, a blur, but which might have become starkly clear had I held my place at the window rather than returning to my work, the line I'd half-written and wanted to complete: *The winds of Extremadura blow* . . .

"I heard her groan," he said. "I heard him say, '*You bitch!*' "

And then, locked in helpless childhood terror, Cody had listened at full volume to the building outrage.

"It was over very fast, I guess," Cody said. "But it seemed like a long time to me, and it must have seemed like an eternity to Katherine."

When it was over, and he knew the unknown man was gone, Cody had gotten out of the car, expecting to see Katherine by the door, but instead found her at the entrance to the garage.

"Her hand was stretched out like she was grabbing for something," Cody said.

"For the guy who attacked her," I said, "according to Arlo McBride."

It struck me that Cody had not actually told me anything new, at least nothing that changed any aspect of what I'd read thus far in Katherine's story or heard from Arlo. He seemed suddenly aware that this was the case and quickly moved forward in time.

"You know what Katherine was like after that," he said. "Closed off. Isolated."

I nodded.

"Her mind changed—that's my point," he added. "It got really dark."

He was moving toward his point, but still reluctant to make it, like a man afraid of the one true thing he knows.

"It's something my mother won't admit about Katherine," he went on. "How angry she was."

He paused briefly, like a man at the edge of a threatening forest, then went on.

"I know that my mother told you that she believes that Maldrow murdered Katherine," he said. "She's told me the same thing. She believes that somehow Katherine found out that he was a con man, that he was just using her. He was afraid she would expose him. So he killed her." He shook his head at what he obviously considered a ludicrous theory. "I don't believe that at all. In fact, I don't believe Maldrow ever existed."

He made a point to pause before continuing, so that I knew he'd arrived at the moment in his story where the screw made a turn.

"I was thirteen when I saw Katherine for the last time," Cody said. "I'd taken a bus from Kingston. Normally, I would have walked from the bus station to her house on Gilmore. But she called and said she'd meet me at the bus stop."

There was nothing unusual in this, I thought. Katherine had walked the streets of Winthrop before, had never been entirely housebound.

"And she *did* meet me," Cody said. "Right at the edge of the park."

They'd ambled away from the bus stop, then up one side of Main Street, to where the Winthrop Hotel stood in its faded grandeur at the corner of Cantibell and Main.

"We went into the hotel and Katherine walked over to the desk clerk and asked if he had the schedule for the Route 34 bus," Cody continued. "The one that goes by where the old slaughterhouse once was." He peered at me intently. "Have you read the part where Katherine mentions the slaughterhouse?"

"Not yet."

His expression turned grim. "You will," he said.

Then he returned to his own narrative.

"Well, the desk clerk had all the local bus schedules, and he found the one Katherine wanted and gave it to her," he said.

He seemed still a bit surprised by the oddity of what had happened next. "Katherine looked at it closely. Then she said, 'Let's go for a walk, Cody.'" He stared at me unbelievingly. "It was getting dark, and Katherine had never liked to be out at night. Not since the attack. But we went on that walk."

They had gone down Main Street, Cody said, Katherine in charge of the pace, which was very slow.

"There was something sad about it all," he added. "She was walking very slowly, and as she walked, she glanced into the shop windows. She'd gone into the shops all her life. Long before the attack. This was her town, and I got the feeling that she was saying good-bye to it."

Occasionally she'd reached out and touched his hand, Cody said, a soft, airy touch, sad and wistful. "Like she was saying good-bye to me, too."

But Katherine's mood had not been all wistfulness. He'd seen a curious sense of purpose, as well, as if she'd had a list of things she had to complete, a person on a mission that had a definite end.

"From time to time, she glanced at her watch," he went on. "And sometimes she seemed to be pretending that she'd found something interesting in one of the shop windows. A pair of earrings, or something like that. But it was all an act, I think, because she was trying to make sure that she got to where she was headed at just the right time. Which was the park. That little stone grotto."

Here—at just the place where Katherine would later last be seen alive—they had sat down.

"We talked for a while, then Katherine sort of went into herself, the way she did sometimes," Cody said. "I've often remembered that the little grotto was where she was last seen alive, and that it was also the place she went to at the end of her story, the place where she departed."

Departed. It struck me as a strange word, but I had no context for it and let it go.

"Anyway, we sat on the bench for about five minutes, and it seemed to me that she was waiting for something," Cody said.

He'd had no idea what Katherine was waiting for until the 34 bus stopped at the edge of the park.

"I didn't even notice the bus until I saw that Katherine was looking at it," Cody went on. "Then I looked over and saw a man get out of the bus and walk into the park."

He was tall and skinny, Cody said, a taut wire of a man who strolled into the park and slumped against a tree, facing the river, smoking a cigarette.

"He was in his forties, something like that." Cody shifted slightly, like a man in the hot seat, feeling the pressure to be exact. "He didn't look like he was just hanging around, this guy. He looked like he had a place to go, but the bus had gotten him there too early. He had a few minutes to kill, so he was having a smoke. He didn't look like he'd come to meet anyone else, and I don't think he would ever have noticed Katherine if she hadn't stood up, almost like someone in a trance, and taken a couple of steps toward him."

She had risen in a slow, steady movement, Cody said, like someone lifted by an invisible hand, and there, by the grotto, with her back straight and her face uplifted, she had stared directly at this man.

"He was about twenty feet away, and he was just sort of glancing around. But at a certain point, he looked over in our direction."

It was then, Cody said, that Katherine had done the strangest thing of all. "She stared at him, really stared."

The air around us seemed to darken suddenly, though I knew that it hadn't, that this perceived change of shade was only the result of the change in tone that had accompanied his words.

"It was like she knew it was him," Cody said. "That this was the man she'd come to see."

"But who *was* he?" I asked.

"I think he was the unknown man Katherine wrote about in her story," Cody answered. "The man she thought had attacked her. I think she'd studied him by then, his movements, tracked him or something, so that she knew he took this bus, and when he got off it."

"But how would she have known this was the man who'd attacked her?" I asked.

"She wouldn't have to know it," Cody said. "She'd only have to *believe* that it was him."

"How did the man react?" I asked.

"He just nudged himself away from the tree, turned around, and headed toward town. Katherine watched him until he disappeared around the corner at the end of Main Street." Cody shrugged. "She never mentioned him or gave me any idea about who he was. He just walked around the corner and vanished."

"Did you ever tell the police about this?"

"I didn't think anything about it at the time," Cody answered. "It was only later, when my mother hatched this weird theory that Maldrow had killed Katherine, that I remembered the man in the park, and that he looked a lot like the guy Katherine described when she wrote about the unknown man. That he was skinny, a smoker." He paused a moment then added, "And I thought to myself, 'She saw him. She recognized him.'"

With this, I thought Cody had reached the end of his story, and felt a vague disappointment that there'd been so little to it, as if only something miraculous could shed more light on whatever it was that had ultimately happened to Katherine.

There was more, however: a twist that brought him back around to the first thing he'd said to me, how with a slight turn of the screw, anyone could do anything.

"And I think she *did* recognize him, Mr. Gates," Cody said. There was an ominous quality to his voice now, a dark undertow. "And because of that I think my mother got the whole thing backwards. The police, too. Maybe everyone was wrong about Katherine. Wrong about her killing herself and wrong about her being murdered. Wrong about what really happened." He watched me silently for a moment, then said, "Because I saw her face when she turned around after looking at that man. And it wasn't the face of a victim. It was the face of a woman who intended to get even."

This was certainly a dramatic conclusion, but it also left something out.

"Then what happened to Katherine?" I asked bluntly. "If she didn't kill herself or wasn't murdered. Why did she vanish?"

He appeared to see Katherine as she'd turned back toward him that day, a vision that affirmed what he had come to think about her.

"Two people usually 'vanish' after a murder," he said. "One of them is the person who was murdered, so that person vanishes into a grave." His gaze intensified. "The second is the murderer, who also vanishes . . . if he gets away with it."

16

So that was Cody's theory, that Katherine had found the man who'd attacked her five years before—or at least convinced herself that she'd found him—and after that, like some black-draped woman in a noir potboiler, murdered him and . . . departed.

It was certainly a twist, as Cody had telegraphed in his opening remark, but I didn't believe a word of it, and because of that I might simply have thanked Cody for telling me his story, filed it away in some corner of my mind, and otherwise forgotten it. There have always been tales in which the unlikely is all that offers itself by way of resolution, the delayed letter, the misplaced note, the unexpected encounter. But unlike those stories, Cody's theory of Katherine's disappearance was one that could to some extent be tested, and for which evidence could be found.

"So, was a middle-aged man murdered in this area around

the time of Katherine's disappearance?" I asked Arlo when he met me for coffee the next morning.

I had just told him what Cody had told me the night before, even emphasized its weirdest implication: that Katherine was, herself, a murderer who'd gotten away with it rather than a woman who'd been murdered.

Arlo shook his head. "Nobody was murdered."

"So what Cody thinks couldn't possibly be true," I said.

"You mean that Katherine killed the man she thought had attacked her, then escaped by vanishing?" He shrugged. "I guess anything's possible, but it's a pretty wild theory."

"Too bad," I said. "Because it would certainly have made for an interesting twist in the story."

Arlo looked at me quizzically. "Why are you looking for a twist?"

"Because of Alice," I said. "She's read a lot of mysteries, and my guess is that most of them have had pretty unsatisfying twists. You know the type, where the murderer reveals all the intricacies of his crime while he holds a gun on the protagonist. Then the hero kicks beach sand in the murderer's face and grabs the gun. The End."

Arlo took a sip of coffee. "I wish I had a better twist to offer," he said. "But facts are facts, and nobody was murdered at around the time Katherine disappeared."

"But there was an assault," I said. "Around the time Katherine disappeared. It happened not far from Gilmore Street. To a guy mentioned in Katherine's story."

"Ronald Duckworth," Arlo said. "How did you know about that?"

I told him about my encounter with the woman with the flashlight, my subsequent trip out to Potter's Lake, the bizarre tale Duckworth had related to me.

"Duckworth told the police the same story he told you," Arlo said.

"Was he in the hospital when Katherine disappeared?" I asked.

"Yeah, he was," Arlo answered. "So he couldn't have had anything to do with Katherine's disappearance."

"Any idea who attacked him?"

Arlo laughed. "Nobody attacked him."

"Nobody? But he says he was beaten to a pulp."

Arlo waved his hand. "Nobody laid a hand on Ronald Duckworth. He was traumatized, that's for sure. But there were no actual injuries. No cuts. No bruises."

"So where did that story come from? It's pretty detailed."

"Who knows? Probably some drugged-up hallucination."

"But he seems to believe it," I pointed out. "Believe that it actually happened."

Arlo glanced out into the town's peaceful streets. "Well, one thing's for sure: He never bothered anybody again." He laughed. "It was like he imagined his own . . . punishment."

"Punishment for what?" I asked.

"For whatever he was planning to do that night," Arlo said.

"Which was?"

"Something unpleasant, that's for sure," Arlo said. "Because when he got picked up the next morning, he had a knife and masking tape with him. You don't carry that around after work unless you're headed for a very bad place."

"Where was he picked up?" I asked.

"He was in the alley behind O'Shea's." Arlo laughed grimly. "With all the other rats."

The blue of evening had settled in by the time I took my stroll from the back of O'Shea's, where the alley began, toward

Gilmore Street, where it ended. I didn't know the exact spot of the attack, but Duckworth had mentioned being thrown against a cement wall, so when I saw that wall, now nearly completely concealed by vines, I knew that I had found the actual location of where he claimed to have been assaulted.

Duckworth had left O'Shea's at closing time, he'd said, so that it must have been around two in the morning when he'd made his way down the alley. He had been headed home, he'd told me, but the location of the attack made it clear that in fact he had turned north, the opposite of where he'd lived, toward the other end of Gilmore Street.

Toward Katherine, I thought with an eerie chill, toward where she lived alone in a little house no more than a hundred yards away from where the attack had occurred. So close, so near to her, that by stepping backward and peering to the north, I could actually see the house Katherine had occupied at the time.

What, I wondered, would Alice make of that?

The Gladwell Hospice was a large Victorian house, painted dark green with white shutters. Potted plants lined the walkway that led from the street to the front door. Inside, there were more plants, along with a couple of idly strolling cats.

"I'm here to see Alice Barrows," I told the man who sat in the building's small foyer. "She was admitted today."

"Yes, Alice," the man said. "She's in Room 12."

"She said she was allowed to go out," I added. "So I thought I'd take her to the park."

"She is allowed to do whatever she likes," the man said quietly. "She'll need a wheelchair. There's one in her room."

"Thanks."

He smiled. "Enjoy the park."

She had fallen asleep over her laptop when I arrived, her

hairless pate glowing softly in the eerie blue light of its small screen. A notebook lay open beside her, and her wrinkled hand still held a red felt-tipped pen.

"Alice," I said gently.

She didn't move.

"Alice."

She stirred slightly, and with that stirring, released a small moan.

I moved to her bedside and touched her shoulder. "It's George."

She lifted her head, and squinted. Then a spark lit her eyes and she seemed to urge herself back to life. "Are we going to the river?" she asked.

"Of course," I said. "But I have something to tell you first."

With that I told her about going to the alley that led from O'Shea's to Gilmore Street, how Duckworth had clearly *not* turned toward his home the night he'd been attacked, how it seemed to me that he had been headed for Katherine's house, no doubt with evil intent, since the cops had found a knife and masking tape on him when he'd been picked up the next morning.

It was an intriguing little sidebar I expected to add an element of interest, but Alice seemed hardly to take note of it.

"I found out that sometimes they work in teams." With those words, she made a few taps on her keyboard, then turned the screen toward me. The heading read *Evil Pairs*.

The photographs were arranged in malignant couples, with a trickle of blood luridly connecting one picture to another: Leopold and Loeb; the Moors Murderers, Hindley and Brady; the Hillside Stranglers, Bianchi and Buono; the Bunker Killers, Ng and Lake.

"Sometimes it takes two people," Alice explained. "They

make one personality. Alone, neither of them would do anything really bad. But together, they can do anything."

This was nothing new, but neither did it seem relevant to anything in Katherine's story. Nor was it a subject I felt the inclination to pursue.

"Okay, let's go to the river," I said. I drew a flashlight from my jacket pocket. "I brought this so we could read."

We were in my car only a few minutes later, Alice a tiny figure on the passenger side. The cool of evening had settled over Winthrop, and since she was easily chilled, she'd bundled up in a heavy turtleneck sweater and pulled a purple woolen cap down over her ears.

At the river, I took her wheelchair from the backseat, brought it to the passenger side of the car, then lifted her from the seat and lowered her into the chair.

"Okay?" I asked.

She shifted about a little, then, once settled, peered down Main Street.

"Katherine would have come down that way." I pointed toward Gilmore.

Alice looked in the direction I indicated, but said nothing.

"And there's the grotto," I added, now pointing in the opposite direction, to where it rested near the river.

"Let's go there," Alice said.

I pushed her forward, along the winding sidewalk that led to the grotto. On the way, we passed a large family, all of whom stared at her as she passed, a curiosity Alice pretended not to notice.

"It's better not to stare back," she said when we reached the grotto. "It makes them feel strange." She looked out toward the river, and I expected her to say something about Katherine's story, but instead she asked, "What did Teddy look like?

There's a picture on the Internet. But it's in black and white, so I don't know the color of his hair or—"

"He was blond," I said, hoping to end the discussion there.

"How tall was he?"

"A little over four feet."

"What did he weigh?"

"Seventy pounds." I shook my head. "Alice, I really don't want to . . ."

"Did he like to read?" Alice asked.

"He was dyslexic, so it was hard for him to read. But he liked to be read to." I looked out over the river into which some forever-unknown man had sunk the body of my little boy. "And he liked to play ball. He played in the Little League."

Alice released a slow breath, and seemed to feel that some secret goal had been reached. "You can read to me now," she said.

NOW

The Chief releases a labored breath. "All right, let us continue."

Maldrow smiles quietly. Years have passed since they first met, but he has no trouble remembering the dreary town where the Chief found him, the muddy street he'd seemed to drift across, drift weightlessly through a pelting rain to where Maldrow leaned against a wooden post. As if no time at all had passed, he heard again the Chief's first words to him: "Sorry about your little girl."

Maldrow hears the spatter of rain on the muddy streets, then feels the warm fire inside the saloon where the Chief later led him, hears again the old man's quiet voice: *Do you recognize this?* A little gold cross glows from the Chief's pale palm. *He didn't get away with it.* The pale fingers curl back around the cross. *So many like her.*

Now Maldrow sees Sasha led into the thickening undergrowth, yanked across a small bridge and into a makeshift shed where she sits, terrified, in a rusty metal chair. Then he is with Yenna in the aftermath, Yenna wrapped in her dark shawl, deep green eyes peering toward the indifferent wood, across the icy stream, to the tar-roofed shed. After Yenna, the others come to him in a riot of grief-stricken faces: mothers and fathers, sisters and brothers, husbands and wives, eyes locked in frantic search of the unknown man who arrived in an instant, stayed but an instant, yet never really left.

Then a world of malignant beings crowds his mind. He sees Countess Báthory with her exquisite tortures, the poisons of Marie de Brinvilliers. He sees Kürten primly dressed for a stroll through Düsseldorf, Vladimir Ionosyan selecting just the right cobbler's bodkin for his evening out. How long have these been his sole companions? Gein and Haarmann and Haigh stand briefly before him, then vanish, leaving him with nothing but the cold vision of their bloody acts, the broken lives they left behind. He has shared every meal with them, every moment of enforced leisure. They trail behind him in a leering throng, rippers and night stalkers. Their signs crowd the night sky with tridents and zodiacs. Their scrawled notes are his literature, words written in blood or pieced together crudely from magazine cutouts. For him, Bach is the final gurgling of a strangled child, Renoir what murderers splatter on mirrors, walls, and doors.

The Chief sees the horror show that plays continually in Maldrow's mind. "We must finish with Katherine," he says.

Maldrow sees Yenna disappearing into the darkened alleyway where Stanovich waits in an even-darker corner, waits for she who had been chosen, and was well prepared to face her fate. Now he thinks of Katherine: how she is made of the same stark fabric. He recalls the way she'd approached the blood-splattered apron, known with a terrible exactitude the nature of the man, all the women who'd lie whimpering on their backs, a man towering over them in his muddy boots. Nothing but death would stop her.

"Do you want Katherine to live forever?" the Chief asks pointedly.

Maldrow lowers his head before what he knows is inevitable now.

"Then you must carry out the plan."

I glanced up and saw the look in Alice's eyes, as if she were watching a dark scenario unfold within her mind.

"Do you want to talk about this section?" I asked.

She shook her head. "No, just read the next one."

THEN

Maldrow got out of the car and stared about with a wistfulness that seemed mournful, like a soldier peering toward the beach he is about to storm, taking his last look at the gently swaying palms, the tumbling surf, the circling birds.

"This is what I wanted to show you," he said.

It was a tiny, nondescript house, on a dirt road that ran off Route 34, where the old slaughterhouse had once stood and which still gave off a wave of intense suffering, dazed creatures going to their doom, though the terrible squealing that had once rung through the adjoining fields was now silent.

"This is where he lives," Maldrow said.

The house itself was covered in aluminum siding and had a roof in need of repair, a house which, despite the bright morning sun, gave off a terrible gloom. A badly cracked cement walkway led through a weedy yard to a small porch. On the porch, an empty swing rocked slowly, as if in response to a ghostly push. The windows of the house were dark and unlighted, and the adjoining dirt driveway was empty.

Maldrow stepped toward the house, then looked back when I didn't follow him.

"We're going in?" I asked.

"Yes," Maldrow said. "I want you to see his bed and his toilet, how physical he is."

With that, he turned and headed for the house, walking in full view, at a slow pace, utterly indifferent to the old man who rocked on the porch of the neighboring house or the teenage boy who worked on his car in the driveway next door. Neither of them glanced toward us as we made our way toward the door.

At the threshold of the house, I stopped suddenly. "Do I have to do this?"

I was trembling now, fear at once ice and fire, a deeper terror than the thing itself, the terror of a terror yet to come.

"It's required of you," Maldrow said.

With no further word he opened the door and stepped aside, so that I was the first to enter the cramped living room, feel the stenchlike aura of the place, the corruption of its air.

"Through here," Maldrow said.

I followed him down a narrow corridor, where we stopped at a closed door.

"He sleeps in this room," Maldrow said. He opened the door and stepped away, leaving me to face the room's grim details alone: a mattress on the floor, its bedding spilled over the edge; a single pillow, folded in the middle and squeezed together, as if by invisible thighs. There were scores of photographs strewn about the bed, ripped from magazines: women tied to beds, strapped to posts, hung from ropes, women cut and bleeding from the wounds in their arms and legs.

For a moment, I labored to imagine the man sprawled across the disordered mattress, his hairy legs wound in the bedding, dirty feet protruding from the sheets, but hard as I tried to envision him, I saw only the empty bed, the gloomy light. And so I finally turned and walked back into the living room, where Maldrow awaited me.

"We can go now," Maldrow said.

He turned and led me toward the door, where I saw a long white apron that was covered in the pinkish stain of washed-out blood hanging from a wooden peg.

I felt all my courage drain away, and with it, my knees buckled and I swooned, staggering as I swooned, so that I would have collapsed onto the floor had not Maldrow reached for me and pulled me into his arms.

"Enough," he said. "For now."

I stopped and looked up from the manuscript.

The light in Alice's eyes faded briefly, then brightened, like a candle briefly snuffed, then relighted. "Why is Maldrow doing this to her?" she asked.

"Doing what?" I asked.

"Putting Katherine through these steps. Making her go places, relive things."

"I don't know," I answered.

Alice remained silent for a moment, then said, "Katherine is going to die soon, and she knows it."

"But she couldn't have known that, could she?"

"Maybe not," Alice said. "At least, not the way I know I'm going to."

She had said this matter-of-factly, but I fled the cold reality of it by glancing away from her out toward the river, a gesture Alice clearly saw, but chose to avoid.

"We can go now," she said. "It's getting dark and cold."

Back in her bed, Alice tried to retrieve her laptop, but it was too heavy. I took it from her shaky hands and put it on her lap.

"Thanks, George. I'd like the pages, please." I gave them to her, then watched as she tapped at the keyboard.

"Countess Báthory was a niece of the King of Poland," she said after a moment, holding her gaze firmly to the screen. "She was born in 1560."

From there she went on to give the other details that shone from the screen, how the Countess had married at fifteen, a man who was often absent, and in whose absence, the Countess's behavior became more and more erratic. Eventually she'd taken up the practice of torturing servant girls for sport, she told me, and this inevitably had ended in murder.

She tapped in another name, waited briefly, still careful not to look at me.

"Marie de Brinvilliers was a poisoner," she said after a moment. "She murdered invalids, along with a few relatives and friends."

From there, she proceeded down the list of the other names we'd just read about in Katherine's story: Vladimir Ionosyan, Carl Panzram and Peter Kürten, all serial murderers, as were Fritz Haarmann, John Haigh, and Ed Gein.

When she'd finished with the last of these, she looked up from the screen, her eyelids drooping slightly, a clear sign that her strength was ebbing.

"We'll start again tomorrow," she said.

"Okay." I rose. "I'll be back tomorrow night."

She smiled softly. "No hurry, George," she said softly, as if to reassure me that she would still be here. "I have plenty of time."

But I knew there wasn't plenty of time for Alice. There was no assurance that we would even be able to finish Katherine's story together. For as I also knew, the end often came suddenly to such children, each breath won against steadily building odds.

It was perhaps the feeling that Alice's time had grown as abruptly short as the sections of Katherine's story I'd read to her that same night that sent me back to work rather than to bed that evening. I don't know exactly what I was looking for, nor even how to proceed, save that I recalled the one name, other than Yenna's, that had often been repeated: Stanovich.

I had no idea if this particular character might later prove important, or even if he had the slightest significance to Katherine's story, but in some way—and this I *did* know—I felt that in returning to this research, I was at least continuing to fulfill my promise to Alice, playing a somber Archie Goodwin to her dying Nero Wolfe, two amateur sleuths following the trail of an elusive mystery.

And so, for the next few minutes, I delved into the comfort of work, digging up whatever facts I could locate about Andrei Stanovich. The information I found was exactly what anyone would expect to find in any criminal biography. Stanovich had been a man in his mid-forties when, in the fall of 1956, he'd first begun to kill. By then he'd secured a job as a railway inspector, and so had no doubt been seen hundreds of times by passengers in trains and waiting rooms throughout the Ukraine. Over the years he'd killed again and again, but his job—the way he rode the rails from one village to the next—had provided a highly effective cover. Added to this, his features had been so ordinary and indistinct he'd seemed hidden within the folds of Everyman.

As to Stanovich's crimes, they were hideous: his victims found with their eyes gouged out, tongues cut off, disemboweled, these outrages inflicted upon some of them—as later became apparent—while they were still alive.

Stanovich's reign of terror had certainly lasted longer than most: a full eighteen years before the murders finally stopped with what was roughly calculated as the twenty-second victim. By that time, nearly twenty-five thousand suspects had been questioned, but not one of the long line of men who'd been summoned to various police stations throughout the Ukraine, many of them tortured—a few to the point of making false confessions—had been Andrei Stanovich.

In the end, it was Stanovich who had revealed himself, though oddly, at least insofar as he appeared to have suffered a "complete physical and mental crumbling," according to one report, as if his body had finally collapsed beneath the weight of his own malignant mind.

A school janitor had found him curled into the corner of the chain-link fence that surrounded the school. He'd been locked in a fetal position with no visible wounds, but whimpering and gasping, his eyes bulging and foam boiling from his wildly trembling lips. No identification had been found on Stanovich, either, save for a single square of torn paper that had been pinned to the front of what remained of his jacket. The word that had been scrawled on the paper was "Molech," a name, as authorities later discovered, that was derived from Melech, "king," and Bosheth, "shame." Molech, as it turned out, was a god the ancient Israelites had once worshipped, and to whom the Canaanites had sacrificed their own children.

As if yanked to my feet and propelled across the room, I suddenly found myself at the window of my apartment, staring down at the street. It was deserted, but I could hear a car in the distance. Like a man who hears something in a dark room and rises to confront whatever it is, I opened the window and leaned out. By then the car was closing in, the lights growing brighter and brighter as it approached, then slowing suddenly, as if now moving through crystal-clear water, so that as it passed beneath my window, I saw that the driver was Hollis Traylor.

Then quite without willing, I heard my mind repeat Max's admonition, *Always remember, George, the Unseen,* and at that instant glimpsed the profile of a woman sitting motionlessly in the backseat, her back straight, her head erect, her arms folded over her chest in what seemed an unearthly patience, as if she'd long been a passenger in this car.

But was it a woman at all, I later wondered, a figure seen or only imagined, flesh and blood or pure phantasm, as real as Alice was and Katherine had once been, or as mythic as the Kuri Lam.

I will never know, though it became quite clear that death was most certainly abroad that night in Winthrop, striking silent and unseen with its old familiar hand.

17

IT HAD STRUCK early in the morning, but I'd learned nothing of it until I reached the *Winthrop Examiner* at just after nine. "I guess you heard about Hugo Tanner," Charlie said.

"No. What about him?"

"He died last night. A neighbor found him curled up in that nutty house of his."

Hugo Tanner had been one of Winthrop's best-known eccentrics, a man who dabbled in "the black arts" as I'd melodramatically put it in the profile I'd done of him. He'd lived in a small house on the outskirts of town, its rooms piled high with a vast collection of psychic paraphernalia. He'd turned his basement into an alchemist's lab, complete with hundreds of beakers and jars. An entire wall was given over to various chemicals, both liquid and powder, many of which, as I'd noticed at the time, were simply spices: cumin, turmeric, cayenne pepper and the like. One whole table had been strewn with the Bunsen burners Tanner had purchased from the old

Depression-era Winthrop High School, before it was torn down.

"He managed to dial 911," Charlie added. "But by the time EMS got there, he was gone."

Charlie had picked the news up on his scanner, recognized Hugo's address, and followed the exchanges until he'd heard an EMS worker report to Winthrop Hospital that the ambulance would be arriving with a DOA.

"Poor bastard!" Charlie shrugged. "He had nothing at all."

"Except his passion," I said softly, though I had little sympathy for the way Hugo had lived his life, squandering what had quite clearly been a good mind on occult studies, a fruitless pursuit that had gained him nothing but a certain local celebrity.

"Yeah, his passion," Charlie said. Then he shrugged. "But what did that get him in the end?"

Nothing, I decided.

Nothing at all.

And so, for the rest of the day, I went about my usual duties, in this case, interviewing one of Winthrop's most prominent matrons about the upcoming Flower Festival, one she hoped to invigorate by having a parade with a surprise celebrity.

"I was thinking maybe Kathie Lee Gifford, or someone like that," Mrs. Lancaster said. "Do you know anyone like that, Mr. Gates?"

I shook my head and moved in mental lockstep to the next question: "This parade you're planning: Will there be floats?"

The interview ended at just before noon. I drove to a local sandwich shop, ordered my usual ham on rye, then went to a corner table. It was warm inside, so I took off my jacket and draped it over the back of the chair. Then I sat down and unwrapped my sandwich, now scanning the room idly. The local high school was only three blocks away, so quite a few teen-agers trickled in and out of the shop while I ate. Many were in groups, but from time to time a couple would stand, holding hands or with their arms slung loosely about each other.

"So naïve," I said absently, more or less to myself, so that I was surprised when a voice came from just behind me—little more than a whisper—but uttering a few words I have not since forgotten.

"At some point in life, we should all be fiercely wrong."

I turned to see a woman standing in the takeout line beside my table. She was tall and quite striking, her long, dark hair streaked with silver.

I had no doubt that she had addressed me personally, so I said, "I suppose so, yes."

She started to speak again, but as she did so, the book she'd been holding slipped from her fingers. She retrieved it and held it gently in her hand, in such a way that the title was clearly visible: *The Turn of the Screw.*

"Are you fond of ghost stories?" she asked when she saw my attention lingering on the book.

"I might be if I believed in ghosts," I answered. "But people don't come back from the dead." I thought of Teddy, Celeste, the long line of the Never-to-Return, Alice soon to join their vanished ranks. "So a ghost story can never be about real life."

The woman's eyes seemed unearthly still. "That's true," she said. "Ghost stories are about hope."

She smiled sweetly, one of those smiles poets call "serene," and I thought she might add another comment, but the line moved forward abruptly, taking her with it as if on a smooth current, so that within seconds, or so it seemed, she had vanished.

I finished my lunch and left the shop, but the woman's ini-tial words to me kept circling in my mind: *At some point in life, we should all be fiercely wrong.* Perhaps they lingered because I suddenly thought of Hugo Tanner, the life he'd frittered away in ludicrous pseudo-scientific research, a waste that by the unknowable windings of thought returned me once again to lives taken prematurely: Teddy's life and Celeste's, and at last to the one that Alice would lose soon.

A dark mood settled over me, one that had only deepened by the time I got back to the office.

Charlie was sitting at his desk, working the phones. "Yeah, got it," he said, then hung up. His eyes blazed with a happiness that I'd rarely seen in them.

"They caught Warren Maizey," he said. "Can you believe it? After all these years, he didn't get away with it." He clapped his hands. "It's a great day for Eden Taub."

Eden Taub.

She'd been found in a basement, lying on a bloodstained mattress, Eden Taub, eight years old, left in the care of a next-door neighbor her parents had paid to keep her while they sought work in the fruit orchards of the Salinas Valley. It had gone on for nearly three months, a systematic torture that included packing Eden in ice and submerging her in boiling water. She'd been lashed with a jump rope, pinched with toolbox pliers, burned with cigarettes, an agony inflicted in what appeared to have been diabolical relay games by Warren Maizey and his two imbecilic daughters, Gwen and Rhonda, aged fifteen and seventeen.

Maizey had left his daughters to fend for themselves after Eden's murder, and with no capacity to provide for themselves or to consider the consequences of their own crimes, they had finally called a social worker who'd taken one look around the house and immediately called the police. I could still remember the answer they'd later given reporters about their father's whereabouts, both of them grinning into the cameras: *Daddy, he just vanished.*

Which he had done, until now.

"Fifteen years, but they finally got him," Charlie said happily. He gave his old familiar wink, the one that always seemed to say, *Told you so.* "I guess miracles do happen, don't they, George?"

I shook my head and thought of all the ones who were never caught, and on that thought, felt the old wrath strike me once again, fierce and shattering, and from which I knew I would never be released, so that "I don't think so, Charlie," was all I found to say.

And so the eddies of my mounting anger rippled on through the day, and were still rippling through me later that afternoon as Wyatt read my piece on the Flower Festival. While I sat silently in front of his desk, I recalled a question my father had asked as he lay dying, the look on his face when he'd asked it, along with the details of the hospital room: the scent of the air, even the small, blinking lights on the machines that monitored the steady ebbing of his life.

"Why are we here, Georgie?" my father asked. "To suffer? To bear witness? That's what Chekhov says." For a moment, he added nothing more. Then, very slowly, his eyes opened and he seemed to be staring at me from a great distance, as from behind the starry curtain of some far galaxy. "Nobody has the answer but me." He smiled. "I have the answer, Georgie."

"Then what's the answer, Dad?" I asked indulgently. "Why are we here?"

Suddenly the serenity into which my father had briefly settled dropped away, leaving nothing behind but his blazing anger. "We are here to correct God's fucking mistakes!" he cried.

"To undo His goddamn screwups!" For a moment, he glared at me with a rage that seemed too vehemently deathless for a dying man. "He had no right," he snarled. "He had no right to take Teddy!" Then he turned and faced the wall, a gesture so abrupt and oddly violent I knew that he meant it as a complete rejection, the cold shoulder he offered to the scheme of things, wordlessly his last word.

"Not bad, George."

I looked over to where Wyatt sat, my piece on the Flower Festival on the desk before him. "But awful purple at the end." He found the lines he meant, underlined them, and handed the page to me:

> The festival floats will be composed of living flowers, according to Mrs. Lancaster, none that have been cut, none that are dead, each bloom a colorful victory, as she seems to feel, over mortality's black hand.

"Yuk, if you don't mind my saying so," Wyatt said.

"You're right," I said. I took a pen and crossed the line out. "Something came over me."

Wyatt took the page from my hand and gave me a pointed look. "Anything wrong, George?"

Suddenly I thought of Eden Taub waiting as Warren Maizey moved toward her, listening for their footsteps in the corridor or clumping down the stairs, hoping for some miraculous rescue, and in a jangling instant, I knew Teddy must have hoped that the figure coming toward him as thunder rolled and the rain swept in, the figure he must have seen draped in a yellow rain slicker, that this figure, drawing ever more near, was his father come to take him out of the rain.

Everything, I thought. "Nothing," I said.

• • •

I have no doubt that some of the raging sadness that had swept over me as I'd thought of Teddy was still in my face when I handed Alice the photographs of Katherine later that same evening.

"This is Katherine," I said. "I thought you might want to see what she looked like."

Alice stared at me silently for a moment, then drew the pictures from my hand.

I walked to the window and stood beside it, watching as Alice went through the pictures slowly, her drooping lids almost closing as she squinted. "Why aren't there any pictures of her after she was hurt?" she asked after she'd looked at the last one.

"She didn't want any after that," I said. "She stayed in her house mostly, as you know from her story. The neighbors said she never turned off the lights."

As I spoke, I could see that Alice was fully imagining the terrible loneliness of those endless nights, Katherine curled over a small desk, writing feverishly.

"Sometimes I wonder if her story is a desperate note," I said quietly. "A plea for someone to save her." Another wave of anger hit me, and as if blown forward by its heat, I strode over to the chair beside Alice's bed and dropped onto it. "But in the real world," I said sharply, "no one comes to save you."

Alice glanced at the pages I'd taken out of my briefcase, and as if prompted by the tone of my voice or the look in my eyes, drew them from my hands. "I'll read to you this time," she said.

NOW

The Chief smiles. "Of course," he says, "we can leave no evidence." He opens his right hand. "Nothing at all."

175

The Chief's hand is empty now, but for a moment, Maldrow is back again in that distant time, a drenching rain outside the saloon, turning the town streets to mud. The stark loneliness of all the years that have passed since then falls upon him. He cannot calculate how long it has been since he last was called "father." He knows only what he knew at the moment of destruction: that his blood would forever run hot and that it was this searing inner heat that had risen into the overhanging sky, flaring out and out until somewhere in the impossible distance, the Chief, himself, had felt it.

"Maldrow?" the Chief asks.

Maldrow blinks himself back into the present. "There will be no evidence."

Maldrow sees flashes of his past labors: women floating in ponds, lowered into wells, buried in ravines, covered over with stones. All the many ways they had been made to vanish.

"There will be no evidence," he assures the Chief again, this time more emphatically.

He recalls the dark glimmer he caught in Katherine's eye at the moment the horror was made clear to her.

"Except a story," he adds. "She's writing a story."

The Chief waves his hand dismissively. "Let her write it. No one will believe it."

"No," Maldrow says. "No one."

The Chief catches the melancholy tone in Maldrow's voice. "Was there anything about the work I did not explain to you?" he asks.

Maldrow feels his mind whirling backward, racing through vast stretches of lost time, years and years and years of fleeing down midnight streets, across open fields, along secluded trails, down narrow alleyways, destined to remain unknown.

"No."

"Have you selected the place of sacrifice?" the Chief asks.

Maldrow knows that this is part of the necessary recitation, part of the buildup for action, its relentless drive, without which, as he has learned, the grim task cannot be completed.

"Yes."

The Chief looks satisfied. "Then her fate is sealed."

Maldrow recalls Katherine's gaze as she stood, facing his approaching car, stood still and firm even as he bore in upon her. He sees the beam from his flashlight sweep over her, a sickly yellow wave that illuminates yet more fully the nature of her condition.

"Sealed," he says. "Forever."

The Chief nods slowly, then reaches over and places his hand on Maldrow's, the insubstantial substance of the one sinking into the false substance of the other until they meld perfectly and are one.

Alice placed the last page of the section at the bottom of the stack of pages in my hand, and with no further pause, read on:

THEN

I headed out along the river, toward the state campground where Maldrow had asked me to meet him. To my right, I saw the deserted fairgrounds. In the river beyond it, a few boats drifted toward the town marina, their running lights glowing softly in the dark air.

I reached the campground a few minutes later, turned and passed beneath the stone archway, then wheeled to the right and followed the road into the deepening woods.

Lawson Road lay at the far end of the campground, just as Maldrow had said, well beyond the bike path and the last of the walking trails. It was unpaved, and cut at an angle through deep woods, part of the old forest, I supposed, that had grown wild and untended through the years, and whose floor lay covered in a thick undergrowth.

I followed his directions and headed down the road, looking for the trailer he'd described, but saw nothing until the road narrowed abruptly and began to twist and turn as if it were alive.

At last I entered the pine brake through which it appeared suddenly, like an apparition, a small, boxy trailer eerily illuminated by the final fractured rays of moonlight. It was even more modest than Maldrow had described, and as I closed in upon it, I noticed how unsightly and poorly maintained it was. Its aluminum sides were flecked with mud, and its window screens were torn and drooped outward like slices of metal flesh.

Closer still, the trailer gave off an even-less-welcoming sense. There were yellowish stains here and there, and the aluminum door slumped loosely to the left, like a man with a hunched shoulder. The entire undercarriage was badly rusted, and the top was carpeted in pine needles, so that it looked as if it had been in this place forever, part of the forest landscape that continually encroached upon it.

I pulled into the empty driveway and waited. The trailer was dimly lighted, its door slightly ajar, so that I could see the edge of a sofa, a small table, a red Japanese lantern dangling from a faded white cord.

I sat in my car and let the minutes pass, thinking now that I should not have come, not have followed the impulse that had urged me to come, fearing that Maldrow was a man to whom I had attached a fantasy, and thus, in the end, unreal, a fear that doubt redoubled, and which reverberated ever more violently within me, like a tremor growing into a quake.

In that state, shaken by those fears, I came to realize that there is a terrifying uncertainty in every oddly open door, in every object that appears in a place different from where it was last set down, in every disappearing key and earring. But stranger still is the play of mind that asks of every ordinary object, every fork and tweezers, *In what dark ways might these be used?* and by that turn imagines every drop of water as a drowning pool and every falling leaf as cover for a shallow grave.

But for all that, I had come this far, forced myself to address these fears, and so felt bound to proceed.

I got out of my car and headed toward Maldrow's trailer. A wind rose around me as I closed in upon his door. It was sudden and I felt curiously stirred, like an animal awakened. It blew a low, tumbling wall of leaves and forest debris over my feet, then twisted and coiled upward with such violence I thought of the dust devils that blew up in the desert wastes, spun viciously for a moment, then tore apart in their own furious gusts.

I stopped a few feet from the door, now feeling even more like an intruder. But Maldrow had summoned me here, and I could not turn and leave. Suddenly I felt a force like a hand at my back. It pressed me forward, so that step by reluctant step I closed in on the trailer's threshold, its interior now coming into view, revealing its own spectacular oddity, walls that fluttered like the wings of a thousand faded yellow butterflies. I thought what I saw must not be real, but merely a weird vision thrown up by my mind. And yet I inched closer, straining for a better look, the open door revealing more and more of the trailer's bizarre interior, my body growing more tense and fearful as I moved closer, so that suddenly, when the voice stopped me, I felt a wave of terror pass over me.

"Katherine."

I whirled around to find Maldrow standing behind me, a flashlight in his hand, its beam washing over me in a yellow wave.

"You found me," he said.

His jacket was slung over his shoulders like a cape, a pose that allowed the luridness of my own imagination full gallop, Maldrow now a leathery, night-bound creature, a vampire of popular myth, pale and fanged.

"Good," he said softly.

I felt my lips part, but no sound came from my mouth.

Maldrow glanced down toward my still-trembling hands.

"You must be cold," he said, then stepped around me, lifted himself onto the trailer's cement step, and opened the door. "Come in."

Come in.

Such simple words of invitation, and yet I suddenly envisioned legions of vanished women, the endless female slaughter, their bodies thrown in ditches, over bridges, eased from the sides of gently weaving boats. I saw them tossed into rushing streams, over granite cliffs, down dusty wooden stairs, saw them rolled up in carpets, blood-soaked quilts, glistening black plastic bags, saw them rudely covered with debris, stuffed into trunks, buried under slabs of hardening concrete. As from the end of an impossibly long tunnel, I heard their echoing pleas for help.

"I can't," I told him. "I can't."

Maldrow pressed the door farther open and stepped back to give me a full view of the interior of the trailer. "You have to see them all."

At first it was revealed in tiny dots of color, like a pointillist painting. Then the separate dots came together, and I saw a strange mosaic of women's faces, all of them bearing the mark of their pain, the depth of their wounds, the sign of the slasher still in their eyes, a jagged scar left on their souls.

"Come," Maldrow said quietly, then stepped back to let me enter. "Come and see what I have done."

Alice looked up from the page and though her voice was weak, it seemed full of certainty. "Now I know the twist," she said.

"What twist?"

"In Katherine's story."

I stared at her silently.

"There were pictures in the man's room, remember?" she explained. "The room Maldrow took Katherine to see."

"Yes, there were."

"Pictures on the floor," Alice continued. "And around his bed. Pictures of women who . . ." She stopped and I saw a terrible revelation swim into her eyes. "I know who Maldrow is."

I leaned forward. "Who?"

Alice appeared surprised that I had not yet guessed the dark twist she had uncovered. "Maldrow," she said with that sparkle of discovery that follows the moment when one believes he has found a story's solution, "is the unknown man."

PART III

"Ah, so I was right, your story is really about Alice," Mr. Mayawati says with a broad smile. "How she solved Katherine's case." He laughs. "An excellent tale. And Alice must have been quite pleased with herself."

Several parrots burst from the trees across the river, alarmed by something they sense or see, but which remains invisible to me.

Mr. Mayawati follows their flight. "But it is sad, is it not, that Katherine fell victim to such a one as Maldrow?" He takes an immaculately white handkerchief from his pocket and swabs his neck and face. "Still, I think Alice must have been quite pleased when she discovered that Maldrow was the unknown man." He laughs deeply, sonorously, like the beating of a great drum. "Such a clever girl, your Alice. And such a clever resolution, no?"

"A familiar one," I tell him.

His face takes on the expression of one who thought himself clever, but now is not so sure. "Familiar? In what way?"

"In that the presumed hero is revealed to have been the villain all along," I answer.

"As Maldrow betrays Katherine," Mr. Mayawati says thoughtfully. "Ah, yes. Familiar." He returns the handkerchief to his pocket, though almost instantly his face blossoms again with tiny beads of sweat. "But there must be a solution, is that not so?" he asks with an overheated mournfulness. "And what can one do when one reaches the end of a story?"

"But we haven't reached the end," I tell him.

Mr. Mayawati is clearly surprised. "So Alice didn't find the—"

"No." I glance ahead, over the boat's gently surging bow, to where a red post marks the extent of our inward journey. "There is more to the mystery."

"More to the mystery." Mr. Mayawati removes his hat and fans his face. "So Katherine's story has a better solution than the one little Alice thought she had uncovered? A better ending?"

"It depends upon who hears it," I tell him.

Mr. Mayawati glances toward the front of the boat, the steadily narrowing river. "But we will soon reach the central station," he says anxiously. "And I have preparations to make."

"Then make them."

He appears to think that in some way he has offended me.

"It is not that I don't wish to hear the rest of the story," he assures me. "It is just that I have so little time left to kill."

"So little time left to kill," I repeat. "Yes."

"But I *do* wish to hear the end," Mr. Mayawati adds quickly. Then, in a broad gesture of polite accommodation, he eases back in his chair, lifts his legs, and rests his feet on the boat's rusty rail. "So, tell me more of Katherine's tale. Or is the story really about Alice, as I suspect it is."

"It is about both of them," I tell him.

Mr. Mayawati brings his large hands behind his head and leans it back into their sweaty cup. "Then continue, please," he says.

18

"YOU ALWAYS LOOK for walls," Arlo said as we strolled down Main Street the next morning. "I noticed that in your book."

He was right. There was always something about walls that intrigued me. Other travel writers loved towers, castles, cemeteries, found something more evocative in them than they found in other structures. But for me, as Arlo had correctly pointed out, it was walls. I recalled the thick defensive ones of Avila, how they rose like one vast shield out of the barren plain that surrounded them. The walls of Londonderry were gray and impenetrable, like the religious hatred they'd kept both out and in. The short, irregular walls of Inishmore mirrored the island's ragged poverty, so vast a labor, in such bone-chilling cold, with no end but bare survival. I'd even liked fallen walls, the ones that had enclosed Loudon, for example, where a doubter and a witch-hunting priest had once sat in the same room, as Huxley wrote, but not in the same universe.

"Why is that, George?" Arlo asked.

"I guess it's because they seem so real to me," I answered.

"Of course, some are invisible," Arlo said. "Mental walls."

We reached the bandstand and as we sat down on one of the benches that faced it, I thought of the night before, Alice's bleak revelation of Maldrow's villainy, the slow torture through which he seemed to be putting Katherine.

"I had a mental block about Maldrow," I said. "It never occurred to me that he might have been the unknown man."

"Who thinks that?" Arlo asked.

"Alice."

I knew that it was a melodramatic turn one either believed or didn't, as I went on to tell Arlo, but in Alice, I feared that it might have struck deeper than a story, and in that way touched upon the cat-and-mouse cruelty of life itself.

"But life is cruel in that way," Arlo said.

"Yes, it is," I agreed. "But I don't think a dying child needs to be reminded of it."

"So what did you do?"

"I reminded her that what Katherine had written was just a story. I told her that there was no evidence that any of it was true."

Arlo looked at me darkly. "Then where is Katherine?" he asked.

"I don't know," I admitted. "No one does, or ever will."

Arlo made no argument against the hopelessness of this conclusion, and we moved on to other matters, mostly talk of Warren Maizey's capture, a case he'd never expected to be solved. Then, quite suddenly, he said, "Let's talk more tomorrow."

He had never made an appointment before, and I wondered why he'd chosen to do so now.

"At the diner, around noon?" he added.

"Okay."

With that he rose and headed out into the park, where, I noticed, he paused at the little rock grotto.

I had just drawn my gaze away from him and settled it on the river when my cell phone rang.

"George? Wyatt. I have a story for you."

I assumed the new story would have to do with some new store opening, or a lost dog, or perhaps a cat that had shown up suddenly after having been missing for days or months or years.

"It seems that Hugo Tanner wanted to be cremated," Wyatt said.

I saw nothing particularly newsworthy in this.

"He wants his ashes scattered, and I thought you might be the guy to scatter them," Wyatt added.

"Me? Why? I barely knew Hugo."

"Well, he didn't have anybody else, evidently," Wyatt said. "And you wrote that profile, so I thought if you wanted to do the obit, it'd make a good ending. You with his ashes, scattering them to the wind."

Wyatt was right. A somber, ash-scattering scene would make a heaven-sent ending for the obituary of a nut. The problem for me was that such rituals had always struck me as the vain attempt of a transient creature to seek a famished immortality by mingling its powdery remains with the permanence of a planet that, if truth be told, was not permanent, either. That Hugo would embrace such a mystical contrivance with all his madly searching heart did not surprise me. There'd been hardly a fruitcake trail he hadn't followed to its bleak end, every paranormal idiocy, by his blurred lights, worthy of full investigation. Still, there'd been a likable quality to him, along with a curious lack of guile, and he'd been generous enough to allow me to write my profile of him despite the cold skepticism he must have seen in my eyes.

"Okay," I told Wyatt. "I'll do it."

"You can pick his ashes up tomorrow morning," Wyatt said. "They'll be at Robinson's."

"Where does he want them scattered?"

"In the river. By that little rock chapel."

I glanced over toward that same location, expecting to find Arlo still lingering there, but he was gone.

"The grotto?" I asked. "Why there?"

"Who knows?" Wyatt answered. "Air. Water. The Elements. Reason wasn't Hugo's thing."

He'd called himself a seeker, and the next morning, on the way to pick up Hugo's ashes, I remembered the way he'd met me at his door, then ushered me into the Sanctum.

It had never been more than an old farmhouse, with a predictable warren of small rooms. There was a large enclosed porch, where, in the old days, a traveling stranger could find refuge for the night. Hugo claimed that strangers did occasionally make use of his porch, and for that reason he kept it stocked with a porcelain water bowl and clean towels, along with packs of beef jerky and a box of Ritz crackers.

He had been an indefatigable forager of the town dump, gleaning clothes and furniture and bottles and pans on an almost-daily basis. From its smelly mounds, he'd retrieved, it was said, everything he needed, save for the food he ate. This he bought in bulk, enormous bottles of ketchup, for example, and huge cans of green beans and corn, along with family-size packages of preformed hamburger patties. He'd toyed with vegetarianism, he told me, and had briefly even been a vegan, an experience that had taught him only that he was a shameless omnivore. Nor had Hugo exhibited a particularly benevolent attitude toward those fellow creatures he did not actually eat. He swatted flies with delicious abandon, and once during our interview hurled a book at a scampering cockroach.

"I'm not a goddamn hippie," he blurted at almost the moment I'd taken out my notebook. "Be sure you make that clear. I'm not a hippie. I'm a scientist!"

But it was only weird science that had ever interested Hugo, a freakish fascination with bizarre forms of cosmic energy, the healing power of various rays of light. He'd studied hypnotism, he told me, and levitation and paranormal communications. "I go where others dare not go," he told me grandly, "into the Invisible."

And then, of course, there was the matter of ghosts, all of whom were restless, according to Hugo. He called them Residuals and claimed that they were created by a force he'd named the Unresolved, an energy produced by the lingering pain of their unsolved murders. "There are no happy Residuals," he said. "Their substance is formed by violent death, and their job is to get even, make things right." He smiled. "I'm not New Age, George, I'm Dark Age."

But for all that I remembered about Hugo Tanner, I knew that there was much I had forgotten, so I decided to revisit his house as a way of refreshing my memory of the place, and of him, before writing the obit Wyatt had just assigned to me.

Hugo had made a point of telling me that he never locked his house, having nothing to steal, so it didn't surprise me that I had no trouble entering his Sanctum once again.

Inside, I found the place very little changed from three years before, when I'd first written about him. There was the expected clutter, the stacks of books and magazines, the Dr. Frankenstein lab equipment, all of it scattered about randomly with no visible sign that Hugo had ever actually differentiated between a kitchen, a reading room, a bedroom, or an experimental laboratory.

For a time I paced among the rooms, imagining the endless hours Hugo had spent in his crazed pursuits. Neighbors had long noticed that his lights often burned through the night, so there was little doubt that he had sleeplessly pursued his pseudo-scientific inquiries with a mad scientist's zeal. In one room I found vats of animal parts floating in formaldehyde, along with a vast collection of tiny bones—birds, for the most part—as well as a generous sampling of squirrels and mice. He had ineptly attempted taxidermy, and the reconstruction of skeletons, perhaps seeking the little room in which was sealed the spark of life he'd spoken of in the interview and which, in human beings, became the soul. Another room housed Hugo's collection of plants and seeds, and tray upon tray of withered vegetation, everything from orchids to lettuce, with little labeling done to identify what the now-dead organisms had once been.

I found the remains of other scientific studies, dried animal skins hung on webs of gray cord, in another, a huge collection of what appeared to be soil samples. At the far back of the house, I opened a door to find scores of plastic models of various parts of the human body, the sort one saw in doctors' offices or bought in model shops. Visible Woman stood practically holding hands with Visible Man, the tiny model of a human fetus lying at their feet.

It was not an illuminating tour, of course, but it had served its purpose in refreshing my memory of Hugo's place, and so for that reason, was worth the effort. Still, I found no reason to linger after this brief tour, and so I turned and headed back toward the front of the house, idly glancing into one of Hugo's many overstuffed closets, which is where I saw it, dimly lit among the otherwise-indistinguishable clutter.

A yellow rain slicker.

There is such a thing as an arctic moment, when one not only feels the cold blast of a sudden shock, but that one's life has been blown around a corner by it, a coincidence so profoundly unlikely it seems both impossible and plotted from the beginning of time.

And I thought, *He's found!*

My fingers began to tremble, then my knees, then all of me, every squirming cell. For the prospect before me was both too horrible and too strangely hopeful for one body to contain.

I don't know precisely when, but at some moment I began actually to move toward the open closet door, its packed, bulging contents, the little sliver of shiny yellow that shimmered among the dull dark woolens that surrounded and nearly smothered it.

At the door of the closet, I leaned forward and parted the other coats and jackets Hugo had retrieved from the town dump over the years, reached for the slicker, and with a weird, unsettling tenderness, drew it out and cradled it, almost like a dead child, in my arms.

At last I lifted it up and turned it slowly in the light, first pulling it open, then turning it inside out. What was I looking for? A laundry tag, perhaps. The owner's name sewn in the lining, or written on the inside collar with a ballpoint pen. Or was it some tiny drop of blood I sought? My last touch of Teddy.

I found none of these things. The label was torn out. There was no name inscribed inside it. I found no drop of blood. And so at last I went through the pockets, now looking for a note, a card, a key, perhaps even the little red bird whistle

Teddy had taken with him that morning, a trinket I'd bought long ago in Cracow.

But there was nothing, and in the wake of that nothingness I accepted fully, and for the first time, that I would never know what had been done to my little boy, nor who had done it to him.

With that acceptance, I returned the yellow rain slicker to its place among Hugo's other scavenged coats, and headed for my car. Once there, I paused only briefly to look back at the house, though even then it was only to feel again what I had so powerfully felt a moment before.

Ashes to ashes, I thought, then hit the ignition and drove back toward Winthrop, to Robinson's Mortuary, where Hugo's particular ashes were already waiting for me.

19

CHARLIE WAS ALSO WAITING, though not for me. I found him slumped against the rear bumper of his car when I came out of Robinson's Mortuary a few minutes later.

"What are you doing here?" I asked.

"Checking on funeral arrangements for Warren Maizey," Charlie said.

"He died?"

"No, but they say he's not going to make it."

"Why not?"

"Liver cancer. Eaten up with it." Charlie shrugged. "So I thought I might do a story on what happens to a guy like that once he kicks the bucket. A guy hated by everyone, I mean. You know, will there be flowers, who'll come to see the bastard, a slice-of-life quickie."

"Slice-of-life quickie" was a phrase Charlie had come up with to describe exactly the sort of article he preferred:

short, requiring limited research, but which had a little weird punch.

He looked at the black cardboard box that held Hugo's ashes. "I heard about you doing the ash-scattering thing." He smiled broadly. "I gotta admit, it'll make a great final scene for the obit. You by the river, scattering Hugo's ashes. That's great stuff, George." He glanced at his watch. "Well, gotta run. I want to be ready when Maizey cashes in his chips."

With that Charlie bounded away, and I walked to my car, Hugo's ashes considerably heavier than I'd expected, as if something had been added to them, the full weight, as I imagined it, of his foolish hope that something out there, a sad Residual, perhaps, might one day make things right.

There were several people in the little picnic area by the river when I got there that morning. A few were jogging along the water's edge, others were lounging about, reading the morning paper. None of them noticed me as I made my way past the rock grotto, where I turned to the left and headed out into a somewhat-less-populated area. I found a place on the riverbank that was shielded from view by a high hedge, and it was there, without ceremony, or even so much as a muttered farewell, that I poured Hugo's ashes into the river.

It was just after ten in the morning by then, and I was hungry. I walked back to my car, put the now-empty cardboard box in the backseat, and headed toward Main Street.

Most of the morning crowd had left the coffee shop, so I had no trouble finding a table. There were a few stragglers in various booths, but by the time I'd finished my breakfast, even they were gone, so that I sat for a time, alone and unmolested, quietly sipping the last of my second cup of coffee.

At such moments, the mind can become beautifully unmoored, thoughts and memories twining around and through each other like colored oils. That morning, I let that familiar reverie overtake me, thoughts of Celeste and Teddy easily intertwining with those of my father, my mother, places I'd been, old adventures. Voices rose from their deep wells. I heard Max, *Always remember the Unseen,* and my father, *Why are we here, Georgie?* I heard my mother whispering the rosary and Celeste's quirky *See you soon, Marco Polo,* as she was wheeled into the delivery room. I heard Teddy asking me to pick him up at the bus stop if it stormed, and with the same old pain, my promise that I would, *Don't worry, I'll be there.* I even heard Cody's odd remark, *With a small turn of the screw, anyone can do anything.* Then, as if in the form of a stern command, I heard the woman who'd stood in this same coffee shop a few days before, a book in her hand, *At some point in life, we should all be fiercely wrong.*

None of these remarks took hold, but just at that moment, a picture did. I had probably glanced at it a thousand times, but on this occasion, I noticed the date on the small brass plate beneath it: *1988.* The photograph was like several others that hung on the coffee-shop wall, all of them shot from the same vantage point, a traffic island just to the east of where Main Street ended at the park. Some of the photographs were quite old and showed Winthrop in sepia colors, its unpaved street crowded with horses and buggies and people in period dress. The photograph that had been taken in 1988 showed a bustling Main Street of small shops, the river park recently refurbished. The little rock grotto looked much the same as it did now, but twenty years before, there had been no hedge behind which I'd just concealed myself as I'd poured Hugo Tanner's ashes into the water.

But amid the usual familiar sights there was something that caught my eye. Twenty years before, Main Street had extended slightly farther to the east. There'd been a dress shop where the entrance to the park now stood, and beyond it, a small grocery, and beyond the grocery, a ramshackle building in whose window I could faintly make out, bloody and unappetizing, two large sides of beef.

A meat market.

I felt my gaze lock on the store, hold there firmly, as if a voice had sounded in my mind, real as a pointed finger—*Look there!*—and with those words recalled the white apron that had hung in the foyer of the house to which Maldrow had taken Katherine in the story, and which had perhaps been his own house, either in real life or as Katherine had imagined it, a white apron stained with blood. Then I recalled Cody's story of having waited for the 34 bus, the one that had gone by the old slaughterhouse, his remark that the man Katherine had seen in the park had looked as if he were "killing time," like a man on his way to work.

Suddenly I thought of that moment the night before, when Alice had grimly muttered, "Maldrow is the unknown man," a conclusion that had clearly darkened her already-bleak mind.

But now I wondered if Katherine's story might merely have thrown up a false lead in order to distract us from the real unknown man, or at least a stand-in for him Katherine had once glimpsed in a public park, found something in his look that appealed to her creative imagination, and thus seized upon him as a character she could perhaps track down and explore. And if this were true, I wondered, what would she have done next? I couldn't know what she'd actually done, but as a writer, I knew what I would have done. I would have followed him, tried to hear his voice, perhaps found out where he lived and gone there. It seemed at least possible that Katherine might have done these things, too. But more important than any of this was the troubling fact that Alice had so obviously merged

Katherine's story with Katherine's life, and that a line of demarcation needed to be drawn between what Katherine had actually lived and the life she had made up. And so it seemed to me that if I could show that Katherine's story was pure fiction, her actual disappearance unconnected to it, then I could read the rest of Katherine's story without fear that the dreadful darkness she had imagined for her last days would darken Alice's last days, too.

"Old Man Fuller owned that meat market," Wyatt told me a few minutes later. "He was pretty mad when the town condemned the building."

"Where is he now?" I asked. "Could I talk to him?"

"He died ten years ago." Wyatt looked at me warily, as if he feared that I was on the verge of the unhinged. "What's this all about, George?"

"Just something I want to track down," I answered. "Did he have any employees?"

Wyatt sat back and folded his arms over his chest. The wariness in his expression deepened. "He always had some guy working for him," he said cautiously, like a man giving information to a source he suddenly considered unstable. "You couldn't run that business by yourself, and Fuller didn't have any kids to help out."

"Do you have any idea who that would have been in 1988?" I asked.

Wyatt shook his head, his gaze now very still. "I admit I'm the town history buff, George, but I'm not the *Encyclopedia of Winthrop*."

"Right," I said. "Of course."

I started to rise, but Wyatt stopped me with a question.

"Why are you interested in someone who might have worked for Old Man Fuller twenty years ago?"

"Just something in what I've been reading," I said. "The story Katherine Carr left behind. Her friend's son—the one who was in the car when she was attacked—told me that she once spotted a guy in the park, that this guy looked like he was killing time, waiting to go to work. Then later in the story, Katherine's character goes to a house and sees a bloody apron."

"So you think it might be a guy who worked at the meat market near the park."

I shrugged. "It's probably a wild-goose chase."

Even so, Wyatt seemed intrigued. "Well, I *do* know that Old Man Fuller had an old house north of the town," he said. "He sometimes rented it to whoever worked for him in the market. It was a way for the old man to take back some of the wages he paid him. If this guy didn't have a family or a house of his own, he might have rented it."

"Is this house still standing?" I asked.

"Yeah, it's still there," Wyatt said. "I went out there a few years ago, when this development company was interested in buying the property. But the Conservancy took it, instead."

"Did you go into the house?" I asked.

Wyatt shook his head. "No. I was afraid the roof might fall. It's just a shack now, gutted, everything taken out of it."

"How do I get there?" I asked.

"Easy," Wyatt answered. "Just take Route 34. Turn at the old slaughterhouse."

After twenty years had passed, the house Old Man Fuller had sometimes rented to whoever worked for him was located in an area that was no longer exclusively rural, though it remained mostly so; a region of small farms occasionally bordered by a large estate, the country house of some wealthy New Yorker, or perhaps the trophy house of a local success story. The farms were neat and the houses were grand, at least by Winthrop standards, but it was neither the farms nor the houses that drew my attention. I was looking for the tumble-down remains of the old slaughterhouse, and beyond that, according to Wyatt's directions, an unpaved road that led deep into a thickening wood.

It didn't take long to find that road, and when I did, I followed it until the woods parted to reveal a small wooden house gone almost entirely to ruin, its outer walls stripped of paint, the windows broken out, the roof bare of shingles, posts fallen from its cramped front porch.

For a time, I remained in my car, simply looking at the house, wondering if it might actually be the one Katherine had described. Her portrayal had been decidedly grim—even lurid—and I was sure that it was my having read it previously that now created the sense of something creepily alive inside it or, more eerily, that the house itself was still sunk in the deep malignancy she'd described, and which made me wonder if perhaps she actually *had* come here, made a few careful observations, as any writer would, and from there gone on to write her description of the place.

But whether Katherine had ever come here or not was something I would never be able to prove, I thought, since the house had no doubt had many tenants during the last twenty years, people who might have knocked down walls, added rooms, made all manner of alteration so that even if Katherine had gone inside the house, her description of its interior was likely to be wildly off.

Still, the house as it currently stood was all I had to work with, and it was clearly abandoned, open to my inspection; so, after a moment, I got out of my car and headed up the weedy cement walkway that led to the front door.

Maldrow had found the door closed, but it was wide open when I reached it, so that I felt not at all like an intruder when I stepped inside and, as Katherine had done in her story, briefly stood in the foyer, peering about, looking for nothing in particular, save a sense of the place.

It was in this foyer that she'd seen a stained white coat hanging beside the door, but now there wasn't even a peg to hold such a coat. And so I left the foyer and walked into what was obviously the living room. It was empty now, save for an old sofa, its cushions long removed, the padding rotted, so that there was little left of it but the metal frame and a few strips of moldy cloth.

Next I drifted into the kitchen. A discoloration in the linoleum indicated where a stove and refrigerator had once rested. The sink remained in place, but was nearly rusted through, the spout removed, along with the taps, leaving round holes in the fitting.

It was in the bedroom that Katherine had confronted a terrible evil, though less in human form than as a jangling energy.

I hesitated only briefly at the threshold of that room, then walked to its center and made the same slow turn, taking in the walls, the one window, and finally the door once again, where she suddenly appeared, a figure backlit by the window behind her, her face almost entirely in shadow, her eyes glimmering in the horror-movie way of a cat's in the night.

"I didn't mean to scare you," she said, so that I knew I must have startled visibly.

"You *did* scare me a little," I admitted.

The woman nodded, but said nothing.

"I just came to take a look at this house," I explained. "It belongs to the state now, so I didn't think I'd be trespassing."

The woman continued to stare at me silently, her eyes very still, a glint of light in the silvering hair that hung in a few willowy strands at her ears.

"I came because someone wrote about it in a story," I added.

"The woman in the story said she came here. I thought maybe the author actually had. Writers do that sometimes."

"What was she looking for?" the woman asked.

I hadn't thought to ask myself that question before, but the answer came to me in a way that struck me as being as miraculous as the sudden appearance of a literary image. "Evil," I said. "The feel of it."

"You can feel it in the horror house," the woman said matter-of-factly.

"Horror house?" I repeated.

"Where Eden Taub was murdered," the woman said. "That's what they called it in the paper: the 'horror house.'" Her gaze became oddly penetrating, as if she were conveying a piece of important information. "They just caught him, you know, the one who did it."

"Yeah, I heard that."

"People thought that they'd never catch him," the woman added.

"Sometimes they never do."

The woman nodded. "More's the pity," she said.

I glanced about the room again, took in the peeling wallpaper, the murky water stains that slithered across the ceiling, the windowsill resting place of moths and flies and spiders, and something in the look and feel of it all seared me with the recognition of the worst life had to offer, all its cruelty and ruin, the daily slaughter nature inflicted upon insects and men, and the unnatural one suffered by the Eden Taubs of life, the doomed and luckless ones who, by chance and chance alone, had met their violent fates at the hands of pure malice, and who had no doubt died in just the way Hugo Tanner imagined, tortured by the Unresolved.

"I guess no one's lived here for a long time," I said.

"Not in a long time, no," the woman said.

She added nothing to this as we drifted back down the corridor and into the foyer where, through its open door, I suddenly imagined Maldrow's car as Katherine had described it in her story, parked at the curb, a dusty old sedan, Katherine in the passenger seat, Maldrow behind the wheel, both of them waiting those few charged seconds before they'd gotten out and come down the little path that led to the door, Katherine either the dupe of a man she'd actually met, as Audrey believed, or a character her perfervid imagination had created.

But for all that, I still wondered if my original idea might have some distant merit: that business of the bloody apron, the meat market that had once been at the end of Main Street.

I glanced back into the ruined interior of the house. "I don't suppose you know anything about a man who might have lived there twenty years ago," I asked. "He might have worked at the meat market in Winthrop."

Had I been Archie Goodwin, this question would almost certainly have led to a revelation, the woman before me perhaps a witness to the very events Katherine had described in her visit here that day, one who'd actually seen a strange woman walk up the battered drive, then drift through the house. In such a tale, one remark would have led to another, and at the end, something vital would have been revealed, a lead Archie could take back to Nero Wolfe, a step toward the resolution of the mystery.

But life rarely supplies such neat solutions, so the woman said only, "Hot in here, don't you think?"

"Yes, it is," I said.

With that, we both stepped out into the yard, then walked silently to my car. She was standing at the door as I got in, and even at that late moment, I hoped to get something from her, some little crumb that would lead me farther down the trail.

"Well, nice to have met you," I said.

She eased away, then suddenly glanced upward, and said, "Look there."

I looked up and saw a large bird circling overhead, its wings spread so far they seemed to touch the far corners of the sky.

"They strike at heat," she said. "There's no way to get away from them."

I looked at her quizzically.

"Hawks," the woman added. She pointed up toward the sky. "That's a red-tailed one."

I glanced up to where a dark bird was making wide, slow circles overhead, a little glint of red sometimes winking in the light.

"Beautiful," I said.

She nodded and stepped back toward the house. "Good-bye, then," she said.

Driving away, I glanced in the rearview mirror, expecting to see her still standing in the yard, or strolling away, but like the figure in the favorite poem of Katherine's girlhood, she was gone so quickly that later, when I thought of her, I wondered if, like the figure upon the stairs, she had ever been there at all.

20

"WHY ARE YOU HERE so early?" Alice asked. She'd clearly been sleeping, but even upon awakening, a distressing weakness clung to her, one that signaled the approach of her final days, her heart inevitably growing more feeble, the last of her strength now draining away.

"Do you mind that I'm early?" I asked. "I could come back when you've . . ."

She inched herself upward and lifted her head slightly with what seemed an added measure of effort. "What did you do today?" she asked softly, her voice noticeably weaker, everything about her suddenly much more frail.

"Well, for one thing, I thought I might have found the house—the actual house that Katherine goes to in her story, the one Maldrow takes her to. So I went there. There wasn't much left of it. Nothing that led anywhere, that's for sure."

In all of this I was simply trying to return Alice to our little game of Archie Goodwin and Nero Wolfe. I'd even planned a carefully paced rendering of my visit.

But Alice said simply, "I'm afraid of what's going to happen to her, George."

She meant that she was afraid for Katherine, afraid to face her dire end, certain that she'd been ensnared in Maldrow's malicious web, Katherine's story no longer a harmless little mystery, but a chilling narrative of true crime.

"We can stop reading the story if you want," I told her. "We don't have to go to the end."

Alice glanced at my briefcase, then back up at me.

"Yes," she said, "we do."

"Are you sure?"

Alice nodded softly. "Yes," she said.

And so, like two wayfarers on a boat together, we journeyed on.

NOW

"So, it seems you have guided her well to the final moment," the Chief says.

Maldrow sips his drink silently, reviewing the questions Katherine asked, the answers he'd given.

"And quite cleverly, at that," the Chief adds. "You never lied to her."

"I was afraid to lie to her."

"Why?"

"Because when the time came, she might not have believed the evidence."

"Ah, yes," the Chief says. "The evidence."

Maldrow sees a vast array of objects, souvenirs of their bloody crimes, torn from blouses or snatched from hands, ripped from walls or pulled out of small wooden chests, pins, locks of hair, all of them bearing the eternally recurring panic of their former owners.

The Chief starts to speak again, then stops abruptly as the bartender approaches.

Maldrow catches the Chief's warning glance and waits.

"You want another drink?" the barkeep asks when he reaches the table.

Maldrow lifts his still-half-filled glass. "Not yet."

The bartender eyes Maldrow briefly, then steps away.

"There is so little we can change," the Chief says.

Maldrow sees the endless slaughter, the unquiet graves. He sees Bobby Franks climb into the black sedan, Loeb at the wheel, Leopold in the backseat, fingering the chisel. He sees Fish take Grace Budd's small white hand. He sees young Klara Jessmer reflected in the oversized spectacles of Joachim Kroll, András Pándy stuffing his refrigerator with the body parts of four children. He sees Amelia's body sprawled across the barn floor, the ripped cloth at her breast. Last of all, he sees Yenna disappearing into the darkened alley where Stanovich waits in an even-darker corner.

The Chief seems to see all these things as well. He watches Maldrow a moment, then says, "We are almost done now. And soon it will be time. So let us go on with the report."

Maldrow knows that the Chief is right, that what is done is done. He takes a quick sip from his drink, then returns the glass to the table.

"The final steps," the Chief says.

Maldrow peers toward the window of the bar, his own image superimposed over the Chief's, the features of the one draped in strange transparency over the other. As if they were his own, he watches the Chief's lips as they part in the old final recitation:

"Amelia."

Maldrow sees her as she makes her way through the snow, the

empty milk bucket dangling from her hand, the kitchen fire already blazing in the little cabin a few yards away, singing to herself as she walks, the little gold cross she treasured tucked inside her dress.

"So innocent."

She is in the barn now, moving through its shadowy light.

"And unjustly doomed."

The figure swoops down from the overhanging rafters, arms spread in flight, like the wings of a ravenous bird. He hears the thud of the drop, then the rip of cloth, the whisper of the knife as it tears through the air, the small snap of the necklace as the tiny gold cross is ripped from around her throat. Then, as if from a great height, he sees the broken body dragged through the snow, then tossed into the icebound river that never gave it back, nothing left of his dead daughter, save—

"The evidence," the Chief says softly.

Maldrow remembers the little gold cross glowing softly in the Chief's open hand.

"And now . . ."

The Chief stops and waits for the necessary response:

"Katherine Carr," Maldrow whispers.

"Tell me the best thing about her," the Chief says. "The thing the world will miss."

"Her kindness," Maldrow answers. "The way she looked when I told her about Amelia."

"How did she look?"

"As if she knew the truth," Maldrow answers. "That there can be no solace for a murdered child."

I glanced up to where Alice stared at me silently. There was a strange bleakness in her expression, the glimmer of her initial engagement in Katherine's story now completely drained away, so that she seemed empty, without shine.

"So Maldrow's daughter was murdered," I said. "And the Chief found out the one who did it, and brought Maldrow the evidence. That little gold cross."

Alice's face was a mask of dread. "But it's all a lie," she said. "That story is all a lie, the one about Amelia."

I was stunned by so dark an interpretation of the section I'd just read. "Then why are Maldrow and the Chief talking about it?" I asked.

Alice's eyes seemed to shrink back into her head as small creatures back into their burrows, retreating ever deeper at the predator's approach.

And yet she said, "Go on."

THEN

We drove through town, then along the shaded lanes on its outskirts. The homes were large, with wide front lawns, and as we drove, Maldrow glanced from house to house, his gaze casual, but at the same time deeply concentrated, like a man who could see through walls, but found nothing particularly extravagant in such a power.

We continued on, Maldrow still silent, though I could sense a growing tumult within him. It was like the distant stirring of a storm, of building winds and tides. He held his gaze firmly ahead, and this, too, appeared a matter of careful calculation and control.

"The stop is over there," he said finally.

He nodded straight toward a bus stop, then pulled over in front of it.

"The 34 should arrive very soon," he told me.

"But the 34 just goes back into town."

Maldrow glanced away, like one concealing the perilous details of a dreadful mission.

"All right," I said and got out of the car.

I didn't look back as I walked to the bus stop. By the time I got there, Maldrow was gone. I sat down on the small bench, alone in what seemed a desolate place, and waited for the bus. A few yards away, a green metal Dumpster rested on a weedy patch of ground. A few sparrows fought over the garbage scattered around it, and just above them, perched on a bare limb, a large crow sat staring off into the distance, motionless and haughty, indifferent to their small wars.

There was little traffic this far out, no more than an occasional passing car, sometimes laden with family, sometimes with a single driver. Once, a lone man slowed as he drifted by, glancing over with a grin and a nod, to which I returned an icy glare.

I looked at my watch. It was just past six, the evening shade now falling all around me, darkening the air.

A terrible wave of dread passed over me, and I might have rushed away, returned to the old shadowland of my former life, had not the bus arrived at just that moment. I got in, walking briskly now, past a young woman with a baby and two girls in white blouses and checked skirts, and finally an old man with a white beard, who sat with a wooden cane grasped shakily in one hand.

The bus moved on toward town, and I recognized that this was the same area through which Maldrow had driven me the day before, the same barn and the wide fields, the hint of a stream through the trees, one whose course I was following idly until the old slaughterhouse came into view, the bus slowing steadily as we closed in upon it until it finally stopped, and another rider came on board.

He was tall and very thin, and he wore a baseball cap with its brim facing backward, like a cocky boy.

"'Bout time you got here," he said to the driver.

My skin tightened and my muscles grew taut, and I felt the air inside my lungs go hot and dry, as if I'd breathed in a draft from the underworld.

The man craned his neck as he lurched forward and I saw the rounded knob of his Adam's apple bob slightly between the bulging ligaments of his neck.

He took a seat near the front, the back of his head all that remained visible to me as the bus moved on.

The woman with a baby got off at the next stop, and at the one after that, the old man left the bus as well. A mile onward, the girls bounded off the bus, laughing as they hopped out into the evening shade.

The bus moved on for a time, the man in the cap faced forward, his body very still, so that it seemed almost lifeless. Then, as if animated by a sudden charge, he turned toward me. His eyes glimmered and a thin reptilian smirk slithered onto his lips. He said nothing, but I heard the little buzzing engine of his malice, and saw the terrible thing he had done, the long ordeal of the one whose hands he'd tied and whose mouth he'd closed with masking tape, whose ankles he'd strapped to the legs of a wooden chair, saw the slow, prancing circle he had made around her, dousing her naked, trembling body drop by drop, saw with what demonic joy he had struck the match.

I felt my knees tremble, my skin liquefy. A terrible sensation of melting seized me. For an instant, the bus seemed to tilt to the right, and I felt my fluid self spill out and begin to flow across the floor like a runny, sizzling egg. Then the bus righted itself, as if directed by an unseen hand, and I realized that I'd stepped briefly out of time, and during that lost moment, the man had risen and moved forward and was now closing in upon me.

"Got change for a dollar?" he asked.

"No," I said.

"You look familiar," he said. His lips parted and I saw lines of jagged yellow teeth. "Yeah, familiar," he added with a sudden wariness, like a man who'd abruptly heard something rustling just beyond the firelight. He nodded brusquely, wheeled around, and moved back up toward the front of the bus, where he took a seat a few rows back from the driver. He didn't move again or look back at me, and when we pulled into the center of town, he left the bus so quickly that he seemed almost to dissolve into the man who stood before its open door, one older than his years, dressed in a dark suit and blood-red tie.

"Hello, Katherine," Maldrow said. "I've come to take you home."

I looked up at Alice, and it seemed to me that a dreadful chill had suddenly struck the air around us.

"That's the end of the section," I said softly.

Alice said nothing, but only turned and stared out into the night.

"Do you want to discuss anything about this section, or should I just go on?" I asked.

Her eyes drifted over to me. "I'm tired, George," she said. "I think I'd like to rest." A faint smile fluttered onto her lips, briefly held, then faded. "Sorry."

"Don't be," I said. "Just get some rest. I'll see you tomorrow."

Her attention had already drifted back to the window by the time I gathered up the pages and headed for the door. When I reached it, I looked back to where she lay. She was still peering out into a wall of night she must have considered utterly faceless and indifferent to her, so that I thought again of nature's old murderousness, how much like Katherine's list of killers it actually was, like them a cruel slaughterer of innocents, Alice but another of its helpless victims, chosen at random, tortured for months and years; then, with a sudden, casual shrug, reduced eternally to ash.

I closed the door softly and headed down the corridor. Most of the doors were open, and glancing into various rooms as I went by, I saw patients in their beds, some unconscious, some staring listlessly at wall-mounted televisions.

These were always sad glimpses of the human fate, but there was nothing unusual about them, so that it was only the sudden appearance of a uniformed policeman that drew my attention.

He was young, barely beyond a recruit, and he came out of the room at the end of the corridor with a quick, youthful stride. There was a nurse a few yards away, young and quite attractive, and as he approached, he said, "The bastard's still alive."

The nurse waited until he reached her, then the two of them inched around a near corner, where I could see just the shoulder of the policeman's uniform, and the hem of the nurse's skirt.

The bastard's still alive.

Suddenly the words stopped me, and I looked at the name outside the room from which the young policeman had just emerged: *Warren Maizey.*

The door was partly open, which offered a narrow view into the room. I could see the foot of the bed, the vague outline of feet and legs beneath a single sheet.

For a moment I hesitated, but my brief talk with the woman I'd met at the house returned to me, her mention of the "horror house" she'd visited. Surely that, too, had been an evil place, Maizey not unlike the hideous villains that were referenced in Katherine's story and seemed to reside like dark tenants in Maldrow's mind, figures of pure malice. Katherine had made the odd claim that she could feel this malice as a "buzzing" in the air, and it struck me that in a strange way Warren Maizey on his deathbed offered me the chance to experience the actual presence of the same unadulterated evil she had written about in her story . . . if it actually existed.

It was a far-fetched notion, of course, but I thought, *Let me try,* and stepped into the room.

21

"Jesus, you went into Maizey's room?" Charlie asked, clearly excited by the opportunity chance had given me. "Did you get a deathbed interview?"

"I wasn't thinking about an interview," I told him.

"Then what were you after?"

I recalled the last section I'd read of Katherine's story, its grim prospect of actual evil, fearful and ubiquitous, configured in a thousand shapes, and which she'd felt as a jangling in her own nerves, heard as a sinister buzz. "Evil," I said. "Its actual presence. Katherine Carr said she felt it."

Charlie laughed. "Felt it?"

"As something real in that way," I said. "Unseen, but real."

Charlie laughed again. "Sounds like Katherine was off her nut."

"Maybe so," I said. "But she's not the only person who's felt evil in that way."

I recalled a particular evening I'd planned to have dinner with Sarah Byrne, an old friend who'd dropped into town, a fellow traveler whose journeys, like mine, had tended toward the dark side, though in her case specializing in tombs, the beauty of mortuary art. I'd hired a babysitter for Teddy, who was three years old at the time. He'd been recommended by neighbors, and arrived punctually. One of Sarah's contact lenses had fallen out. She'd recovered it and retreated to the bathroom to put it back in. During that time I'd shown the babysitter Teddy's room, given him all the relevant emergency numbers, all the things a parent does before leaving a child in another person's care. Teddy had been sleeping at the time, and so once these preliminaries were completed, the boy had returned to the living room and had sat down on the sofa.

He'd still been sitting there fifteen minutes later, when Sarah came into the room. She'd been dabbing at her eye, but she stopped instantly, and I saw her gaze fix on this silent boy, her features suddenly concentrated and wary and troubled, something in the hunch of his posture or the vacant look in his eyes, or perhaps in the twining of his fingers, or the way he sat with his feet pointed inward. Or was it the crook of his neck that alerted her, or the slant of his nose, or the fact that he'd buttoned the top button of his shirt? Did his socks not match? Was he too thin? Was his Adam's apple too prominent?

Sarah never knew, could never explain, called it "the strange part," then laughed and noted that all Truman Capote's villains had hair sprouting from their ears. Perhaps, she said, it was something as silly as that, but whatever it was, it had sounded the alarm, and she'd immediately drawn me into another room and said, "We're not going out, George."

And we didn't.

And three months later the news flew through the neighborhood that this same boy had been arrested for exposing himself to a child in a public park.

I hadn't thought of this incident for many years, but now, as I faced Charlie silently, I knew that I'd also felt some measure of Sarah's dark intuition, and of Katherine's, palpably felt the evil of an incontestably bad human being.

"A friend of mine once felt it," I said, hesitated briefly, then added, "And I've felt it, too."

"You?" Charlie asked. "When?"

"The day Teddy disappeared."

It was as I'd stood by the window, watching the first wave of rain pass over Jefferson Street, I told Charlie.

"I saw a man in a yellow rain slicker," I said. "And out of nowhere, I just felt . . . uneasy."

But because it was day, the middle of the afternoon, and raining, and because my line about Extremadura was waiting to be finished, I'd merely watched as he drifted past my house, then dismissed the eeriness that had washed over me, and returned to my desk.

"But you don't know, do you?" Charlie asked when I finished my story. "I mean, you don't know if it was him."

"No, I don't," I said. "And I never will."

Charlie must have seen the old hollowness settle over me because he moved quickly to change the subject.

"Okay, so you didn't get an interview with Warren Maizey," Charlie asked. "But you saw him, right?"

"Yes."

"So, what did he look like?"

He was lying on his back, I told Charlie, his body covered by a single white sheet that had been drawn up to just beneath his chin. Unlike the man Katherine had encountered on the bus, he didn't have a lean and hungry look. He wasn't tall, nor in the least imposing. Just the opposite in fact: a white-haired old man with what must have once been a handsome face. His eyes were closed, as were his lips, and his breathing was slow and even, the rhythm of a sleeping child.

"Okay, so what did you do?" Charlie asked.

For a time, I simply waited, I said, staring at the plump, peacefully sleeping figure in a bed, waited like one expecting some sort of revelation. But no revelation came; so, after a moment, I slipped back into the corridor and headed down it, past where the young policeman stood enthralled by the equally youthful nurse.

"I'm guessing you didn't get anything out of him, then?" Charlie asked. "No comment from Maizey? No story?"

I shook my head. "Only the feeling that I'd done something ludicrous."

And it *had* been ludicrous, I thought now, my little detour into Warren Maizey's room, and for that reason I'd awakened the next morning with a sense of having been the victim of a fierce chicanery, like a man who, against his better judgment, bets his life's savings on a single lottery ticket and, quite predictably, loses.

Charlie made no more of my visit to Warren Maizey's room. We went on to talk of other things, the story he was still working on about prostitution in Kingston, but which had been cut short by an odd disappearance.

"Who's disappeared?" I asked.

"Hollis Traylor," he said. "There's been no sign of him for a few days."

"That's strange," I said. "I thought I saw him a couple of nights ago."

"Where?"

"He was driving past my window," I said.

Charlie laughed. "Well, he must have kept on driving." He

shrugged. "But people come and go all the time. Who knows where they went?" He smiled. "That's the strange part when it comes to a disappearance, don't you think? If they don't leave some clue, then you'll never know."

The strange part.

Sarah had used the same phrase, which was probably why I found myself turning it over in my mind after I left Charlie a few minutes later, and which finally took me back to my first trip to Kilimanjaro, how I'd trudged up its slowly rising slope like so many younger Americans before me, with a copy of Hemingway in my backpack.

In "The Snows of Kilimanjaro," he'd written about a leopard that had been found near the very summit of the mountain, a place the Masai called *Ngaje Ngai,* the "House of God." Harry Black, Hemingway's dying hero, asks himself what this leopard was seeking at such heights, and in the way the question is formed in the story, the meditative, near-terminal voice in which Black poses it, it does seem strange that a leopard would journey so far up the slope of Kilimanjaro, where there was no food, nothing to hunt. Black clearly finds it inexplicable, one of life's insoluble mysteries, the strange part we can never fathom.

But, in fact, as I'd subsequently discovered on that first trek up Kilimanjaro, the leopard's presence on its upper slopes was no mystery at all. In fact, it was so wholly without mystery that a single question had settled the matter. *Why do you think a leopard would come up so far?* I had asked it of a local guide, and when I did, he laughed in a way that made it clear he was familiar with Hemingway's tale, and had been asked the same question by other fools like me. The leopard hadn't climbed toward the summit at all, he said. It had not been seeking anything because it had been long dead by the time it reached the higher elevations of Kilimanjaro. Masai tribesmen had carried it up the slope and left it as a sacrifice to mountain gods. They did this regularly. It was no more than a superstitious religious ritual. As for Hemingway, he could have solved the mystery of what the leopard was seeking simply by asking, the guide told me. Or perhaps Hemingway had asked, he went on, still laughing, but not liked the answer because it didn't fit his story.

Possibly, I thought, both—at the time I'd met the guide, and later, when I'd written up the experience for a travel magazine. But now I wondered if Hemingway's posing of an almost-mystical question was evidence of a greater failing than simply that of a writer who for the sake of a story had decided to fudge the facts. Maybe for all his clear-eyed realism, Hemingway had been seduced by the need for a "strange part," or at least by the possibility of some unseen element of existence that remained hidden to us, but which animals might sense, and for which they might even "seek," as the Buranni by rituals and festivals sought the benevolent intervention of their cherished Kuri Lam.

The problem was that I had sought it, too—this touch of the unseen—and that it was this seeking that had propelled me into Warren Maizey's room. But what had I been so intently hoping to find in that room that I now felt cheated in not finding it, and embarrassed that I had even tried, as if I were the dupe of some vast sleight of hand?

For most of the morning I pondered that question, though it wasn't until I met Arlo for lunch that I brought it up again.

"So what was I actually looking for when I went into Maizey's room?" I asked, after relating the entire tale of my visit there.

"You were looking for evidence," Arlo answered flatly.

"For what?" I asked.

"That it's more than a story."

I shook my head. "I'm not fooled by a story that easily."

Arlo looked at me as if I were a child, easily misled. "You've already been fooled," he said. "Me, too."

"What are you talking about?"

Arlo shifted slightly. "Because we both thought Maldrow promised Katherine that he'd find the guy who attacked her."

"He did."

Arlo shook his head firmly. "No, George, he didn't. We got the idea he did. So did Audrey, I guess. But it doesn't really say that in the story."

I didn't buy it. "But in the story Maldrow takes her to the fairgrounds," I said. "And to this house that—"

"Maldrow never says whose house that is," Arlo said.

"What about the guy on the bus?" I asked. "Isn't that supposed to be the actual unknown man?"

"The guy on the bus is never identified," Arlo said. "And besides, the man she sees is a man who burned a girl to death. He's not the one who attacked Katherine."

"Then who is he?"

"I don't know," Arlo answered. "Maybe just her fantasy of a man who got away with something horrible like that."

22

KATHERINE HAD PLAYED AN INTRIGUING little trick upon her few readers, and I expected Alice to find Arlo's discovery of it at least somewhat interesting. But at the end of my narrative, she merely drew in a long, oddly hollow breath, then said, "What's the strangest thing that ever happened to you, George?"

I knew instantly what the "strangest" thing had been. In fact, I'd told it to Charlie only a few hours before. Still, I wasn't sure if it was the right story for Alice under the circumstances because it was so hopelessly grim.

Her gaze was insistent, however, and so I did.

"I thought I saw him," I told her. "The man who killed my little boy."

And he was there again, vivid in my mind, wrapped in a glistening yellow rain slicker, moving effortlessly down Jefferson Street toward where Teddy waited for me in the pounding rain.

Alice's gaze was now quite intent. "When?" she asked.

"The day Teddy disappeared," I said. "I was standing at the window, and I saw this man in a yellow rain slicker. He was walking down Jefferson Street, in the direction of the bus stop where Teddy was last seen."

"You didn't see his face?" Alice asked.

"No," I answered. "I was supposed to pick Teddy up at the bus stop. Before he left the house that morning, he'd said something about a storm coming in, and I'd told him that if there were a storm, I'd pick him up. But it was just a few blocks he had to walk, and I figured the storm would blow over. So I turned away from the window before the guy got close enough for me to see his face."

Turned away from the window and went back to my desk.

"I'd been trying to come up with the first line of an essay on Extremadura," I told Alice, "a region of southern Spain that's very spare, very poor, mostly dust and scrub plants."

A landscape so bare and monochromatic, as I went on to tell Alice, that it had always struck me as ironic that it was from these barren wastes that Pizarro had drawn the young men who would later chop their way through the steaming jungles of South America. Almost none of these young men had ever returned to their desert homes, and it was the expression of that irony I'd been struggling with all that afternoon, the first half of a single line filtering endlessly through my head. *The winds of Extremadura blow bitter, dry and piercing, like . . .*

The end of the line was still eluding me as I'd stood at the window, watching the storm, thinking I should retrieve Teddy, my eyes briefly following the floating blur of a yellow rain slicker.

"Why do you think it was this man who killed Teddy?" Alice asked.

"I don't have an answer for that," I admitted.

"What makes it strange, then?"

"That I've always believed that it was him," I answered. "Without any evidence, I mean. Just a feeling."

Alice looked at the pages that remained of Katherine's manuscript. "Something you couldn't be sure of," she said.

"That's right."

"And so he got away," she added with a strange sad finality that seemed perfectly to anticipate the next words I read.

NOW

"Last call," the bartender says.

The Chief looks at Maldrow gravely. "It is time," he says.

Maldrow considers the ones before Katherine, the ones who'd almost reached this point, but who, in the end, had proven unfit. What was it they'd lacked? Some had loved life too little. Some had loved it too much. But the final failure had been a failure of belief. How many had mistrusted him? How many had whirled away at his approach? How many had not been able to take the horrors that had to be endured, and at the point the cup was finally passed, had refused to take it from him, drink the final draft.

And in the end, he wondered, would Katherine do that, too?

"The time has come," the Chief says.

Maldrow sees the great hall again, the robed figures he has so many times imagined, taking in the Chief's eloquent argument that only those who had experienced the full measure of loss and grief, the towering fury of the unjustly injured, could be selected.

"The passing," the Chief says.

Maldrow feels a terrible weight press him flat against the hard ground, press his face into the pavement. Fingers close around his neck, sharp as talons. His screams rake the air, and in those screams he hears all the anguished panic of the slaughtered, the burned and scraped and cut and beaten, screams that ignite the

224

air, bathing his skin in a lava flow of sound. The earth turns to quicksand, sucks him down and down into its suffocating depths so that he feels the hollow oblivion of the million million graves, the shivering cold of their untimely deaths, the hellish flame of their rage.

"Last call," the bartender says again.

Maldrow looks at the clock, considers the timetable, knows that Katherine should be leaving her house on Gilmore Street.

He glances at the empty seat across from him, the Chief already fled, the final signal that the time has truly come.

He rises as if lifted by a current of hot air. On the way out of the bar, he looks at the clock again to assure himself that there is such a thing as time. Then he steps out into the street and peers to the left, where at the end of Main Street he can see the little grotto in which Katherine Carr will meet her fate. He glances at his watch. Strange what they call it, he thinks. The witching hour.

At the end of the section, I stopped and looked at Alice. She was staring at the pages with a curious intensity, as if something unexpected had occurred to her, something she couldn't be sure of. "Go on," she said.

THEN

I startled slightly when the wind threw a scattering of raindrops against the window, then got control of myself, marched to the small table in the kitchen, sat down, and peered out into the night. I thought again of Maldrow, the way he drifted through time, weightless as the memory of something that never was. Could one live that way, I asked myself, forsaking all the promises of life, embracing darkness only, abandoning all one loved, and all by whom one had once been loved?

The nature of what Maldrow had loved had been revealed to

me only the night before, a long night of talking in the dark front room, shades drawn, as they always were, a cave of walls, drapery, tightly closed blinds.

He told me of Yenna, the task he'd offered her, a dark mission she would have taken up without hesitation, and carried out without fear. Stanovich had foiled all that, striking before the moment came for Yenna to be taken up.

"Did Stanovich get away with it?" I asked.

Maldrow shook his head. "And neither did your unknown man."

"How do you know that?"

"I have evidence," Maldrow answered.

"Show it to me."

"I will, when the time comes."

"I want to know now," I demanded. "You don't know what it's like to know he's out there, that this man who did this thing, that he—"

"I *do* know, Katherine," Maldrow said.

It was then he spoke of Amelia, his murdered child, the man who'd killed her so brutally, a man who, in the end, had not gotten away with it.

"How do you know he didn't?" I asked.

"The same way *you* will know," Maldrow answered. He started to speak, then stopped, waited a moment, then said, "Amelia. Innocent."

A terrible sadness fell over him, all the weight of the world, or so it seemed, the memory of his daughter's death a bitter draft he had to drink again and again.

Captured in that memory, he lowered his head. His body seemed to deflate, all his strength drain from him, so that he leaned to the right, as if toward an invisible pillow, a gesture of such brokenness that I gathered him into my arms.

He rested there a moment, then lifted himself again. "Tomorrow night," he said. "At the grotto."

"I'll be there," I said.

And I will be, I told myself now.

With those unspoken words, I stood up, walked into the living room, and sat down on the sofa. Rain fell noisily beyond the window, but I paid no notice. I could think of nothing but the eternal night that engulfed him, his mind a labyrinth of blood-soaked rooms. To live as Maldrow did seemed the most dreadful of fates: forever friendless, childless, without love, a figure cloaked in night—not just dark, but composed of darkness.

The rain stopped suddenly, and I knew the time had come. I didn't bother to get a coat or an umbrella. There would be no need for anything save for the long dark shawl that would briefly protect me from the cold. At the door, I glanced back into the room, the desk in the corner, the small folder where I'd placed my story along with a final poem, my true core.

I walked onto the porch, drew the shawl more tightly over my shoulders, then made my way down the stairs. At Gilmore I turned left onto Cantibell, then continued on until I reached town. The pale neon sign of the Winthrop Hotel swam into my view, and after it, around the near corner, the green shamrock that swung over the entrance of O'Shea's Bar. *The time has come,* I told myself. *The time is now.*

On the dark wings of that thought, I lifted my head and steeled myself for what was to come. It was still lifted when I reached the river, drew in a determined breath, then made my way toward the grotto where, beyond it, I could see the steadily encroaching fog.

I looked up from the pages, trying to gauge Alice's mood.

Alice said nothing, and in that silence appeared deeply engaged in a strange contemplation. Then she said, "Not much left."

"Just a few pages," I said. "We can finish it tonight."

Her eyes widened, like a child caught in the grip of some terrible foreboding. "No," she said. "I'm not ready."

"But we're right at the end," I said.

Her head lolled wearily to the left. The light seemed to have dimmed around her, so that her eyes were very nearly in shadow. Beneath the bedding, her body appeared impossibly thin, and as I gazed, a rush of searing rage swept over me, the burning, bitter certainty that we should never have lived at all if we had to live like this.

"Not yet," Alice said softly. "Please, George, not yet."

I tamped down the blazing wrath that seized me and swallowed it like a lump of coal. "Okay," I said. "We'll finish it tomorrow night."

She nodded heavily. "Tomorrow night, yes," she said weakly. "Tomorrow night you can read the end."

With that, she dropped her head, and seemed almost instantly to sleep. I came over to her gently, needlessly straightened her bedding. She gave no sense that she had felt my hands.

I left her at that point, and headed down the corridor. The young policeman was at his watch, but as I passed I noticed that the door where he'd stood guard was flung open and that the room was empty.

"I guess the bastard finally died," I said.

The policeman nodded. "Natural causes," he told me with a hopeless shrug, "so I guess you have to say he got away with it."

I glanced into the room, the bare walls and floor, and its emptiness seemed mine.

23

I HAD A RESTLESS NIGHT, and the next morning, blearily going through the usual routine, I felt somewhat like Katherine in the opening scene of her story, surrounded by her disturbing visions of the unknown man, save in my case it was not the man in the yellow rain slicker, but Alice who seemed everywhere around me, at my desk when I fumbled with a drawer, across from me at the breakfast table, waiting at the door when I grabbed my jacket and went out, her ghostly image so vividly in my mind that it seemed little more than a haunted house through which she roamed sleeplessly.

Charlie was already at his desk when I arrived at the office a few minutes later.

"Morning, George." He took a single sheet of white paper, crumpled it in his hand, and tossed it in a perfect arc toward the wastebasket a few feet away. "I was once pretty good at basketball," he said, though he seemed surprised that he'd actually made this latest goal. "But not pro material." He stared almost wistfully at the wastebasket, the paper he'd thrown into it clearly visible through its wire mesh. "Not even close to pro material." He appeared to pull himself out of an old dead dream, gripped his knees softly, and rose to his feet. "So, what are you working on now, George?"

I shrugged. "Just Hugo Tanner's obit."

Something in my tone clearly focused his attention. "What about that profile of Arlo McBride?"

I shook my head. "It didn't go anywhere."

"And that little girl with—"

I recalled the way Alice's head had lolled the night before, almost too heavy, it seemed, for her to hold up. "She's almost gone."

Charlie nodded. "You know, George, if you don't have anything on your plate, how about covering Warren Maizey's funeral? Wyatt tossed it to me, but I just got a great source on that prostitution ring in Kingston, and I'd already arranged for a meeting."

"Where are they burying him?" I asked.

"The town cemetery." Charlie glanced at his watch. "You'll need to be there in ten minutes."

It would be a distraction, I realized, a way of chasing Alice from my thoughts, however briefly. "Okay," I said.

A rather large crowd had already gathered by the time I arrived at the town cemetery, mostly reporters and local officials, but also a withered old couple who huddled together beneath a large elm and whom I recognized as the parents of Eden Taub. I'd seen their picture in the *Winthrop Examiner*, of course, but I think I would have recognized them anyway because they had a look I'd often seen in my bathroom mirror: grief that is also an accusation, a child death's for which, however inadvertent and unintended, one must finally be held responsible. I had little doubt that there were mornings when they rose from their beds and saw Eden as I'd so often seen Teddy, standing in the hallway or by a window, pale, silent as Teddy always was, though with a terrible question in his eyes: *Why didn't you come for me?*

I felt a deep inner quaking, but suppressed it the way I always did, by concentrating on this latest assignment, the same means by which I held the ground I retook each morning, like a soldier in a battle that never ends.

The crowd was raggedly composed, as I noticed, reporters idling together, officials huddled with their own kind. There was the usual scattering of the merely curious as well, townspeople who'd no doubt followed Eden Taub's case through the years, and had now come to see this bleak but final resolution of it.

I took out my notebook and was scribbling various observations into it when the hearse bearing Maizey's body appeared in the distance. It passed slowly beneath the cemetery's iron gate, an old black relic from Robinson's Mortuary that probably had been selected for its sheer lack of elegance. Who, after all, could possibly care how Warren Maizey was delivered to the little slit in the earth that would eternally contain him?

The crowd watched as the hearse made a wide turn, then circled around to where a group of gravediggers waited for it, all of them in ordinary work-clothes, open-collared shirts with the sleeves rolled to the elbow, laborers who'd probably been unloading bricks or lumber only moments before, Maizey's burial just another job.

When the hearse came to a stop, the gravediggers closed in upon the rear door, then waited for the driver to come around and open it. When he did, they unceremoniously hauled

Maizey's plain wooden coffin out of the back, heaved it onto their collective shoulders, then bore it to the grave with something a good deal less than military precision.

At that point, the crowd closed in upon the grave. I did the same, and it was then I saw Arlo take his place at the head of what appeared to be a small contingent of retired detectives.

He didn't see me in the surrounding crowd, or if he did, gave no indication of it. His head was bowed slightly, though clearly not in prayer. Instead, he seemed to be following Maizey's descent into the ground, for it was only after the coffin hit bottom and the lowering ropes had been pulled up that he lifted his head again.

I'd expected a priest or some other religious figure to step forward at that point, offer a prayer, ask God to forgive even Warren Maizey's blackened soul. But to my surprise, it was Arlo who evidently had been designated to speak, probably by Eden's family since, as I now recalled, he'd been the lead investigator in their daughter's case. At any rate, as he stepped forward, his face was suddenly caught in a ray of sunlight.

"I don't know why a man like Warren Maizey was ever allowed to live," he said. He glanced about the crowd, stopping from time to time at what I took to be a familiar face, perhaps some old veteran of the force, or one, like me, whose life he'd touched. "And more than that, I don't know why, given what he did to Eden Taub, he's been free all these years, became an old man, and finally got sick and died just like anyone else." He shook his head. "But when I think about Maizey never getting caught, I make myself think of something I once read. It was about a couple of young men. They were named Leopold and Loeb. They were an evil pair who killed a little boy, took his body out into the woods, stripped it, and dumped it in a culvert. At some point during all that, Leopold dropped his glasses near that boy's body, and because of that, he got caught." His gaze suddenly settled upon me. "Could it be that some unseen hand reached into that boy's jacket and flipped out that pair of glasses?" He held his attention on me a moment longer, and in that brief interval his eyes took on an odd twinkle. "That's my hope, anyway, and hope—or at least the hope for hope—is the one thing we should all still have at the end."

"It comes from Katherine's story," Arlo said. "That Leopold and Loeb stuff."

"It must be near the end of it, then," I said.

"Yes, it is," Arlo said.

We'd walked from the cemetery, taken a table at the small coffee shop, ordered, and after that talked briefly about Warren Maizey, which had finally led me to mention his talk at the gravesite.

"We're almost at the end," I said. "Alice and I. Just one more section to go." I shrugged. "I hope it has a good ending, Arlo. Alice would be disappointed if it had some phony twist."

"Phony twist?" Arlo asked. "Like what?"

"Like if Maldrow ends up trying to kill her, and she knocks the gun out of his hand and kills him instead. *That* sort of typical mystery ending. Or somebody shows up to save Katherine in the nick of time. Somebody you wouldn't expect. The guy on the bus, maybe, who ends up the hero, somehow. Or even that creep, Ronald Duckworth." I thought a moment longer, then added, "Or Cody. Or Audrey. Maybe it turns out they've been running relay, keeping an eye on Katherine, so they're there to save her just in time. An ending like that would really disappoint Alice."

Arlo peered at me silently.

"It's worse, isn't it?" I asked. "Katherine's ending is even worse than the ones I've just mentioned."

Suddenly Arlo seemed very weary, like a man who'd failed a vital mission. "Maybe you're not the right man to have read Katherine's story after all, George," he said. "Maybe you never were."

For the rest of the day, I worked on Hugo Tanner's obit. First I reread my earlier profile; then I looked through the photographs I'd taken during the tour Hugo had given me of his place. The interior of his house had looked far different then, less cluttered and certainly less chaotic, though the first hints of Hugo's incontestable OCD were already beginning to show in five-foot towers of old magazines and milk crates overflowing with all manner of small bottles.

I thought of all the bizarre formulas Hugo must have tried, the potions he'd concocted, always trying to prove the existence of paranormal communications, magical cures, unseen worlds. In the end, it had been an obsession that had expelled him from society, made him a freak. And yet, as it seemed to me, it was a freakishness whose starry mantle he'd worn defiantly to the end.

It was late in the afternoon before I finished the piece and took it in to Wyatt.

"The curtains were sprinkled with glitter in Hugo Tanner's house," Wyatt read, "star-lit and sparkling . . ." He stopped, completed the first line silently to himself, then read it aloud, ". . . like the robes of Merlin." He smiled. "You're always good at first lines, George."

"Sometimes they come quickly," I said, then heard that long-ago rumble of thunder and the thud of rain, along with the dry winds of Extremadura. "Sometimes they don't."

Wyatt returned to the piece, read it through silently, then placed it in what he called the Ship and Bill file, which meant that it was ready for the copyeditor.

"What do you think Hugo was looking for in all his crazy experiments?" he asked lightly, with no expectation of an actual answer, as one might ask why a particular lunatic had chosen to think himself Christ rather than Napoleon.

And yet, I thought I had an answer, so I gave it.

"He was looking for proof," I said.

"Of what?"

"The usual nonsense," I answered. "Angels, goblins, little people." I thought of Arlo's talk at Warren Maizey's grave. "The unseen hand."

Wyatt shook his head. "But he never found any proof," he said. "So what, for all his effort, did he leave behind?"

I looked at the one page I'd written: Hugo Tanner's fate recorded in a few short paragraphs.

"Just the story of his search for it," I answered quietly, thinking of Katherine's story now, oddly dreading to read the end of it. "Nothing more."

24

ALICE WAS SLEEPING when I came into her room at just after eight that night, and I chose not to wake her. Instead I slumped down in the chair a few feet from her bed and waited. She now seemed smaller than ever, her wrinkled face barely visible in the depths of her pillow. Her breath was very weak and a little ragged, not unlike my father's, who, at nearly eighty, had been dying of the same terrible confluence of diseases that were killing Alice at twelve.

In my past visits, she'd appeared quite calm, her body for the most part still; but that night, as I sat in the shadowy light of her room, she was quite visibly fretful, constantly jerking her legs or clenching her fists, so that she seemed tormented, either by dreams or by her body's unconscious-but-continuing desire to live.

It was perhaps an hour before she opened her eyes, first languidly, then with what appeared to be a pure act of will.

"Hi, George," she said softly.

I nodded. "I didn't want to wake you."

She labored to pull herself upright. I stood up, walked to her bed, took one of the pillows, and tucked it behind her back.

"Is that better?" I asked.

She leaned back into the pillow, her body so light it hardly made an impression in its folds. Her breathing was very soft, like her voice, and seemed hardly to carry the words she said: "Did you bring the end of the story?"

"Yes." I pulled the chair close to her bedside and took the last of Katherine's pages from my briefcase. "Shall I read it now?"

She nodded slowly, and I began:

THEN

At last I arrived at the little grotto beside the river where Maldrow had asked me to meet him. I'd vainly hoped to find him there waiting for me, but the place was deserted. I was alone in the river's mist.

I don't know how long I waited, but it could not have been very long, certainly not long enough for me to doubt that Maldrow would come.

But when he came, he seemed older than before, slightly hunched, his eyes sunken, his face a web of wrinkles.

"How old are you, really?" I asked.

Layers of secrecy seemed to peel away from him like old skins, and yet he made no effort to answer my question, but instead drew me beneath his arm and gently turned me toward the river. "This way," he said.

We walked a few paces, then stopped. In the distance, through the gloomy mist, I could hear the lapping of the river, very soft and rhythmic, like a heart.

For a little while, we stood in silence, facing the blank screen of the unseen river. Then Maldrow lifted his arm and pointed out into the thick, rolling fog that approached us. "Look there," he said.

With that word, both fog and river vanished, and we stood in a shadowy wood.

"Look there," Maldrow repeated.

I looked in the direction he indicated and there, in the distance, saw two young men laboriously carrying what appeared to be an unruly bundle that shifted inconveniently as they hauled it forward, and which, at one point, caused one of the men to stumble.

"Come on, Nat," one said. "Get a grip on the thing."

The other did as he was told, reached firmly under the bundle, and drew it up again, this time almost to his shoulders, so that the mass inside shifted yet again, and from out of the covering, a small white hand suddenly emerged, the fingers still and curving inward toward the palm.

"Got it?"

"Yeah."

"All right, let's go."

They came forward again, tromping awkwardly through the tangled undergrowth, unused to such heavy labor, and resentful of it, but still closing in upon the shallow culvert where Maldrow and I stood watching them. They passed within a breath of us, but gave no notice of our presence, so that I knew we were as silent and unseen as a bird circling overhead.

"You know who they are," Maldrow said.

And, of course, I did, for he had told me of this moment many times: the look of the young men as they went about their work, undressing the boy, screwing the top off the jar of acid they'd brought with them, pouring it over the boy's face and genitals, the taller laughing as he did this, the other dancing away, slapping at his trousers.

"Don't get that stuff on me!"

The smaller young man's face soured. "It's hot." He stripped off his jacket and slung it across a fallen limb. "Come on, let's finish this up."

Together the two completed the task, then stepped back to admire their work.

"Perfect," the taller one said. "A perfect crime."

Maldrow stretched out his hand as the smaller of the young men reached for his jacket and, with an invisible finger, he tapped at the pair of glasses that hung loosely from the pocket. The glasses slid smoothly from the pocket as the young man lifted the jacket, falling and falling until they came to rest in a bed of grass, the lenses glinting in the afternoon sunlight as the young men strolled away.

I stopped reading, placed the latest page behind the others I had yet to read.

"Do you get what's happening?" I asked Alice. "Do you get what Maldrow does?"

Alice nodded gravely, her once-absorbing gaze now barely able to focus. "He makes sure people get caught," she said weakly. She seemed hesitant to add anything to this, but also compelled to add the thought that had so obviously come to her at that moment. "Bad people, like the man who took Teddy."

"But he was never caught," I said in a tone considerably more bitter than I'd expected, and which I labored to control. I rustled the few remaining pages of Katherine's story. "There's a little more," I said, now so disappointed with where it was going that I wanted only to be done with it. "Shall I?"

"Please."

And with that I began to read again:

The two young men continued to walk away, one of them laughing haughtily as the river fog drew in upon them and finally covered

239

them, the blank wall of its thick mist now fully recomposed before me.

"But that is not your mission, Katherine."

"What is?" I asked.

"To feel murder."

A wave of cold swept out and enveloped me, a cold that deepened with each passing second, colder than an arctic blast, a cold that seemed to come from the unfeeling core of cruelty itself.

I gasped as one might struggle to breathe in the last atom of oxygen from a block of ice, but the cold pressed in, my body paralyzed, as if already frozen in place, so that I could only watch as the air thickened into a wall of ice.

"To feel murder a million million times."

The wall of ice exploded like a mirror, filling the air around me with tiny shards of razor-thin glass, a swirl of glittering fibers, each point of light a single, dreadful image: Socks stuffed into a drainpipe. A freezer leaking water. Blood swirling in a toilet. A slimy pool. A murky well. Bleach on a tiled floor. A strand of blond hair caught on a briar. A half-filled sack of lime.

And still the flashing images continued: The jagged edge of a shattered bottle. The dripping needle of a syringe. Hooks on a conveyor belt. Wet leaves scattered over plywood. A mound of clothes in a basement furnace. Rope hanging from a wooden beam. Wires dangling from a battery.

The mirror shifted: A small white ankle lashed to a chair leg. A mouth stuffed with a red handkerchief. Trembling hands tied, chained, bound tight by black tape. By the millions, I saw the murdered where they lay in cellars, barns, attics, basements, their bodies dropped into mine shafts, tossed over cliffs, rolled into ditches and ravines, sunk in rivers, streams, and ponds.

The mirror now flashed with desperate messages scrawled on mirrors, walls, doors; notes written in crayon or drawn on mist-clouded windowpanes, interrupted in their pleas, *Help m—*

"Help me."

The cloud vanished and became Maldrow.

"And you will," he said.

I felt a profound loosening of inward bonds and at the same time a sense of myself sweeping out and out, like a child stepping into a book and entering its world. At that instant, all the poisons of human life drained from me, all its bitterness and wrath. My earthly bonds released, and as their weight dropped from me, I felt myself slip beyond the downward pull of mortal life, felt a new gyroscope spin within me, a movement that seemed to fling silver droplets in all directions, filling both my inner and my outer space with a magisterial scope.

I didn't speak, but Maldrow knew that I'd accepted the mission, that I would carry it out forever, vanish from my present life and step into a new one.

For a long moment, we stared at each other silently and without motion, until Maldrow finally reached into the pocket of his jacket.

"There must be resolution," he said, and with those words, drew out his closed hand and opened it.

"He didn't get away with it, Katherine," Maldrow said.

I stared at the gold ring in his hand, and knew absolutely that it was the one that had been stolen from me.

"Take it," Maldrow said.

I drew it from his hand, but had no need to look inside the band, for they were undoubtedly there, my initials, carved roughly as I had seen my grandfather carve them. For a time, I stared at the ring, knowing that it would be the last of my earthly possessions, the last of my human connections, the last I would know of true touch, this ring the only object I could take with me in my vanishing.

"He didn't get away with it," Maldrow repeated. "Any more than Stanovich got away with it, or the man who killed my daughter. Any more than the man on the number 34, who burned that young woman. He will not get away with it because it will be you who comes for him."

I felt as if a pair of dark wings had sprouted from my shoulders, a keenness in my eyes, the way they required neither sound nor movement nor color to find my prey, but only the heat of the one who was to be punished.

"I'm ready," I told Maldrow.

Maldrow touched my back. "Depart now," he said, "and restore the balance."

Then, as if carried on a river of air, we moved toward the dark, flowing water of the river until we reached its bank. My feet were bare, though I had no idea where my shoes had gone. I could feel the cool water lapping at my toes, along with a great beckoning force, the end of my earthbound story, the stars gathering around me as I rose toward them, the earth now far below me, small and blue and streaked with clouds, until I reached the miraculous apogee of this flight, and from its zenith began my return to earth, knowing as I made my dark descent that somewhere out there, in ever-changing shape, unseen by the human throng, I would strike tonight.

"The End," I said, then simply stared at Alice silently for a moment before I added, "*I* was hoping for a better ending, too."

In fact, it seemed to me that the ending Katherine had concocted for her story could hardly have been worse: a scene of magical levitation that was ludicrous on its face, the sort of ending I would have expected from some cheesy fantasy writer, and because of which, I suddenly felt a deep disappointment in Katherine: not just as a writer, but as a person. Until this point, I'd admired the way she'd faced life with the starkness of one who, having faced it squarely, had every right to walk into the river, as I felt quite certain she had. Then, in a ridiculous, supernatural turn, she'd wrapped herself in the mantle of eternity, turned herself into a woman made more for rapture than reality.

These were not thoughts I would have kept to myself, but before I could speak again, Alice released a long, weary breath and said, "I'd like to be like Katherine."

"Like Katherine?" I asked. "In what way?"

"Just let it go, the way she did," Alice answered.

"Let what go?"

"Life," Alice answered in a voice that was little more than a whisper. "Leave it all behind."

At that moment, I realized the very different ways in which Alice and I each had received the ending of Katherine's story. For me it was one of supernatural transcendence, easy to dismiss and even hold in contempt. But for Alice, the ending had spoken of acceptance and surrender, so that I suddenly recalled my father's last days, the way he'd fought to take just one more breath. He had struggled on by will alone, or perhaps simply the brute intransigence of this organ or that one, a heart that against all odds just kept on beating, lungs determined to pull in just one more gasp of oxygen.

I knew that this was the kind of death Alice wanted to avoid, but I could find nothing that might move her closer to the letting go she sought, and which I found myself idealizing as an instant of complete serenity, her eyes and lips closing in some final, welcomed peace.

She moved slightly, and with that movement, winced.

"Do you need something for that?" I asked.

For a moment she watched me thoughtfully, eyes very intent and oddly searching, though she also seemed reluctant to reveal what was on her mind.

"I don't want to finish yet," she said finally. "With Katherine."

"But we've read the whole story," I said. "There isn't any more."

"You said there was a poem," Alice said. "A poem she left behind."

"Yes, there was. But I don't have it."

"I want to read it," Alice said. "I want to know . . ." She stopped. "I want to know what happened to her."

It was a futile ambition, I knew, Alice's hope to move from guessing the ending of a little mystery story to solving the actual case of its vanished author. But she was dying, and I wondered if perhaps in these final desperate hours, she was even suffering from a vague dementia, so I said, "All right, I'll see if I can get it."

My pledge clearly eased her. She drew in a long, delicate breath, and on that breath, closed her eyes. "Thank you, George," was all she said.

She was quite obviously exhausted, so I left her a few minutes later, went to my car, and headed home.

On the drive to my apartment, I considered Alice's passionate need to solve Katherine's case. I knew there was no possibility of her doing any such thing, so for a time I'd actually entertained the notion of fooling Alice in some way, at least to the extent of providing a solution of my own. Various schemes occurred to me. I could claim that something she'd said had led me to investigate further and that I'd miraculously uncovered new evidence, evidence I would provide myself: undiscovered chapters of her story that I myself would quickly write. The chapters would tell all, and thus resolve Katherine's story. Or I might claim that Katherine's lost ring had been found among the effects of some criminal who'd suddenly died in a neighboring town, proof that she had been murdered. If Alice appeared doubtful, I could use Celeste's ring as proof, say that Arlo had managed to get hold of it for me.

But every scheme I came up with proved more ludicrous than the one before it, so I finally gave up and called Arlo.

"We finished reading Katherine's story," I told him. "Alice isn't satisfied with the ending."

"I see."

"She wants to know what actually happened to Katherine," I added. "She wants to read the poem. You said she left a poem behind."

"Yes, she did."

"Alice wants to read it."

"I'd have to check with Audrey before I could give it to you, George."

"Could you do it now?" I asked.

He heard the urgency in my voice. "She's that close, Alice?"

"Yes."

"Okay," Arlo said. "If Audrey says it's okay, I'll drop it at your place."

"Good. Thanks."

"Just don't get your hopes up, George, because that poem doesn't have anything to do with what happened to Katherine." His voice grew curiously taut. "It's not about her at all."

25

THERE ARE TIMES now when I let slip the reins of what I know is real, and release my own best hope like a white horse into a limitlessly open field. At those moments, I imagine Katherine watching from high above, like the soaring bird she wrote about, looking down, looking through, watching patiently as her plan unfolded, this most tender of her schemes.

But that night, waiting for Arlo to arrive with Katherine's last poem, I felt only my great desire for Alice to find a satisfying conclusion to Katherine's story, one I couldn't find myself, any more than the police had found it, or Audrey or Cody, or anyone else who had tried.

I had hoped it would be only a few minutes before Arlo slipped the poem through the slot in my door, but an hour passed, then another. After a time, I headed for O'Shea's.

In some strange way, O'Shea's was where it had all begun,

I thought, as I settled into my usual booth. It was here Arlo had first approached me, here we'd had our first quiet talk, here where he'd first mentioned a young woman who had vanished twenty years before. It was the place where Katherine's story had begun, as well, with Maldrow and the Chief seated in a back booth that might well have been the same one I was seated in at that very moment.

I took a sip of my drink, my gaze moving about in the way Katherine had described Maldrow's, from the window, to the patrons at the bar, then back to the seat just opposite him, where the Chief had suddenly appeared, speaking the first line of dialogue in that melancholy way of his: *You look tired, Maldrow.*

I'm sure I looked tired, too, though it was Alice's weariness that was my chief concern at that moment, the heaviness of each breath, how much she wanted to let go of life, simply step back into the fog as Katherine had.

"Hello, George."

I looked up to find Stanley Grierson standing at the booth.

"Hey, Stanley."

He had been my neighbor when I'd lived on Jefferson Street, a widower who now seemed locked in perpetual grief. His wife Molly had died a long, slow death seven years before, and after that, Stanley had kept pretty much to himself.

"I like your stories in the paper," Stanley said. "It's a good job, being a reporter."

I remembered when Bill Daugherty died. He'd been my father's best friend, an old hand at covering wars both hot and cold. At his wake in New York, a slew of aging reporters had come tottering in to pay their respects, foreign correspondents mostly, wearing trench coats and smoking Gauloises or some equally smelly foreign cigarette. One of them had come over to me and asked what I did for a living. I'd told him I was a freelance writer, but he'd seemed to hear something more august. "Reporter," he said, "comes from the Latin. *Reportare,* to bear away." He'd yammered on about something or other, but I'd looked over his shoulder to where Celeste stood across the room, pregnant with Teddy, careful about what she was eating, not drinking at all, because of the child she was carrying. And I'd thought, *She knows. She knows what's worth bearing away.*

"I wouldn't go that far," I said. "But it puts food on the table."

Stanley shrugged and took a sip from his beer.

I would normally have said nothing more, but the expectation of Alice's death, the return to solitariness that would inevitably follow, urged me forward just enough to say, "So how have you been, Stanley?"

Stanley seemed genuinely surprised that I'd opted to continue the conversation. "Okay," he said. "You know, missing Molly."

There was little to be said in response to this, so I let my gaze drift away from him and down toward the table, old and scarred as I noticed, punctured and gouged out, sometimes words, sometimes numbers, and there, somehow more prominent than the others, more deeply and more violently dug, as if carved into the vital organs of the wood, a name that might have been the one Katherine had written of in her story, the one "Maldrow" had seen, carved angrily, as she'd described it, the carver's lips curling down with each dig of the knife.

"What have you been up to?" Stanley asked.

"Following the Flower Festival, the Chamber of Commerce," I answered in the idle way of simply keeping the talk going. "Reading a story this woman left behind after she vanished."

"Left behind?" Stanley asked. "You mean, like a clue?"

I realized that I hadn't thought of Katherine's story in that way before, and it all suddenly seemed terribly "genre" to me, a reporter with a tragic past reading a story written by a mysteriously missing woman that a retired detective had given to him. I wondered if I might find myself a character in some romance story next, or worse, in some fantasy, riding a winged white horse through starry worlds.

I took a quick sip of scotch. "And writing a profile of a dying girl," I said. "She's sort of gotten to me."

Stanley nodded heavily. "It never fills up, does it?" he asked.

"*What* doesn't fill up?" I asked.

"The space they leave," Stanley said. "The ones who've been taken."

I heard Teddy's voice: *Can you pick me up if it rains?*

"No," I said. "It never fills up."

We talked on for a time, though not about anything I could later remember. Then Stanley rose and headed back to his empty house on Jefferson Street.

As he left, it struck me that if real life worked like an inspirational story, then he'd have left me with some little nugget of wisdom he'd garnered from his hard experience, some life-affirming little lesson he'd learned from Molly's death, a remark that I could ponder, reshape, perhaps fashion into a plan of action with regard to Alice. But Stanley had had nothing of that sort to offer me, or if he had, he'd kept it to himself.

I watched him leave, ordered another drink, then another, so that I was never able to say exactly when I left O'Shea's that night, or be certain—absolutely certain—of what happened after that, save that I headed home on foot, as always, and that at some point, I noticed the lights of the coffee shop at the end of the block, a woman in the window, reading to herself, noticed how her long silvering hair fell in a thick curtain over her shoulders and down her back, and how, when she saw me standing groggily in the rain, she closed her book and sat with her hands in her lap, so that she seemed to be waiting for me to come inside.

I nodded toward the empty chair opposite her. "Do you mind?" I asked.

"Not at all."

I sat down and nodded toward the book she'd been reading, but which now lay closed before her.

"Good story?" I asked.

She looked down and one pale hand rose from her lap and tapped the book. "They're like ghosts, don't you think?" she asked.

I took a sip of coffee and felt a little of my mental haze lift a bit. "In what way?"

"Because they're the voices of the dead," she answered.

"You could think of them that way."

A smile played delicately upon her lips. "Yes." She turned the book toward me, opened it at where she'd placed a dark red ribbon, and pressed it toward me. "I'm reading this story at the moment."

I took the book and glanced down at the title. "'The Last Leaf,'" I said.

"O. Henry. Do you know it?"

"Yes," I said. "It's about a dying—" I stopped, because something in her gaze stopped me.

"Go on," she said.

"A little girl who's dying," I said.

"As are so very many," she said quietly.

"More's the pity," I said, as if called upon to say it, so that the two of us now seemed to be speaking in the coded language of a long-familiar couple, one we by some arcane means mutually understood.

I handed the book back to her. "It's a sentimental story. Sort of a lie."

"I prefer to think of it as a hopeful fraud," the woman said. She tucked the book firmly under her arm. "Forgive me, but my bus is here."

I glanced out the front window, and saw the Number 34 glide over to the curb.

"It must be the last bus of the evening," I said.

"It is, yes." She smiled. "Good-bye, then."

I got to my feet. "Good-bye," I said.

She offered a hand that seemed ivory in its whiteness, in its smoothness, with nothing to add to its ghostly pallor, as I noticed, save the slender glint of a plain gold ring.

Arlo had still not dropped off Katherine's poem when I got home, so I grabbed my book on the Buranni and began to read about their belief that it was the unseen things of life that were most powerful. Life was invisible, as was Death, they claimed, nor could anyone see the force that allowed pain to radiate from one person to another, so that people could feel the loss and sorrow of others.

I'd been reading for only a short time when I heard a car pull up outside. I went to the window, and looked down to see Arlo get out of a dusty old sedan. He had a plain white envelope in his hand, no doubt the poem Katherine had left with her story.

I retrieved the envelope a few seconds later, took it back upstairs, opened it, and read the poem, hoping that Alice might have been right, that something within its few lines actually revealed Katherine's fate.

But Arlo was right: The poem had nothing to do with any of that. Not one word about Maldrow, or Katherine herself, or anything that might remotely suggest the circumstances of her disappearance.

And so I folded the page and returned it to the envelope, convinced now more than ever before that there could be no solution to her case.

26

I DELIVERED KATHERINE'S poem to the hospital the next morning. Alice was still sleeping, so I left it on the table beside her bed, then went on about my day.

As usual, I filled the hours with work, writing my piece on Warren Maizey's funeral first, an article that did not include my bizarre little visit to his hospice room, but focused on his crimes instead, how he'd been apprehended at last, though already dying by then, so that he'd quite clearly escaped punishment, Eden Taub's terrible death forever unavenged.

By noon I'd turned it in, waiting as always while Wyatt read it.

"Good," he said when he finished it. "Love the first line." With that he read it: *"Warren Maizey's coffin was borne to the grave coldly and indifferently, with no sign of human feeling, as if in imitation of his life."* He smiled. "Ouch!"

"He didn't deserve any better," I said dryly.

Wyatt slipped the pages into the Ship and Bill file. "So, who's next?"

"Alice Barrows," I said. "When she dies."

"And after that?" Wyatt asked matter-of-factly.

I felt something very small give way within me, the crumbling of a little wall. "After Alice?" I said. "I don't know."

For the rest of the day, as I worked my next assignment, a piece on the town's upcoming exhibition of local painters, I was seized with odd thoughts. They came the instant I was not otherwise occupied, came like bats, fluttered insistently. I thought of the Third Man, with his tale of diamonds stashed in tiny graves, the elfish name he'd manufactured for his tale, how eerie it all was. Then Max came to mind, my night in the Viennese demimonde, his injunction continually echoing in my mind, warning that I should never forget the Unseen. I thought of Celeste's encounter with a stranger who turned out to have shared her surname. In remembrance, I took again my long, winding drive up the Amalfi Coast, recalled again and again the eerie expanse that swept out from the Terrace of the Infinite. But each of these thoughts and recollections returned me inexplicably to Alice, so that by the time evening fell and I headed back to Gladwell Hospice, I felt that in some way I'd been with her all day.

She struggled to lift herself when I came into the room, but failed, so that her head lolled backward into the pillow. "Can you just . . ."

"Sure," I said as I rushed over and helped ease her upright. "Is that better?"

"That's fine," Alice said. She drew a long breath, and seemed to deflate when she released it. "I had a bad night," she said.

The simple act of speaking appeared to be a burden to her, a weight she found difficult to lift. She gave off a sense of utter exhaustion, deep and irrecoverable, a tiredness with being tired.

"I could come back later," I suggested.

She shook her head. "Did you read it?" she asked.

"Katherine's poem, yes, I read it." I shrugged. "It has nothing to do with her story, or what might have happened to her."

Alice handed me the poem. "Read it again, George."

And so I did:

> *Why credit only what we see,*
> *Believe what only seems to be,*
> *Choose the Visible's dark mire*
> *Over what our hearts desire?*
>
> *Better let our dreams remake*
> *A world not made for Evil's sake,*
> *But open to the tender hand*
> *That offers hope to hopeless man?*
>
> *What serves us better, doubt or hope*
> *As we walk the darkling path,*
> *Bestows on life an unseen scope,*
> *And offers us an end to wrath?*

"What do you think?" Alice asked after I'd finished.

"It's singsongy," I said dryly. "And the beat goes off."

"I mean, about what it says," Alice said.

"It's silly," I said. "She wants us to believe in things we can't really believe in."

"Like Maldrow," Alice said. "That there are these 'entities' out there who track down bad people and make them pay."

"Exactly."

Alice drew in a long, faintly wheezy breath, and shifted again. "Supernatural. Like Katherine becomes at the end."

"That's right," I said. "People like to believe crap like that."

I went on to describe the weird beliefs of the Buranni, the intervention of the Kuri Lam.

Alice listened attentively, but pain and weariness continually distracted her, so that it didn't surprise me that she asked for no additional details.

I handed the poem back to her. "How about you? What do you think about it?" I asked.

"I didn't like it much," Alice answered. Her head drifted to the left and seemed to be almost too heavy for her to keep upright. "Sort of silly, like you said."

"So we agree?" I said.

"Not exactly."

For a moment, I feared that Alice had done what anyone might in her condition: grasped at the straw Katherine offered at the end of her story, its vision of immortality, or a world beyond this one, Katherine sailing out among the stars.

But what she said next put that fear to rest.

"Katherine's not some kind of immortal," Alice added. "Not like she becomes in her story. But maybe she wants us to think she really is like that, off in the clouds with Maldrow."

I was relieved to hear this, but since I had no idea where Alice was going at this point, I remained silent.

"But maybe the poem tells us what really happened to Katherine," Alice said. "A better ending. Not that she was murdered or committed suicide."

"Then why did she vanish?"

"Because it was her only chance." Alice's voice was thin, but she was clearly determined to press forward with her discovery. "It wasn't much of a chance, but it was the only one she had."

"Her only chance for what?"

"To make us believe her story," Alice answered. "Maybe that was all she cared about. Maybe it was like her child, so she wanted it to live forever."

"I don't know what you mean," I said.

"That's what her poem says," Alice went on. "She wanted people to have hope that there were these things out there that helped people. Immortals who made sure people didn't get away with murder."

"Like the Kuri Lam?" I asked.

"Like Maldrow," Alice said. "Immortals like that. Which Katherine became, too, at the end of the story." For a moment, Alice remained silent, as if letting me think all this through. Then she said, "Maybe that's why Katherine disappeared."

I looked at her blankly.

"Maybe Katherine wanted people to believe that her story could be true," Alice said. "But she couldn't do that if she killed herself because her body might be found. And so she vanished. She *had* to vanish in real life because she vanishes at the end of her story. So for her story to be true, she had to disappear."

"But where did she go?" I asked.

"It doesn't matter where she went," Alice said. "The only thing that matters is why she did it." She sat back and drew in a long, difficult breath. "It's a fantasy she wants us to believe in, and so to give us a little evidence to hang on to, she went away." She smiled for the first time—a quick smile, but crowned with satisfaction. "What do *you* think?"

I knew that in the usual mystery, a different ending would have been required, one far more dramatic and revelatory, Alice somehow able to discover what had actually happened to Katherine, whether she'd been murdered or committed suicide, her true end. But as I watched Alice rest contentedly, clearly pleased with the "solution" she'd come up with, I realized that no matter what had actually happened all those many years ago, it had ultimately been the fate of Katherine Carr to offer both the gift of a mystery and the satisfaction of its vaguely plausible resolution to a dying child.

I smiled. "You're a true detective, Alice," I said quietly.

I expected her to take this in the way I meant it, as a compliment to her powers of detection, the little elements she strung together from Katherine's poems, but instead she continued, "Teddy. You told me you were trying to finish a line the day he disappeared."

I wondered if she were now trying to turn the tables on our own story, almost in the way of a sentimental tale, a dying girl's attempt to provide soulful balm to a tortured man.

"Yes, I was."

And like a figure in a science fiction novel, spiraling backward in a time machine, I returned to that earlier time and place. As if perched, birdlike, at the top of a bookshelf. I saw myself seated at my desk, staring at the opening line, half completed, needing an ending that would set the tone, struggling to find it as the first rumble of thunder passed over Jefferson Street and the first stormy rain lashed at the window.

"The line was about Extremadura," I told Alice, "the very bleak arid part of Spain that sent so many of its young men with the Conquistadors. I'd written the first half of it."

But I'd failed to complete the line, as I went on to tell her, so that it remained truncated, dangling, as disturbing to me at that moment as a half-severed arm.

"When I heard the thunder and the rain, I got up and walked to the window."

Where I'd stood, staring at the rain and listening to the thunder, recalling the promise I'd made to Teddy, but stymied by the uncompleted line, feeling it form somewhere within my mind, but still foggy and insubstantial.

"I knew the end of the line was about to come to me. They come out of nowhere. You can't just summon them. I knew this one was coming, but I needed time . . . just a little time."

And so I'd turned and gone back to the page, turned just as from the corner of my eye, a slash of slick yellow swam out of the fog.

"And so I didn't go get Teddy," I said. "Instead, I went back to my desk and reread the half-line I'd written." I could see it form in my mind, that still-uncompleted opening line: "'The winds of Extremadura blow bitter, dry and piercing like . . .'" I quoted. "That's where it stopped."

Alice closed her eyes and drew in a ragged breath, one that seemed painful, an aching in the chest. "And you never found the end of the line?" she asked.

"No, I didn't."

Then the end of that long-sought line suddenly appeared like a ghost down a long corridor, always there, but invisible before now.

"I just thought of it," I said quietly.

Alice watched me silently, clearly awaiting my discovery.

"'The winds of Extremadura blow bitter, dry and piercing like . . .'" I recited, "'. . . like the memories of lost sons.'"

Alice was silent for a moment, and I expected her to make a comment about the line, tell me she liked it, or didn't. But instead she said, "I'd better get some sleep now."

"Okay," I said.

I started to rise, but she lifted her hand to stop me; then, with slow, heart-wrenching grace, she patted the side of her bed. "Just until I go to sleep," she said.

I lifted myself onto the bed and gathered her into my arms.

She remained in my arms, and if real life were a sentimental story, a peace would have settled over her during this time, and the many pains that afflicted her would have grown less pronounced and finally vanished altogether.

But in fact, Alice never went to sleep, but continually awakened herself at the border of sleep, and from that border peered fretfully out into the darkness beyond the window, so that by morning, she seemed still to be searching through infinity itself, past moons and stars and planets, as if, in her final moments, she had grown dissatisfied with the very ending she had herself proposed, found it conjectural and implausible and so had ceaselessly continued to probe beyond it, reaching out and out into the nothingness that surrounded her, out and out until she herself was stretched infinitely thin, a tiny string of light that grew more frayed with each breath until —at last—it broke.

27

ALICE WAS BURIED the following Sunday, and a week later the piece I wrote about her was published in the *Winthrop Examiner*. In it, I connected the two stories that had each come to a strange conclusion with Alice's death. They had been oddly intertwined, and finally flowed together, I wrote, so that they'd finally become a single small stream of hope against hope.

After that I took whatever trivial assignments Wyatt tossed me—a pet-shop opening, a wine tasting—and in that way resumed my life.

Over the following months, Arlo and I met occasionally at the diner or O'Shea's, but after a time there was little reason to discuss Katherine or her story any further, so almost all mention of her came to an end.

In October the creepy house off Route 34—presumably the one Katherine had used as a model in her story—was bulldozed to make room for a state tourist center. Later that same month, the single white post and small bench that had marked the bus stop where Maldrow had left Katherine off to face pure malice was replaced by a Plexiglas waiting area festooned with advertisements.

Thus, by summer, only two physical reminders of Katherine remained in or around Winthrop: the house on Gilmore Street, which I never revisited, and the rock grotto I sometimes glimpsed as I drove through town, but to which I now gave little notice. For it had surely come to an end for me, I thought, Katherine's tale, an end so utterly final that by fall I rarely thought of her, nor had the slightest expectation that I would ever hear of her again.

And so it came as a great surprise when, in July of the following year, one Anthony Ray Carmine was arrested in nearby Kingston. He'd lived in Winthrop some years before, he said. He'd worked at the marina that bordered the park, mostly washing boats. He'd always had a strange obsession for what he called "mysterious women," and by which he seemed to mean women who ignored him. He said he had murdered at least six such women in various towns throughout the state. He knew the names of his victims and the order in which they had been murdered. They had all been women who had been reported missing, and never subsequently found. The fourth name on his list was Katherine Carr.

"Carmine claims to be a thrill killer," Arlo told me when we met to discuss this breaking news on the afternoon following his confession. "He doesn't beat his victims up or rape them. The thrill is in the killing. Always with a rope."

I didn't need to hear any additional details, though I had no doubt Arlo had them.

"In a way, I guess it's a relief to Audrey," I said. "Since the most important thing to her was that Katherine didn't kill herself."

Arlo nodded, but there was doubt in his eyes. "Providing Carmine really did it."

"You think he didn't?"

Arlo shrugged. "I'd like to see the proof."

"What would be proof?"

"Her body. He says he took it downriver in the dead of night. No one saw him because of the fog."

"And threw it overboard?"

Arlo shook his head. "No, he says he knew the cops would drag the river, so he finally headed back to shore, waited until there was just enough light, then dragged it into the woods and buried it."

"Where?"

"That's what he's going to show the cops tomorrow." Arlo took a sip of coffee. "Do you want to come along?"

I wasn't sure. It was the same dark journey I'd made after Teddy had been found, and the prospect of repeating the experience brought back the utter hopelessness that had come upon me that day like a change of weather, a storm that never lifted or in any way moved on.

But there are mysterious compulsions, a door we must unlock, a drawer we must open, because to do otherwise would be a dread admission that we do not want to know.

Still, it was hardly an easy decision for me, one I thought over a moment before I finally resolved the matter.

"I think so, yes," I told Arlo.

He didn't seem surprised. "I thought you would. After all, you're a reporter."

And to report, as I recalled the words of the reporter at my father's wake, is to bear away the truth of what actually is, dark though it may be.

• • •

We left the next morning, Arlo at the wheel of his car, part of a law-enforcement convoy that included a crime-scene laboratory van. In near-military formation we wound north along the river, taking this turn then that one, often quite abruptly, with Carmine in the front car, no doubt enjoying his brief authority as leader of the pack.

At a place called March's Crossing, we swung east and headed along the river's twining course until we reached a break in the wood, turned right, and moved a little farther on to where we finally came to a halt at the muddy edge of the embankment.

Up ahead, a contingent of state troopers instantly surrounded the lead car so thickly that I was nearly upon it before I caught a glimpse of Carmine standing, legs shackled, but with his hands cuffed at the front, so that he could lift and lower them as he puffed a cigarette rhythmically. Clothed in an orange prison jumpsuit, he appeared somewhat smaller than I'd imagined, and very thin, so that he looked oddly starved of some vital element men needed in order to be men. "Ready, boys?" he asked with a crooked grin.

Even in shackles, Carmine strutted like a little bantam rooster as he led us toward the riverbank. Two enormous troopers flanked him on either side, but beyond their orderly ranks utter chaos reigned. There were plainclothes detectives in summer suits, deputies from the sheriff's department, and lawyers from the district attorney's office, along with a select group of TV and print journalists, cameras and notebooks in hand, firing questions Carmine answered with smiles and winks and shrugs and nods, but without ever saying a single word.

He didn't stop until he reached the water's edge, at which point he glanced left and right like a man trying to determine his position.

There was a moment of suspension, Carmine silent on the riverbank, his head cocked first to the left then to the right, like a bird on the watch, until something caught his eye, and he said, "There it is." He grinned. "I wasn't sure it would still be there."

For it had been twenty years, after all, and weather is weather, and time is no respecter of landmarks, nor of evidence, nor of permanence of any kind. And yet it was still there, according to Carmine, a metal sign that had been fresh-painted at the time, but which was now so rusted that its simple injunction could barely be read: NO DUMPING.

"I thought that was funny," Carmine said with that same twisted grin. "'Cause dumping is exactly what I done."

I looked at Arlo and saw that somewhere deep within the recesses of his own quiet reason, he'd wanted to believe that some element of Katherine's story had been true, that somehow she'd managed to escape so common a fate as murder, that he and Alice had shared in that spectacular hope for hope he'd earlier described.

"You really don't want it to be Katherine, do you?" I asked.

He turned to me and shook his head sadly. "No," he admitted. "No, I don't."

We followed Carmine south along the embankment, past the ruined sign, and through a stand of reeds beyond it, where we at last arrived at a spot he appeared vaguely to calculate as the right one. "I don't know how deep it is," he said, "I dug it fast." He laughed. "Had to do something with the goddamn thing, right?"

The diggers assembled on the spot and began their work, unearthing mounds of dark earth, everyone else to the side, watching. Carmine stood with his beefy escorts, smoking one cigarette after another. On occasion, his eyes would drift over in my direction, but they never lighted on me. From time to time he would follow the flight of a bird or glance toward some sound from the depths of the undergrowth, but otherwise he appeared hardly to be present at all until a question from the ranks of the idling reporters suddenly seemed to return him to a lost moment in his life.

"So, Ray, tell us about the murder."

He tossed his cigarette into the flowing water, and laughed at a joke that seemed to be only his. "She died like the bitch in heat she was."

He started to say more, but one of the diggers called, "Got something!" At that instant, I saw Arlo's doubts dissolve in the same way my hope for Teddy had dissolved into the featureless mush that time and the river had made of him. Even so, he simply turned back toward the diggers and waited for them to complete their work.

There is a raggedness in such recoveries, of course, small bits of nearly rotted cloth, and a duskiness as well, the sad powder of disintegration. Beyond these, there is nothing but the brutal nakedness of bone. Arlo and I saw all these things during the next few minutes, but we saw something else as well, bits of dark fabric.

Arlo released a desolate breath. "I guess they've found her at last," he said.

Then one of the diggers reached down into the pit and came up with a skull. It was caked with mud, but its shape was clear.

Carmine's laughter pealed over the river, into the woods, cut like a knife through all of us. "Just like I told you," he cried. "A bitch in heat."

The digger lifted the skull into the light, and with a cautious finger, probed its canine fangs.

• • •

"So we'll never know what happened to Katherine," I said to Arlo as we sat together at O'Shea's that same evening.

By that time, Carmine had admitted that it had all been a lie, his confessions only a playful ribbing of authority, Carmine himself guilty of nothing more than a bleak little joke.

"I guess not," Arlo said. He took a sip from his glass. "Or Hollis Traylor, either."

"Still nothing on him?" I asked.

"Nope," Arlo said. "But the cops found some horrible pictures in a fishing shack he had on the lake."

"Women?" I asked.

He shook his head. "Little boys. Tied up. Hanging. Internet-porn stuff. Tons of it." He shrugged. "Wouldn't it be nice to think that Katherine got him?"

"Katherine is long dead," I said starkly.

Arlo stared at his glass for a moment, then glanced up at me and noticed the desolate hopelessness that must have settled over me at that moment. "What are you thinking about, George?"

"Alice."

"What about her?"

"That she deserved a better ending," I said.

A chill had settled in by the time we left O'Shea's. Arlo pulled on the old trench coat he'd worn to countless murder scenes, the bloodied rooms and dank cellars and silt-laden streams and weedy ravines in which, for all time, the hapless dead have been laid to rest.

Arlo glanced into the cloudless sky. "Nice night."

"Clear as a bell," I said.

I offered my hand and we shook in silence, then turned away from each other and back into lives from which, as we assumed, both Alice Barrows and Katherine Carr would slowly but inevitably vanish.

My car was parked on a side street, but I wasn't in the mood to go home, and so, despite the chill I headed farther into town, then all the way down Main Street to where it ended, as it always had, in a park with that little rock grotto.

I sat down on a bench across from it and imagined Katherine on her final night, standing alone in the darkness, surrounded by mist. How strange, I thought, that it was in the most obviously fictional part of her story that she had predicted her actual end.

As I turned this odd circumstance over in my mind, I suddenly heard the sound of hydraulic doors.

I looked toward Main Street where the 34 bus had halted at a small white post. The windows were coated with a thin layer of dust from its mostly rural route, but still clear enough for me to see a single figure moving toward the front of the bus, head down, hooded, and who, on a cloudless, starry night, wore a yellow rain slicker.

And I thought, wildly and irrationally, like one suddenly lifted on an unseen wave, *Could it be him?*

I rose and stood motionless, like a man simultaneously jolted into action and frozen in place, half convinced that such a thing was possible, half convinced that it couldn't be.

By then the figure had stepped out of the bus and turned into the park, a yellow splash weaving among the trees in a shifting pattern that, for all its evasiveness, seemed oddly meant to compel my attention. For a few seconds, I watched as the figure swam in and out of view, still undecided as to what I should do. For what were the chances, after all, that this was indeed the man who had taken Teddy? No chance, I thought, no chance at all, and yet I couldn't rid myself of the steadily building but illogical hope that it was truly him, that the man who killed my son had by sheer coincidence come within my grasp.

And this time, I thought, *he will not get away.*

On the wave of that wholly unreasonable thought, I made my way into the deeper reaches of the park, watching as flashes of yellow weaved in and out of the shadows.

By now the figure had reached the river and was moving along its bank, though at a pace that had clearly slowed, so that I was suddenly no longer sure if I were pursuing the yellow rain slicker or if whatever evil coiled inside it had set a trap for me.

At that point I might have relented, since I was quite aware that I was being moved by an unreasonable impulse. But there are moments, stripped and pure, when your deepest pain asserts itself again, demands payment, explanation, or relief, so that you suddenly feel the kind of heedless passion that lovers feel, or men in battle, or those drawn by the pull of some great cause.

And so I continued on, quickening my pace, now closing in, as we both reached the stone jetty that stretched out into the night-bound flow of the river.

Suddenly an awesome rush overtook me, an anguished urge I could not explain any more than I could control it, a desperate need to make one final, frantic effort to set some small portion of things right not only for Teddy, but also for Alice in her fierce last hours, for my father in his deathbed rage, for Celeste in her early death, for everyone and everything on earth that had ever been caught in the web of life's immemorial injustice, the gharry horses and the gray-haired rickshaw pullers, the slaughtered slaves of Alaric and the desolate girls of the African road.

"Stop!" I cried. "Please stop!"

The figure in the yellow rain slicker stopped cold at my command, then turned to face me, standing motionless, waiting, as I approached.

The only light was a harbor light, its occasional flash a very poor illumination, so that I could make nothing out until a smooth white hand reached up and drew back the hood.

"Oh!" I breathed. "I'm sorry."

The woman's face remained in shadow, the revolving harbor light revealing one small feature at a time, an eye, a hint of lip, so that her face came to me in facets, as one sees bits and pieces in a cubist portrait, the whole connected more by the imagination than by anything actually seen.

"I hope I didn't scare you," I said.

"No," she said. She drew back a strand of streaked gray hair. "You didn't."

She glanced out toward the river, and I saw a shadowy profile that struck me as oddly familiar, then not familiar at all.

"It's just that I thought you were someone else," I said hesitantly.

The woman looked at me distantly, and yet with what seemed a terrible nearness, as if intimacy were a wave that traversed illimitable reaches of time and space in a single, incalculable instant.

"Who did you think I was?" she asked.

"A man I saw once," I told her. "He was wearing a yellow rain slicker. I've been looking for him for a long time." A shudder ran through my soul. "Because I believe he killed my little boy."

The harbor light swept over her, and in its rotation I saw she was regarding me quite fearlessly, as if I were someone with whom she had been long familiar.

"I know how you feel." The tone of her voice was like the touch of an unseen hand on my shoulder, soft and sympathetic.

"You want to know he didn't get away with it."

An odd, internal illumination now brought the woman's

face into a vaguely bluish light and in that face I saw a great abundance of emotion: grief, pain, loss, pity, and at that moment, every weird, fantastic tale, every ghostly touch and freakish circumstance, every bizarre coincidence and inexplicable twist of fortune congealed in my mind so that I now felt myself poised at the edge of a strange precipice, facing out and beyond it into an unseen infinitude of possibility.

Katherine? I thought.

I never voiced the question, but in that impossible instant of suspended disbelief, I felt a great loosening of bonds, a terrible heaviness falling away from me, the vast weight of the real lifted momentarily on the wings of the miraculous.

I started to speak, but couldn't. I simply stood in the utter calm of this curious suspension, unable to move, unable to speak, as helpless as a glass figurine turning slowly in the wind.

From her place in the darkness, the woman watched me with what seemed a kind of love, though not that of a wife for a husband or a mother for a child. It wasn't the love of a sister for a brother, or even a friend for a friend, but that strange, wholly invisible sense of connection the Greeks called *agape*, and without which, they said, one could not live a balanced life.

She lifted her hand and touched the collar of the rain slicker delicately. "The man it belonged to doesn't need it anymore," she said finally.

She stared at me silently, moving her fingers lightly over the lapels of the rain slicker, movements that seemed a kind of invisible writing, all our communication now like waves on a beach, moving into and over and around each other.

"Do you want it?" she asked.

She meant the rain slicker, and I suddenly thought of the little cross the Chief had offered Maldrow in Katherine's story, then of the ring Maldrow had given to Katherine, and as I let my gaze move to the yellow rain slicker, I felt utterly and beyond all understanding that here, being offered to me now, was the same dark proof.

"No," I answered, like one rejecting the pelt of a once-raging beast.

The woman nodded softly. "Perhaps we'll meet again."

"Perhaps."

She started to turn, but I drew her back with a question. "What happened to him?" I asked. "The man in the yellow rain slicker."

Her voice took on the hardness of metal upon metal. "He went for a drive one night. He was never seen again."

With that she stepped back with what I can only describe as an unearthly grace, turned slowly with no sense of effort, as if rotating in the air, then strolled away from me, deeper into the night, wisps of fog suddenly gathering around her, a mistiness that gave her a look so ghostly and insubstantial, she seemed hardly made of flesh at all.

Mr. Mayawati stares at me like one stricken, his gaze deeply troubled, like one no longer certain of the world, nor secure within it. His lips part, then seal, then part again. Finally he says, "The woman in the yellow rain slicker . . . she was . . . Katherine?"

When I don't answer, he starts to speak again, but falls silent, and remains silent for a long time, like a man pondering the consequences of a terrible miscalculation. Then, like a coward concealing a seizure of fear, he laughs loudly. "You did not see such a woman."

I offer no defense of my tale, make no gesture in regard to proof.

My silence only heightens the agitation I see in him.

"So it is your own story you are telling," Mr. Mayawati says, like one seeking to impeach the honesty of a witness. "Not Katherine's or Alice's."

When I only stare at him silently, he shrinks back like a

small creature from a threatening predator. "But there are loose ends," he adds hesitantly. "For example, the woman in the coffee shop. And the woman at that house, and that other woman, the one on the street where Katherine lived. You do not tell us who they were."

I neither confirm nor deny this.

I sense the inward squirm of Mr. Mayawati's wormy soul, but give no sign of what I see in the fearful glint of his eyes, nor feel in the heat that comes from him, nor the horrid pungency it carries, the smell of bodies in decay.

Mr. Mayawati yanks his handkerchief from his pocket and swabs his neck and face violently. But it does no good; the sweat returns, so that he seems to be melting in the heat of a hellish inner fire. "You deceived me," he says in the slightly offended tone of a guileless man badly used. "You made me believe it was Katherine's story."

He rocks back in his chair like a man pushed by an unseen hand. "Then you made me believe it was Alice's story." Suddenly his eyes flare with an anger that is all bluster, a shield raised against his fear. "But it is *your* story, is it not?"

"No," I tell him quietly. My voice goes cold. "It is *your* story."

Mr. Mayawati laughs, but it is the panicky laugh of one gripped by a terrible anxiety. "*My* story? How could it be *my* story?"

I rise abruptly and walk to the rail of the boat. The water that flows beneath it remains impenetrable, the bow a blade that slices through only the thinnest layer of its opaqueness, reveals almost nothing of what lies beneath.

"Still, it is a very strange story, I will give you that," Mr. Mayawati says. He laughs again as he mops the relentlessly pursuing moisture that consumes his face. "Too strange to be believed."

I peer out into the jungle. Beyond the central station, the Buranni are already preparing for my visit, laying out their evidence, proof, they say, of the unseen, though it may only be evidence of how ardent it is, the human hope for miraculous intervention, relief, real or not, from injustice's anguished sting.

Mr. Mayawati squirms in his deck chair, starts to rise, then eases himself back into his seat. "The heat has made me . . . uncertain of my . . ."

I know now that Mr. Mayawati's fear is not the fear of the innocent, for the innocent have no fear of justice, celestial or otherwise, of tribunals held in vast white halls, of sentences handed down.

I turn to face him and when our eyes meet Mr. Mayawati's features take on the frozen alarm of the suddenly recognized, those who stumble out of fields, wiping blood from their hands, to find not the empty road ahead, eyeless and uncaring, but a little boy glancing back at just the right instant, tugging at his father's coat. *Look there.*

"Uncertain of my . . ."

Mr. Mayawati falls silent, and beneath that silence, like a voice behind a curtain, I hear a little girl reading in the park, the one who was so lovely.

For a moment Mr. Mayawati stares at me with a strange recognition, and in the following stillness, I see his flabby shadow as it falls over the child, the sniff of her nose at the mingled smell of sweat and curry that came from him, the putrid, confident, ruthless, brutal smell they all have, the ones who think they got away.

"I do not believe your story," Mr. Mayawati declares firmly. He waves his hand. "Of course, I do not believe it." He rises as if rudely jerked to his feet and moves heavily away, toward the back of the boat, his eyes rising as he walks, lifting into the sweltering sky, where high above, a dark bird makes a long lazy circle.

"You don't have to believe it," I say softly, knowing that he freezes at the sound of my voice. "But then . . ."

He turns, his eyes all but liquefied by the terrible inferno of his own inner heat.

"But then . . . what?" he asks hesitantly, fearfully, as if no longer certain of his fate.

I do not face him, but only smile. "But then . . . you may be fiercely wrong."